TROUBLED SPIES

Deception is the only language
they understand

ARUN MATHEW

notionpress
.com
INDIA · SINGAPORE · MALAYSIA

Copyright © Arun Mathew 2025
All Rights Reserved.

ISBN

Paperback 979-8-89906-613-9
Hardcase 979-8-89854-982-4

This book has been published with all efforts taken to make the material error-free after the consent of the author. However, the author and the publisher do not assume and hereby disclaim any liability to any party for any loss, damage, or disruption caused by errors or omissions, whether such errors or omissions result from negligence, accident, or any other cause.

While every effort has been made to avoid any mistake or omission, this publication is being sold on the condition and understanding that neither the author nor the publishers or printers would be liable in any manner to any person by reason of any mistake or omission in this publication or for any action taken or omitted to be taken or advice rendered or accepted on the basis of this work. For any defect in printing or binding the publishers will be liable only to replace the defective copy by another copy of this work then available.

Contents

1.	House of Cards	5
2.	Trouble in Paradise	18
3.	Currency of Trust	25
4.	The Indian Station	31
5.	A Cold Handshake	39
6.	The Orchestrator	47
7.	The Moscow Station	54
8.	Otto and Tesla	63
9.	The Troubled Spies	72
10.	So It Begins	79
11.	In Plain Sight	86
12.	Sleight of Hand	93
13.	The Big Three	95
14.	Missing in Action	102
15.	The Safe House	113
16.	The Plot Thickens	122
17.	Post Hoc Ergo Propter Hoc	126
18.	Spanner in the Works	133
19.	Bon Voyage	138
20.	Circle of Trust	146
21.	The Request	152
22.	The Game's Afoot	160
23.	The Face Off	167

24.	Hook, Line, and Sinker	174
25.	Wheels in Motion	182
26.	SpyGames	188
27.	So It Begins	198
28.	Man Down	204
29.	The Joker Card	212
30.	The Butterfly Effect	223
31.	The Queen's Gambit	232
32.	One-Man Cavalry	242
33.	The Man in the Yellow Tie	248
34.	Needle in a Haystack	253
35.	Bus to Vyborg	258
36.	The Wrong Man	262
37.	Bait and Switch	270
38.	Old Dog, New Trick	278
39.	Homecoming	286
40.	Occam's Razor	293

Chapter 1
House of Cards

September 26th, 1982

Century House-SIS Headquarters, London

Simon Henley stared at the prominent facade of Century House—the fabled MI6 headquarters nestled right into the bustling streets of Westminster Bridge Road. The headquarters gained notoriety and recognition as the place where British surveillance and counter-surveillance employees worked. It was the citadel of the espionage business in the Cold War. Over the years, it became London's worst-kept secret, almost laughable, with everyone from a KGB agent to a taxi driver knowing this was where the British intelligence officers worked. Yet, the show went on unabridged.

Henley thought the building was crying for a fresh coat of paint. The shops and establishments next to the headquarters offered a contrasting view of the new London, new businesses, thriving communities, and the influx of migrants from Asia and the Caribbean islands. This societal change was not the London where he started his career three decades back, and he was pleased to see this change, of new cultures, new ideas, and possibly a new way of conducting espionage right in the heart of the capital.

Simon had barely slept, courtesy of the long-winded flight he had taken from Moscow—all just so Archibald Cumberbatch, his boss at MI6, could deliver a thunderous rundown of everything wrong with Henley's Moscow Station operations over the last couple of years. But Henley had been in the service long enough to grow a thick skin and a shallow conscience. *Make sure you come prepared*; Control had mentioned in his last cable. Henley went through his brown leather duffel bag and quickly checked for the blue file—the front section, a roster of their failures or challenges as he would like to call it, and the back section with a series of pages with arguments, case histories, that he could use to defend his team. *A neat red nylon strip partitioning the file into failures and challenges.*

Roslyn had carefully prepared Henley with footnotes and rehearsals of the responses he could give in their defense. In front of Control, a moniker for the chief of British intelligence's clandestine operations abroad, there was no we, us, or the team. It was just him alone. Roslyn was the oil that kept the wheels of his MI6 outpost moving. What would they do without her, Henley thought?

Henley caught his reflection in the glass panels of the newly constructed Marks and Spencer. He could easily have been part of the hardworking middle-class landscape of London, who bustled around on the streets. He looked pale, tired, and had the mood to match. It was still early in the day, but the street was already turning into a marketplace. Newspaper vendors had opened shop, and the papers—heavy stones barely keeping them in place—were flying off the poorly arranged tabletops. A long line of daily wage laborers was awaiting instructions on the heavy lifting they were to partake in in the coming hours. A few immigrants were forming the queue to shop for their daily groceries at the delicatessen—telltale signs of newfound wealth in the melting pot of cultures that London was. The classic bakeries of the yore had made way for French-style delicatessens. *Tea,* he thought. Nothing else could solve his problems that morning. It would do for now. He wouldn't put it past Control to force his hand toward a glass of cognac at their showdown. *Control knew of his vices.*

The waitress at the Parisian-styled cafe was a sight for his sore eyes. She greeted him with a radiant smile and warmth, almost making him forget the arduous task ahead and the pains of the grueling long distance he had traveled. He ordered an English breakfast tea and scones. He looked through the large transparent windows and saw the streets filling up with a medley of people—school-going children, mums walking the dogs through the side pavements, and sharply suited men speed walking to work. Spooks, Henley thought as he saw the men in suits rushing toward the building with leather briefcases. Henley conceded that hiding in plain sight wasn't the strongest suit for those in the intelligence service.

Henley walked toward the lobby and, with every few steps, looked around for any familiar faces, both friendly and those from behind the Iron Curtain. He had been long gone from the London station and was not used to plying his trade in the middle of a bustling city center. *The spy game behind the Iron Curtain was a covert and intense affair.* The street was too busy with itself to bother an entourage of spies and employees of the Secret Service Intelligence, some loafing and the rest scampering their way into the building.

The inside of the building had been refreshed. There was a smell of fresh leather, British racing green painted walls, a large mahogany wood front desk, and a plush new seating arrangement for visitors. Henley walked up to the reception and presented his details. The crisply dressed receptionist quickly checked his ID and belongings, and Henley found himself waiting for the lift that would take him to the twenty-first floor—Control's office. Control sat at the top of the *Circus*—a much-maligned but widely used moniker for the MI6. Much like the nations England colonized, Circus had its way of discriminating against its members. The higher your standing in the service, the higher the floor.

Henley waited as a rush of recruits barraged through the corridors—their fresh trims, affordably tailored suits, and faces full of excitement giving them away. Not for long, Henley empathized. *One proper field assignment or an outing with the scalp hunters, and they would be thrown into the deep end and expected to swim back alone.* That should give them a taste of the service and what it meant to be a secret service officer—a reality check; it was not all suits and codes behind a computing machine.

A familiar face walked toward him.

"Simon Henley! What a pleasant surprise! Moved back to London, have we?" It was Dick Engels, the Chief of Accounts and one of the Big Three at the Circus.

"Not likely with the meager wages and the extortionate house prices here, Dick," Henley retorted.

"How are you?"

"Oh, come on; you're in it for Queen and country, not for yourself, right?" *True to his name, after all*, Henley thought. Money was the primary motivator for spies and counter-spies—Engels held that opinion. Money was the strongest motivator for recruiting double agents, with hatred as a distant second. Sex came third. Wright, his flamboyant case officer in Moscow, knew a lot about the third, Henley thought with a smirk.

"Is that a new Jaguar I see you driving around?" Henley asked. It was a guess; Henley had seen a swanky new car drive into the building as he walked toward the lobby.

"Henley, you slippery bastard. Nothing skips your eye, I see. Thanks to the missus, we make a decent living," Engels quickly defended himself.

The lift finally arrived, and Henley and Engels joined a few junior staff. Henley pressed the button for the top floor.

"Ah, so Control's called you in?" Engels remarked. A young recruit in a navy blue suit looked up to Henley with adulation and awe—Henley's towering presence had that effect. Henley gave him a wink.

"Who else? Unless you have an operational field bonus for me to collect?" Henley wasn't in the mood for small talk. He was already expecting the worst outcome and didn't need Dick Engels to give him a push over the ledge.

Engels got off at the eighteenth floor. It made sense now; the Jag, the fresh Savile Row suit, and a pair of Crockett & Jones boots—Engels had made it to the eighteenth floor. The last time Henley went for budget approvals, he had still languished on the tenth. *Henley thought Engels probably played the game much better than anyone else. Maybe I could retire in London with the MI5, looking after domestic troubles rather than running counteragents in foreign lands, better for his health and the bank balance.*

The top floor of Century House had its own aura. For a man with acrophobia, it was intimidating yet offered enough serene views of the city to calm him down. Linda Garvey, Cumberbatch's long-standing secretary, ushered him in and asked him to sit in the reception. To his memory, Control's office hadn't changed. The leather couch had the upholstery redone—the fresh leather scent giving it away.

"Can I get you a cup of tea, Henley?" Linda, a gorgeous blonde pushing into the fifties yet could easily pass off in her early forties, had always been a class act—a welcome change in a business dominated by men.

"Black with two," Henley said, folding his suit into a neat pattern onto the chair next to the couch—a creature of habit.

"Russia hasn't changed you, then," she said, pressing a bell on her desk. No custom orders were placed on the one-way calling bell, which meant only tea was on offer. A few minutes later, a doe-eyed, tall, and beautiful young woman came with a pot of tea and a cup full of sugar cubes. An intern, Henley concluded. Good-looking women like that barely made it to permanent status in the SIS. Linda and Roslyn may just about be the last of their kind. Linda looked radiant as a beam of sunlight through the windowpanes shone on her, her sharp features and curves still by her side. Not that she needed it to survive the travails of the espionage business, Henley surmised.

Remember that we have been the best performing station for the MI6, and make it sound so, Roslyn's last words to him before Henley set sail. Henley tried to control the odd shivers in his left hand. The shivers weren't the cause of the occasion but a lingering health issue he had been carrying secretly. Dr Manning might figure this out in the following health check-up, Henley was sure. But then, even if it was bad news, they had gone back a long time, since their Cambridge days, and he could count on the old doc to keep it tight-lipped. He needed to be in the service for a few more years to earn his big payday upon retirement.

The grand old clock in the waiting room chimed nine o'clock. Henley got up and went over to Linda. He had been sitting for 20 minutes and already had two servings of tea.

"Am I his first meeting of the day?"

"Oh, he's been here since 6."

"Has he?" Henley was not shocked. Control was a workhorse and could pull in odd hours, mostly when things had gone south.

"He's been in a real mood the last few days."

"You don't say?"

"I'd keep it low and easy, Henley," Linda suggested.

The telephone rang. Linda picked up and signaled Henley to go in.

"Good luck, love," she said. Henley looked back with a smile. *What a woman*, he thought.

Henley squinted in the dim light of Control's office and felt his lungs constrict with the deep breath of the cigar smoke that filled the air. Beyond the smoke and yellow lights, a grand tapestry of curtains and wallpapers, part-Gothic and part-Victorian, splashed Control's office walls. Photos and commemorative plaques adorned the walls of the circular office, mementos of Control's time in the field. Long back, Control had run the Moscow Center, the primary seat of all espionage action, now Henley sat on it. Henley wondered if this would be his office someday, if only he knew how to play the game in London and be as ambitious as those at the top of the Circus.

"Henley, have a seat, will you? Stop staring at the walls. No medals here," Control quipped. The Secret Service was a thankless job. *The secret service agents worked under the shadows while the military men took home the medals for keeping the country safe.*

"Not much has changed here," Simon said as he pulled the side arms of the oakwood chair with a plush leather seat in a chestnut brown color and contrast stitching in a shade of mustard yellow. *The man had taste,* Henley thought as he took the chair.

"What did you expect? Flowers and ribbons? Did you meet anyone on the flight on the way home?" Control asked. The stack of files in front of him partially blocked his view of Henley.

Henley knew exactly what Control meant. It was not a courtesy question—it just implied whether someone had followed him to London from Moscow.

"No one worth remembering," Henley said, re-adjusted the chair for a better view. He needed to look Control in the eye.

Satisfied, Control opened a bottle of Yamazaki. Henley quickly recognized the batch—the gold ribbon around the bottle's neck was a golden anniversary edition to celebrate fifty years of Yamazaki whiskey. Henley had a bottle back home in Moscow. Control poured two glasses and pushed one toward Henley. He held his ground. It was early by his standards, and he wanted to keep his best self until the situation warranted that he lean on the Yamazaki.

So, will you tell me why I'm here on such short notice?" Henley said and leaned forward on his chair. It was showtime.

Control opened his drawer, pulled out a red file, and handed it over to Henley. "Why don't you tell me?" he said, getting up and pacing around the office, the glass of whiskey in one hand and an unlit cigar in the other.

Henley picked up the file and ran through the pages. It was a debrief of a handful of agents sent on special assignments—their profiles, previous assignments, family… the works. There were details of their onward journeys, travel routes, cover stories, and, for a couple of agents—an account of their time spent at the Indian station of MI6. The file dated events as recent as the last three months. It wasn't unusual for agents to spend time in the cold before being regurgitated and sent to a new station for a new assignment. All looked fine until he spotted one name: Vince Gilligan.

"Gilligan. He's due to be posted with us," Henley said.

"He was until last week," Control remarked.

"Was?" Henley said.

"He's missing. Presumed dead," Control rarely played in the gray—always black or white. It undoubtedly influenced why he had reached the top and stayed there. The rest could never take sides, always on the fence. Simon Henley himself was prone to that mediocrity. Here was Control, pushing seventy yet still managing to strong-arm an entire legion of agents worldwide.

"If he never reached my shores, what's it to do with me?" Henley asked. It was not that an agent had gone missing in this business for the first time.

"It's possible that in a long time, we have a mole, Henley," Control said, lighting his cigar finally. He shifted the curtains, and a shaft of light ushered in.

"He'd gone rogue?" Henley contemplated an answer to his own question. The ghosts of Kim Philby and the other Cambridge spies were still roaming around in the halls of the SIS.

"Look deeper, Henley. You only spotted the one name that came from a recent memory. The list goes beyond Gilligan."

"You mean the rest of these agents…"

"Missing or dead," Control cut him off.

Simon Henley reached for the whiskey.

One was an anomaly. Four was a trend. All within three years. For a moment, Simon felt a fleeting sense of relief; this was not to be the showdown he had envisaged. But what was it?

Control continued staring through the window, the bare sunlight hitting his face and throwing a massive shadow onto Henley. There was a moment of silence, not to respect the dead or missing, but for each to contemplate their next move. Who would break first? Henley had had this dance many moons ago with Control when he wanted to move on from the Moscow Station. He needed time outside the Iron Curtain, outside the high pressures and politics of running an MI6 station in Moscow. Control had prevailed then. He was sure to prevail now.

Control closed the curtains and took to his leather-upholstered chair. Grand, old, and still with a bit of class, the chair reflected its owner. It only got better with age.

"We had something similar during the war before Philby turned traitor," Control said with a measured tone, framing his following sentence carefully. "The Germans seemed to catch every piece of intel coming out of our stables. Even chicken feed went their way. We suspected our comms were being intercepted and changed our communication equipment. That did not stop the leak. It was not out of the realm of possibility that someone within MI6 could have been turned. It was not a battle of ideology but rather one of survival. All we wanted was to come out of the war unscathed."

"Not just Berlin, I presume?" Henley asked.

"You are right. Berlin, London, Vienna, and Moscow—we were bleeding everywhere. We thought we were the best of the lot. But the events from 1940 until '43 threw us down a rabbit hole. Agent movements, covert operations getting burned, and standard surveillance routes chased by counteragents became the norm. It was something new for us. If some of our agents and their ideologies had been turned, the doubts were within. It was like chasing our tails."

Control went back to the bar counter for another round of whiskey. Linda came in with a tray of bread and fruits. Henley was famished but didn't dare to break the mood.

"How did you fix it? Was there a leak? Or a mole in the agency?"

"That's the irony. The combined forces of the greatest spies in the British Isles, and it was not our hurrah moment of fixing the plug or catching the mole. It took the help of a hapless woman from Sussex. She suspected her husband, an MI6 operative, was having an affair. She told the secretary of the Control back then about this. Word passed around, and

Control put a tap on him. That fucker was giving away all the secrets to the woman he thought he was madly in love with."

"All that for sex?" Henley said.

"Men, we never learn," Control couldn't help but laugh.

"Why this story now, Chief? And why me?" Henley asked.

"Because we have a mole, Henley… and it leads straight to your doorstep."

"How? Gilligan? I hardly think that qualifies as a Moscow problem," Simon fought back.

"Here's what you don't know," Control interrupted. "The three before Gillian were supposed to reach Moscow too."

"Why was I not informed?" Henley shouted and locked eyes with Control, searching for the truth.

"You don't need to know everything, Henley," Control asserted, "For your good and of the Circus."

"Everyone's a suspect always, even me." Henley was not having any of this. "I know the playbook, Archie." It got personal for Henley. It was among the few times he called Control by his first name.

"You wouldn't be here if you weren't in my inner circle of trusted people, and you wouldn't be hearing about this problem," Control said and paused. Henley went back to the file and browsed through the pages.

"Hold on. All four went to India for a clean chit and a new cover story?"

"Yes."

"Ever wondered that the problem could lie in India?"

"Now you're getting somewhere, but not completely."

"How so?"

"Because that's where I started. I had Father Samuel in the same chair as you last week."

"And?"

"And I think there is value in you and him figuring this out together."

Control went and took the chair next to Henley. It was now beyond just work.

"Henley, I have known you for decades. I know you are clean, and I trust you with my life—the same with the priest. We are in troubled times. Our American cousins are breathing down our neck, trying to prove their superiority."

"Not bloody likely!" Henley charged up.

"I need you to be calm, methodical, and ruthless," Control said, placing his hand on his back, "I need you to build your inner circle and smoke the bastard out. Could you speak to the priest and work with him? His loyalties are in the right place, and he has a bloody good mind," Control said. It was more of a command than a suggestion.

Henley felt he could trust Father Samuel at Control's persuasion, but he knew little about the workings of the Indian station. He did, however, know the man who had a pulse on every foreign station of the MI6. John Marbury.

"Do you have someone you trust with your life?" It was as if Control read Henley's mind as he thought of John.

"I do, Chief," Henley said.

"Then that's your right-hand man," Control said. "You report to me and only to me. Leave Engels, Maeston, Smith, and their entourage out of it."

"If you say so, but I don't know how, it'll be hard to keep it away from them," Henley warned. Keeping it away from the Control's deputies at the Circus would not be easy.

"Leave that with me." Control said, his voice carrying the air of authority.

Henley was now coming to terms with the extent of this threat. Control's desire to keep it away from his deputies could only be one reason. The Big Three were also on his list of suspects. Anyone could be the mole.

"Well then, if that's all?" Henley said, getting up. He took his overcoat and walked toward the door.

"Trust no one, Henley," Control said, opening his work file. The meeting was over. A siren wailed past the building, leaving a deafening silence for a moment.

Henley stepped out, kissed Linda quickly, and called for the lift heading down. He got into the lift, fighting the tremor in his hand, and pressed a few buttons thoughtlessly. His mind was still racing. His worst fears were being realized.

Henley had harbored his suspicions of a leak for almost a year. Control had just put a stamp of confirmation on that. There is a mole, a traitor amongst their ranks.

This was going to be a long trip back to Moscow.

Chapter 2
Trouble in Paradise

"There are Russian spies here now. And if we're lucky, they'll steal some of our secrets, and they'll be two years behind."
– Mort Sahl

October 1st, 1982, MI6 Station, Moscow, Russia

Winter in Moscow was all about survival. For Muscovites, it was a time of reflection, sustenance, and resilience, followed by slow progress toward growth, sunshine, and hope. For Simon Henley, this winter had been a harsh reminder of the life he had chosen and the challenges that came with it. This winter tested his patience, loyalties, friendships, and even the distant enemies that seemed ever lurking in the shadows of the forgotten sun were circling in. He was prepared for the worst and was silently hoping for the best.

Henley had held the mantle of the station for far too long, his detractors would say. Age was not on his side; he knew it was fast catching up. Moscow Station was the most crucial British intelligence unit outside of England. Working right under the noses of their greatest enemy, Simon Henley and his crew had run a tight ship against the odds. The Cold War between Britain and Russia had been going on for decades and had taken a toll on both sides. Moscow Station had always delivered counter-intelligence that significantly shaped the Cold War.

Henley opened the envelope that Roslyn had brought back from the comms room. He read through the transcript: *The priest is expecting your call. Form your operational team as soon as you can. We need results.*

Trust no one, Control had said. But it was easier said than done.

Henley sat behind his mahogany desk on his perfectly cushioned chair, looking beyond his office chambers' glass walls. Though the Moscow Station was the best functioning MI6 counter-intelligence unit, the building didn't reflect it. Istanbul and Budapest had it much better. Any requests for improvements had been stonewalled. The reply was that the nature of the building and its architecture didn't allow for expansion. *Fuck you, Engels.*

The building that housed the MI6 offices was not far from the bustling industrial town being developed—telltale signs of an improving Russian economy. Henley thought they seemed to be getting the better side of the Cold War. The factory sirens bellowed a screeching sound. Although distant, the sound was thunderous enough to break through the embassy's walls. It broke his train of thought but almost came as a welcome distraction. He had been on the desk for hours, mulling through countless debriefs and reports from the last couple of years.

This was his favorite time of the day. The grand old clock in his office was timed to chime out an alarm at 5 PM. The sound of the hammer oscillating between the bells and sending out rhythmic notes was the perfect antidote for him—a poignant reminder that there was life beyond the walls of the Moscow Station. Henley liked to pour himself a cognac, open the windows to let the northern winds in, and watch the employees from the office buildings and embassies go home and get on with their lives. *Each fighting their battle.* Henley felt a shiver at the thought that possibly one of them could be the traitor—the mole threatening to bring down his operation, his legacy. There was a clear and existential threat of secrets continuing to leak, possibly from his office.

It had been almost a week since his return from London, yet he still hadn't formed his team. He had his Moscow Five, the chosen ones—some by him, some from the Circus—but not all enjoyed the privilege of his complete trust. Some had more, some far less. But none enjoyed an unconditional trust. That was the game, the profession, built on the ability of its operatives to lie.

Henley turned away from the window and looked at the blank sheet of paper on his desk. He drew a simple chart. On the left side were the Moscow Five, the Big Three and their cronies at the Circus in the middle, and to the right, the Indian station of MI6. He would have to cast a vast net to land the traitor. This was too big a list even to consider working through. He needed to trust someone to get started. Control had placed his trust in Father Samuel and seemed a good enough place to start. But he'd also need someone in Moscow to bring in on the hunt.

The station was empty by now. The crew had left a while back, and Henley had his first glass of the finest cognac on offer. *He'd never taken vodka.* Perhaps he was too stubborn. Henley closed the curtains and turned on the green glass desk lamp—a gift from Sara, who was with their sons in Turks and Caicos for a holiday. *What I would give to be with them if not for this mess.*

He had the priest's direct line, thanks to Linda. She was some woman. In the business he was in, it was easy to fall for easy sex and a side gig with a woman, but that's where he drew a line. Henley had made a vow when he entered the service. Thirty years into the job, and he had not faltered. Once, nearly. *Linda.* But he had found his way out of it relatively unscathed.

Henley poured another drink and dialed. The call would go straight to the priest's parsonage, ring three times, and wait two minutes before calling back again. He checked his watch—a

Vacheron Constantin Americane 1921. An expensive watch he gifted himself to mark a personal milestone that marked his start of time as the Chief of the Moscow Station. Two minutes passed, and he rang again.

"Samuel Turner," the voice on the other end said.

"Father, this is Simon Henley from Moscow." Although there wasn't a need to address him as a priest, Father Samuel and his day job as a priest demanded that respect. He was an ordained priest and studied at the parsonage, after all.

"Henley, you old dog, how are you? I was hoping you'd call."

"Things have been better, Father"

"I hear you. What's keeping you up?" Father Samuel asked.

"The same as you, I suspect."

"Control wasn't sure if you'd follow the lead."

"Was there a choice?" Henley laughed.

"You could play the 'getting old' card."

"This could be my last dance for all you know, Father."

"How can I help?"

"I believe you've read the files."

The priest grunted in the affirmative.

"Good, so we agree it's not just a Moscow problem. Where do we begin?"

The two exchanged brief notes on the four agents in the dossier who had been due to make the trip from London to the Indian station. They were all destined to hit Russian shores afterward. But Father Samuel had only had three visitors for R&R (*rest and recuperation*). Gilligan had never made it to the Indian station.

"So, you mean to say Gilligan never came to your doorstep?"

"Positive."

"And the rest?"

"Pete Rush, George Barkley, and… hold on for a minute…" Father Samuel rummaged through the files on his desk.

"Kate Miller, presumed missing. The other two are presumed dead," Father Samuel said as he closed his file. "This could be hearsay as the information post-op is murky, but Pete Rush was assigned to Istanbul from here with a journalist cover story. After a cooling-off period, he should have traveled to Moscow. The scalp hunters reported having found him in the local morgue in Budapest."

"The scalp hunters, you say?" The scalp hunters were a group of agents who did the work no one else wanted to.

"Smith's department, yes," Father Samuel confirmed.

"And he ended up in Budapest? How did the authorities know he was a foreign national?" Simon asked.

"Well, that's a lead worth checking." The veteran spies had circled in on their first lead.

"And Barkley… lovely chap from what I hear coming from Shakuntala, was headed to Budapest as a cultural secretary. He left only a couple of months back. Control planned to build a channel between Budapest and Moscow and he was the man for it."

"Control had an eye on Budapest?"

"So I would presume… Budapest has been a trouble ground for a while, and now, with these deaths… well, I don't need to spell it out, but Control still has his pulse in the game, although the Big Three would want to perch onto his position."

"And I thought *Moscow and India were* the kids that went rogue… What's Shakuntala?"

"Shakuntala is our safe house, tucked in a small town in Central India, away from Pondicherry."

"How did we conclude Barkley's dead?"

"Control told me. Didn't have time to go into the details."

"And the girl?"

"That's the interesting part. She just vanished from the safe house."

"What passport is she carrying?"

"English. We had that on file. But she's a trained spy; if she wanted, she could have got a new one," Father Samuel said.

"How is this just becoming a problem? Four agents missing or dead, and we only look at it now?"

"Your guess is as good as mine, but I'd wager the Yanks raised the alert."

"Control said our cousins were getting nosy."

"You know, Henley, I'm understaffed. Why don't you send someone to help us clear a few loose ends?"

"I suppose I could. But…" Henley wasn't sure who to trust with such an important assignment.

"But you prefer to run an op between us first?" Father Samuel read Henley's mind.

"Preferably. Is there something in the playbook that is a two-person job?"

There was silence on Father Samuel's end of the line. Father Samuel would indulge in a glass of wine or two on those rare occasions when the situation demanded it. Now was the moment.

"Do you remember the Vienna Ruse that Crawley ran in '72?"

Henley wrung the telephone wires around his fingers, trying to remember the play. It had become a part of the MI6 folklore and a case study for young recruits to learn about guile and deceit in espionage. *Crawley, the station chief at Vienna, was stuck with a counter-surveillance problem with the Germans at the Viennese outpost. All his routes were tracked end to end by the Germans, and communicating with his field agents and sending files back to London became untenable. Control had tasked him with resetting the route—a hard reset—so they could start over and build new routes. Crawley and his team then set a simple plan—sending the same communication through all routes and drop sites- that they were moving the Vienna operation to Budapest in about two weeks. The team then set about sending communications back and forth between Vienna and Budapest— all worthless pieces of information, "chicken feed," which the Germans tracked and intercepted. While this happened, a select team set about to develop a few covert drop sites and routes over two weeks and managed to resume covert ops and communications.*

"You think we could run the Vienna Ruse here?" Henley asked.

"Not all of it, but surely a part of it," Father Samuel said.

A few hours in, there was a plan—although a quick fix—that might help to smoke out the mole if they were lucky. Father Samuel agreed to send over the package that could help the operation get on its way.

Chapter 3
Currency of Trust

Henley had a spring in his step the following morning, unfazed by the sleepless night he had, courtesy of his long conversation with the priest. Henley seemed focused and put in the pace, rolling back to 1964 when he had joined the Vientiane station in Laos as the second-in-command. That was Simon Henley at his peak—sharp mind and a youthful body. The body had aged through the years, but the mind still carried the sharpness. He looked through the glass walls of his office as his stellar crew of agents began to populate the station.

Roslyn, his assistant of fifteen years, was brilliant, fiery yet elegant. Few knew of her personal life beyond the fact that she had lost her son during a train wreck. Henley knew he could trust her until Control came calling and sowed the seeds of doubt. She had never given him a reason not to. But before Moscow, she'd had a tumultuous career, quickly moving from station to station. *Did I miss a beat, not wanting to know everything about her past?* Henley reconsidered his position on Ros.

John Marbury, the communications and tech expert, was his best friend and batch mate from Cambridge. Henley couldn't picture Marbury as the mole. Marbury had spent many years at MI5 before Henley brought him to Moscow. This was not a man who could trade his country, conscience, and friendship—Henley just knew. Kim Philby's betrayal was decades ago, but the Philby affair had taught the service that friendship was the biggest deceiver of all.

Charles 'Charlie' Darcy was Marbury's understudy. A well-raised Yorkshire lad, he had signed up for the espionage life at the behest of his catholic parents and was pushed to the service courtesy of the church's influence on MI6. He never had a pretense and kept a low profile, barring a drinking habit that wasn't out of the ordinary for those in the business of espionage. Which soul hadn't crumbled in this severe weather and found solace in the arms of either a woman, a warm pour of cognac, or both? Darcy might have fit the bill outside looking in, but he was just a techie and a low-level functioning cog in the unit. Counter-espionage of this level was well above his pay grade.

Stuart Wright was the prime candidate, more through Henley's prejudice than proof. The larger-than-life, swashbuckling spy had a carefree attitude to life, much to Henley's annoyance, but was a brilliant case officer and an excellent agent runner on the field. Henley handpicked Wright, although it was by an act of conscience and not calculation, probably the last time he followed his heart when he brought Wright from the deep trenches of the Panama station. Wright was the odd one out, yet he was the influencer amongst the others. He had a taste for the rich life: women and cars. Whether Henley agreed with his style, Wright was a bloody effective spy. His numbers spoke for themselves. His eidetic memory often came to his rescue. But was there a dark, brooding, vengeful person behind the fancy facade? History suggested that men of such extravagance and character palette often played both sides to satisfy their vices.

Finally, there was Keith Aldridge, his rising star and second-in-command. A young, charismatic spy brought in a few years back from the Istanbul station to run Tesla—the most significant Russian double agent the station had in its ranks for quite a long while. Henley referred to Keith Aldridge as the conductor. He steered all the information that came in and out of the Moscow Station. It was clear that he was being groomed to take over from Henley, and now, the old spy wondered if his protégé's exemplary rise came because of his talents or courtesy of an external entity running the show. There was reason for doubt.

This was his team, the hand he was dealt with. Henley knew any of his five associates could be the mole, but so could someone from the Indian station or London. Control's words echoed back into his ears: *trust no one, Henley*. But he had to start somewhere. Trust was in short supply.

But he knew he could trust John Marbury the most. Henley had been the best man at his wedding and was godfather to his kids. Had been at his side when Marbury had lost his wife, Mary, to cancer. There was too much water under the bridge and too much history to start rewriting it with an ink of suspicion.

The main section of the office had been a ballroom, then a semi-theater, before finally finding its true calling as Moscow Station. Cracks coursed down the walls, adding character to the sheets of forest green wallpaper that the previous station head had plastered over them. In the center of the room were four cubicles, one each for Aldridge, Wright, and Roslyn. The fourth workspace was free to welcome any visiting dignitaries or agents—one's definition may vary —but invariably was just a table full of files and random stationery. The left section was glass-walled with partitions; one was for Henley to use as his office, and the other was a meeting room. The front right section had the water cooler, the refrigerator, and provisions for tea and coffee. Marbury and Darcy had a separate workspace at the back, the tech room, where one would almost always find them. Well, Marbury, at least. Darcy didn't have the tenacity to warm a chair through the day.

"Where's Darcy?" Henley asked as he walked into the tech cabin. He hadn't set foot in the tech cave for ages; probably the last time had been when he had shown an important visitor around the office. It was small, cramped up with wires and equipment, and barely had enough wiggle room for Marbury and Darcy. Yet it seemed cozy, warm, and personal. Marbury had hung a picture of his late wife, a copy of his honors from university, and a rather old photograph of him and Henley outside Hagia Sophia in Istanbul. Marbury seemed like a loner if one went by the walls of the tech cave.

"Market. We needed supplies. Why?" Marbury said, not turning to look at Henley. He was hunched over a piece of radio equipment, tapping a series of signal patterns that communicated through the box, covertly, with other stations or with the handler of an asset.

"Just checking, not a crime, old sport. Care for a walk or d'you have something better to do?"

"Can I say no?"

The silence that followed was a cue. Marbury got up, took his overcoat, and started leaving the office. Henley was in tow.

The streetlights had just warmed up and glowed on the dark morning; a light powdering of snow had just covered the streets. Men and women dressed smartly in layers of warm clothes to protect themselves from the elements or hide themselves from prying eyes populated the street. The two Englishmen easily blended into the crowd and continued down the pavement toward *Anatoly's* —a Parisian-style cafe in the middle of the bustling business district, ably run by Anatoly, a loud, sweet-tongued baker turned businessman from Belarus.

"What's troubling you, old boy?" Marbury asked, lighting up two cigarettes at once. Henley took one, and the ends glowed, momentarily illuminating the wrinkled faces of the two spies as the dark skies entirely took control of the day.

"We have a problem," Henley said, taking a puff. The two men stood outside the bakery, customarily smoking a few cigarettes before setting up for coffee.

"Control on your arse again, complaining about our operations, work rate, and end product?"

"If only."

"He's gotten under your skin… what did he say?" Marbury said, signaling Anatoly behind the glass windows with two raised fingers. Anatoly got the message—two croissants and coffees. Henley gave him a quick recount of the London trip.

"You're fucking kidding?" Marbury coughed up the smoke that filled his lungs.

"Everyone is under suspicion. Including you, sport."

"Give me a day's notice before you mark me red. Get my assets in Switzerland lined up," Marbury laughed. Henley wasn't in the mood.

"Seriously, you're not considering it might be coming from within the house. Right?"

"Nothing is impossible. You know that."

Marbury could see the pain in Henley's eyes.

"Well, start digging somewhere," Marbury said, stubbing out his cigarette. He looked squarely at Henley, expecting instructions.

"We've been here, Marbury, quite a few times. We could go through every document and every history and dig through the lives of our lot. But it would take ages and do a lot of damage to morale. And it risks alerting the mole."

"True. What's the idea then?" Marbury asked.

Henley had a hint of a smile on his lips.

"Our man in India," Simon said.

"Tell me you are not asking our people to confess to the priest?" Marbury laughed.

"Hear me out. We ask the priest to run a special op and loop all our guys in. It would be a well-orchestrated, believable, high-profile plan."

"Only for it to be a ruse? To smoke the rat out?" Marbury asked.

"You are catching up now, sport," Henley said, taking another cigarette from the box. "We dish out specific information to every station member and look for where the smoke leaks out."

"Only our people?" Marbury asked, offended that they were already considering keeping the mole in Moscow.

"We throw a few bones to those in London as well," Henley said.

"More like it, old boy," Marbury said, his poker face giving away to a far more concerning look.

The two spies went into the bakery to warm cups of coffee, and a bloody big problem to solve.

Chapter 4
The Indian Station

Pondicherry, 1982

October in Pondicherry was the best time to be in this town—tucked away in the southeastern corner of India—every quaint little chapel, temple, or mosque along the winding roads adorned itself with hues of green, tiny lights, and garlands of flowers. After a torrid summer, autumn had arrived early at the doorsteps of the houses and little establishments that the simple people of Pondicherry called home.

If July and its rains stood for somber tones, puddled roads, and the pruning of forestry along the terrains of Pondicherry, October and its cold undertones called for celebrations and embracing the shedding of leaves, making way for new life. For Neil Alvares, October had a different meaning. Decades ago, his parents had left for France one October, leaving him with his grandfather, Martin. When Daniel and Jenny left Neil with him to find and build a better life in Europe, Martin found himself in a new role—that of a grandfather and a custodian. The chirpy kid they left behind replaced the void left by his son and daughter-in-law. Martin and Neil grew up together, one would say, learning the meaning of life in each other's company. Martin reprised his role as a parent and ended up doing a better job the second time around, and Neil grew up in Martin's image—to be a self-sufficient, strong individual. The Alvares family, originally from the coastal state of Goa, had long made Pondicherry their home.

The two shared a special bond. It was a friendship first, parenting later for Martin. They spoke to each other as peers.

Kashif, Martin's friend, had warned that Neil would never find his true calling if Martin didn't step back. He had paid heed to the advice and let his grandson flourish into the free-spirited, adventure-seeking person the kid wished to be.

Ten years back.

Alvares was twenty-five when he had first stepped into what was then a first for Pondicherry— an art gallery. Alvares was required to serve up a full spread of delicatessen at the art gallery—Martin, his grandfather, was the owner and chief baker at Martin's Corner— Pondicherry's most loved cafe and bakery. With eminent art patrons, connoisseurs, and enthusiasts poised to grace the event, Martin's Corner was the only bakery competent to serve good quality croissants, English crumpets, cold cuts, and top-of-the-line breakfast tea. Although a small city by Indian standards, it was a melting pot of cultures with its past of being a French colony in a country ruled by the British for over two centuries. Martin took pride in being able to bring about a culinary experience that was foreign to Pondicherry.

Of the several dignitaries that included state guests, royals, bureaucrats, and officers from the Indian Army, the most prominent—the showstoppers—were two females, Amrita Sher-Gil and Jamini Roy. For Alvares, a young impressionable man back then, women weren't known to be at the top of an industry and art, even less; India was a patriarchal society. Amrita Sher-Gil, who died a year later in 1973, employed a Post-Impressionist style of painting that she had learned at the Art Academy in France. She had evolved into an artist who was leading the Art Déco culture in the Asian continent and was prominent in her display of Indian miniatures in her work. Jamini Roy, another artist at the top of her game, was dishing out her work that involved pat paintings and European modern art with much aplomb and fanfare.

To Alvares, this was a completely new realm. While serving up the food at the event, he could catch glimpses of the artwork on display and the constant crackle, loud banter, and hushed admiration for the *pièce de résistance* from the artists. But what took him aback was the sheer grace and confidence the two female artists exuded as they spoke to each patron admiring their work. Alvares could sense the excitement that the awestruck art fans were feeling.

The galleria that housed the artwork was an ensemble of work from multiple budding artists of its time. The French governor had commissioned the work for developing a waterfront property that would resemble the sensationalism of the French Renaissance yet pragmatic enough to be part of the Pondicherry landscape. The then-resident French governor had asked for a building on the promenade as an ode to the Musée d'Orsay in Paris, his hometown.

The galleria was decked up that night. Adorning the promenade along the French Quarter, the art gallery was a sight to behold. A medley of colors and lights interplayed across the facade of the gallery. Admirers and casual observers alike could relish the visuals emanating from the building and the clear waters along the shoreline. Alvares was soaking up the entire atmosphere as the night progressed. The Chief Patron of the Galleria, Mr. Chatterjee, announced that the last hour of the display was on, and after that, the Galleria would shut down for a few private collectors to speak to the artists. Mr. Chatterjee took Alvares aside and calmly expressed his desire to see through the last hour with no goof-ups and asked Alvares to oversee the food and beverages for the private viewing.

As the clock struck nine and the final hour of the exhibit was underway, Alvares made his way to the private viewing room, where all the principal dignitaries were present alongside the two artists. Alvares took great care to be omnipresent for their needs and ensured that refreshments were offered to these high-profile visitors with minimal fuss. Alvares shadowed the guests in anticipation of learning more about the artworks. He stole a few glances at the portraits and brilliant art on display; he felt a feminine hand wrapping around his waist. The elegant figure of Ms. Amrita manifested itself in front of Alvares. Shortly, he was introduced to each of the fine artworks on display, escorted by Ms. Amrita.

Alvares was star-struck. He followed Amrita around like a schoolboy in a candy store, waiting to see which candy he got to choose from. All poise and class, Amrita, unhinged that she was in the company of Alvares—a complete misfit in the elegant group of patrons, was a sight to behold. The entire scene was artwork in itself, like a patch of film caught in color, while the whole movie was shot in black and white. Alvares drowned in this mysterious world, drawn into it by the most beautiful mermaid herself. *Amrita gave him a telling account of each of her works, how it came to be, and what it stood for. He was in love, with her and her art.*

Alvares realized he could see the entire world with an entirely different palette of colors and shapes. The kaleidoscope of his imagination was at work. He had never envisaged an hour of passionate and enchanting encounter with an incredible woman, and how she saw the world would completely change his perception of life. Amrita had put rose-tinted spectacles on Alvares, figuratively speaking; he saw things in a different color than the traditional black, white, and gray. For the first time in his life, he felt sheer joy, exhilaration, and ambition all the same time.

That night as he lay on his bed, recounting the day's events, Alvares realized he had found his true calling in his life, his Talisman, his Sikandar. Amrita had left him with one great piece of advice. She had said, "Neil, art need not always be expensive or come from a popular artist or has to be a jewel from the crown of a forgotten prince. Art can be found in the deepest trenches and darkest caves if you know what you are looking for. Go, find your Sikandar!"

As a kid growing up, Alvares had been fed with stories of detectives and their bravado. His mother would occasionally send books from France and Alvares would devour them with utmost enthusiasm whilst he imagined a life of high-voltage action. But the small town of Pondicherry was not a place to sate his appetite. But that all changed when Father Samuel walked into his life during a hot, unforgiving summer of 1973. Father Samuel Turner—the deacon at the Sacra Couer Church in Pondicherry. A man serving God and the British Secret Intelligence Service.

That same year, Sacra Coeur Church at Pondicherry, better known as Basilica of the Sacred Heart of Jesus, held a unique service for visitors from America and England who had set camp across a few cities, including Pondicherry. The visitors had been part of a government entourage tasked with scouting locations for a joint research project with the WHO and ICMR to explore areas concerning the health of the general population. They had already set to work in Delhi, Rajasthan, and nearby regions, and Pondicherry was touted to be the next.

In his spare time from his university work and internship at the local newspaper, Alvares often helped the church with accounts and any hand they would need during the weekends. That evening, right after a dinner hosted by the church for their guests, Alvares—together with Venkatesh, his hired help—was preparing for the church mass the next day. Venkatesh was cleaning the dishes, and Alvares was running the weekly accounts across the church gardens. Alvares heard some leaves rustling on the far end of the garden and quietly tip-toed toward the source. The conversation he overheard had his pulse rising.

"Are you sure they are studying the effects of *Aedes Aegypti* and not *Anopheles Stephensi*?" the silhouette of a taller man was reaching out to light the cigarette for the shorter, broader man. Alvares dared not to look at the faces that lit behind the tiny flame of the lighter. He maintained his vantage position.

"I'm sure. I commissioned a special batch of flies to be brought in to test their long-term effects."

"That's surprising. How come the GCMU is allowing us to do so? Shouldn't it have been the other way round?"

"We're in the middle of a Cold War. Any biological warfare starts with a series of experiments, and so does this one."

"What could be better than experimenting on foreign soil and not bearing the risk of affecting your people!" saying so, the shorter man, who seemed to be the other man's superior, started walking back toward the church foyer. Alvares held his position until he saw the two men and their silhouettes fade into the night. Alvares kept repeating the four absurd words he had heard all night. Venkatesh couldn't make any sense and was sure that the devil had possessed Alvares.

Alvares rushed the next day to Romain Rowland Library to research the two sets of words he had heard. He had scribbled the words he understood phonetically, and thus locating the exact spelling and meaning was a tiresome affair. He knew the library would not disappoint him as he struck gold in the zoology section.

Anopheles Stephensi, a type of mosquito, spread Malaria, while *Aedes Aegypti* caused Yellow fever, a deadly disease spreading through Africa. GCMU stood for Genetic Control of Mosquito Unit, created by the WHO and the ICMR. Alvares knew he was onto something. He started writing letters to the ICMU in Delhi but the letters were returned with a *'return to sender'*, which meant the packages were opened, contents read, and the reader conveniently had them sent back. He hit a brick wall every time he tried to force his way open.

Alvares had another shot at glory a few months later when the church hosted another farewell dinner for the same delegates that had visited them the last time around. But Alvares wasn't aware as the farewell dinner was privately hosted and oddly, secretive. Alvares and Jaggi, his best friend, were down a few drinks by the time he found out about the dinner.

With his senses betraying his usual composure when he needed them most, Alvares gatecrashed the party and went ludicrous. As chaos and loud noises ensued, the guests became uncomfortable as Alvares kept shouting, "Anal Stephen and Ass Egypt." In his mind, he was trying to pronounce the two mosquito species correctly, but the alcohol he had in his system betrayed him and his senses. To save face in front of the international guests, the local police had Alvares locked up overnight. Alvares was let off with a warning not to chase the guests again.

A few weeks later, the story was broken by PTI (Press Trust of India), although conveniently leaving out the names of the Brits and Americans, just mentioning *foreign forces*. When Alvares read the news piece, he was crestfallen. He was so near, yet so far from his Sikandar. He had almost unearthed an international controversy with a healthy dose of spy craft, biological warfare, CIA, and the conspiracy to it all by the Indian government. Someone had pulled strings, just in time, to deny him his glory—Father Samuel.

During the second Lent of the same year, Father Samuel had taken the complete reigns of the Sacra De Coeur Church in Pondicherry. His first order of business had been to assemble his crew and he approached Neil Alvares.

Initially, Alvares revolted and rejected the idea, and thought it was ridiculous that a priest could be a spy. But the more he spent time with the enigmatic priest, the more he was enamored and convinced this world was something he could call his own.

He could find the spark he was missing all his life, working for MI6 and Father Samuel. Neil Alvares signed up, and since that hot, brazen summer of 1973, he had been a part of the MI6 station in India. He had found his Sikandar, his true calling as the deputy command at the Indian station of the MI6.

Chapter 5
A Cold Handshake

Pondicherry, India

October, 1982

Sunday mass had finished early, thanks to the upcoming General Assembly elections. The weeks leading up to the elections had already seen loud claims, an odd fight between supporters, and the lavish processions that followed each of the candidates—this was a developing India at its weakest. Posters and wild claims of improvement had completely taken the streets of Pondicherry over from the competing political parties. Probably the days leading up to the election were the only time when the general people of Pondicherry felt any sense of power.

Father Samuel finished his duties at the church and retired early to his parsonage. The parsonage was beyond humble—a lavish two-bedroom house, a fully stocked kitchen, and a private study—all to house one priest. Religion had its sway, whatever the economic condition it presided over—this too was a developing India at its weakest. Over the years, Father Samuel had built one of the bedrooms into a fully functioning file room that doubled up as a communication room filled with state-of-the-art communications equipment.

Earlier in the evening, *La Casablanca*—a freighter from Morocco—had docked at the Pondicherry Port. The head of the shipping company that operated *La Casablanca,* Jonathan Banks, was one of a select few Father Samuel trusted outside the Circus. Banks, an Englishman with a French wife, had struck gold in Morocco and settled there to set up his shipping business and played the role of a courier as and when the MI6 came calling. Banks was the babysitter when Samuel Turner ran an op in Casablanca in the 60s—a high-profile target from German intelligence was spotted in Morocco, and the MI6 had him picked up from the airport and interrogated him for 2 days. Banks was running local shipping operations and gladly arranged for one of his shipping containers to be the holding cell while Turner interrogated the possible German defector. Although the German lead turned out to be a damp squib, Turner earmarked and cultivated Banks as a possible long-term ally. Over the years, Banks widened his shipping routes, and Father Samuel was able to use his ships to transport covert messages and documents across the world.

Mr. Vishwa, one of the few locals Father Samuel employed in Pondicherry as a courier, had called at the parsonage this morning to inform that La Casablanca was due to arrive in a couple of hours. *Package dropped at La Casablanca, arriving at Moscow at 16:00 in three days from now*—Father Samuel had wired Simon Henley. It was unlike the priest to send comms of a covert drop before it happened; he trusted Alvares to get the job done. Now to find Alvares quickly, Father Samuel thought and started his Jeep. But first, he needed to signal to Banks that a drop was to happen later that night.

The mob of people on the roads from the election campaigns had made the journey difficult, and all the prying eyes would make it almost impossible for the live drop to happen around the port. La Casablanca was slated to leave the shores early in the morning.

When he reached the port, Mr. Vishwa escorted him toward the freight ship, and Father Samuel looked around, hoping to spot Banks. But the dock was relatively deserted. Given the time of the day, it was likely the men had hopped into the city for a drink. Father Samuel made his way to the hull of the ship and walked toward the propeller section. He knew the crew would do a routine check, and importantly, Banks would. Father Samuel took out a chalk and made a mark. A cross, and the shape of a mountain with an 'N' and an arrow. He added a small 'S' as a postscript. Hopefully, Banks would understand the signal—*live drop will not happen at the port, but rather at the mountains. Come from the north end. Turner.*

Job done, he headed off to find Alvares at his grandfather's bakery.

※

The warm, sweet smell of freshly baked bread hit Father Samuel as he walked into the bakery. Father Samuel gave a quick wink to Alvares, who sat behind the counter cashing up the till, and took a seat near the windows.

"What brings you here on a Sunday, Father?" Alvares asked as he pulled a chair and sat next to the priest.

"I need you to make a drop."

"When?"

"Tonight."

Neil Alvares looked briefly shocked.

"Hope I'm not asking too much," Father Samuel said, adjusting his glasses. Next to the Bible that he'd placed on the table lay a small package that Alvares quickly retrieved.

"Guessing it can't wait?" Alvares wasn't prepared for an encore so soon. He had been on assignment just a couple of days back to Vellore.

"You know the drill, Alvares." Father Samuel sounded stern. He had this capacity to move from soft to menacing in a heartbeat.

"There's a wedding tomorrow, and the bakery's been overloaded. I was planning to pull an all-nighter to help

Martin and Khan," Neil said, "But I guess I can take a quick trip to the port."

"No can do. Too busy. Elections, remember Alvares."

"Where is the drop, then?"

"Our friend will meet you at the hill from the north end of the beach. His ship is docked for a few more hours and leaves at 04:00. The drop time is uncertain, but I promised him we would keep vigil through the night," Father Samuel lied. He couldn't be sure Banks would see and understand the change of plans. He needed Neil to stay put all night. Father Samuel needed the time to prepare for an alternate option to make the drop if Banks didn't turn up. *Shakuntala, the safe house, would have to come into play.*

"I'd better get going then," Alvares said and pushed the chair back. "Martin, Father Samuel's here. One Bun Maska and chai please!" he yelled and walked toward the till.

"*Merci*, Alvares. Take the day off tomorrow if you wish."

"Oh, I will."

❦

Neil Alvares kept looking at his Omega, constantly reminding himself that this would be a long arduous night. Nervously, he kept fidgeting with the curved end links. His wristwatch was his prized possession, it stood for everything that he wanted to be: refined, elegant, precious, and always on time. The night sky had a black cherry flavor to it with a large expanse of stars overlooking Pondicherry's landscape. Neil tried hard to focus, a long week taking its toll, as the moon rose against the backdrop of the Gothic-Renaissance architecture of the Eglise de Sacra Coeur Church. The church was a long-standing tourist attraction of Pondicherry, with its interiors depicting the life of Jesus Christ through its arcane stained-glass panels. The church gave enough photo opportunities to aspiring photographers and visitors with its twin spires, imposing facades, elaborate artistry, and exquisite craftsmanship.

The church wasn't the only place of worship that found prominence under French rule. All religions found equal status under the almighty French. The only disdain and point of discord for the Indians was the division of the city into *White Town* and *Black Town*. Alvares, being the rebel while growing up, would often scamper to the other side of the town, much to the chagrin of his father. The vagabond he was, Alvares would bike around Lake Ousteri with his friends from school, along the northeastern side of the city, smartly evading any prying eyes, and hop off to Bharathi Park on the eastern side of the town, the French side of Pondicherry. These escapades were his lifeline and his only way of letting out steam, releasing the exasperations that chained the youth of those days.

Alvares drummed up a bit of sound on his Emerson Radio, keeping the volume low to avoid alerting a passer-by or an unfriendly night creature. The midnight program served the needs of the souls that needed it most; *the heartbroken and the ones with unrequited love, of which there were quite plenty in Pondicherry*. Romantic songs, stories of dark desires, forgotten friends, and homages of poets long dead, with an occasional intervention of the local and international news that allowed the radio station to maintain a healthy roster of sponsors.

As the life and times of one of South India's eminent lyricists drew to its conclusion, the news break brought some cheer for Alvares. The squad for the Indian One Day International cricket team for the World Cup to be held next year in England was being announced. The third edition of the competition interested every cricketing nation, mainly because of the dominance shown by the West Indians during the first two. Everyone wanted to beat them, though no one felt they had the slightest chance of doing so.

Alvares had grown up on stories of cricket and how it had picked up in India. His grandfather, a devout cricket follower, instilled in a young Alvares a burning passion for the game. One of his favorite memories was Martin's account of the incredible match between the English and Indian teams—a test match. He could sense the excitement in his grandfather's breath and the sheer joy and exhilaration when he spoke of the fantastic scenes he witnessed at the Bombay stadium back in 1962. The hued fabrics and grandeur spoke of the fashioned upper echelons of Bombay, dominated by the Parsi community during the sixties, and the memory of the expanse of green on the ground adorned by the strip of brown in the center with its players, felt all livid and fresh as Martin recounted those events to him. All seemed incredibly real yet far too imaginative for a boy his age.

Neil Alvares took another look at his watch. It had been four hours since he took cover at the forest's edge. Alvares had been working alongside Father Samuel for a decade now— his able deputy. He ran drop-offs, communicated to the other stations, ran key ops from the safe house, managed the incoming and outgoing agents who were on *R and R,* provided cover when the priest had to be away for days, and managed the communication with the London headquarters of MI6 when needed. He knew what the rest in Pondicherry didn't about Father Samuel. Father Samuel, the chief vicar of the Sacra Coeur was a career spy and the Station Chief of MI6 in India. When Shakuntala, the safe house came to be 6 years back, Neil took over as the trusted deputy and a major voice in how MI6s operation was run in India. When Alvares started off, Father Samuel had taken a big bet on a young man with smarts and guile. But there was a lot to learn and prove. Over the last ten years, Neil had taken over the operations for the Indian station and worked in tandem with the Middle East,

Africa, and South American stations of the MI6. *Europe and Russia were still a larger part of the remit for Father Samuel and the Indian station.*

Alvares opened the package that he had been carrying for the drop. *This was a first.* Inside the box were three sets of maps, machine drawings, and a list of parts for manufacturing. Usually for these drops he would carry a simple letter with coded messages or accompany an agent from the India Station, cash to launder, or sometimes just go with the priest to meet their visiting counterparts. Something big was going down in Moscow, he thought. This was probably the first time he was running an op that involved the Moscow Station.

Just as he was preparing to wrap up and call it a day, he saw a distant silhouette walking toward him. A tall man in a gray overcoat and gum boots greeted him. Alvares rehearsed the sequence of phrases to identify his visitor.

"Morning! The best way to the train station?" the lanky gentleman asked Alvares.

"You could walk or hike; it's about ten miles."

"Boy, that's far. But I could use the exercise," the man said.

Alvares had a sense of relief. The man had just responded with the right identification code—*exercise*.

"About time. I thought this night would go to waste," Alvares said.

"Had to excuse myself from the crew. The lads were pissed as farts and three sheets to the wind and took a while. But here I am!" Banks said.

"I can imagine. The city has been unusually busy; it took me a while to go black, too."

Banks nodded in appreciation. "The priest gave you something, I believe?"

Alvares returned to his hideout, brought the box, and handed it to Banks.

"Thank you, I hope we cross paths again."

I hope so too, thought Alvares. He wanted in on the action that was to go down in Moscow.

Chapter 6
The Orchestrator

Simon Henley was feeling a tad more confident that he could see his station through these tumultuous times. Father Samuel was an able ally, someone he could lean on. It was still his show, but now he had a sidekick. He quickly understood that the role he was to play was that of an orchestrator and let others do his bidding and the legwork involved in the modern iteration of this spy game. He did not have the time or the energy to run the show alone. A cable had come in the morning from the priest. The package that would set the ball rolling was on its way to the Novorossiysk Sea Ports from Pondicherry.

Henley sat in his home office with a stack of files that he had brought back from the office. He worked through Saturday and Sunday morning. He needed to get ahead of the curve and see all the pieces of the puzzle. Thanks to Roslyn, the file room was well-maintained and indexed. The stack of files was everything he could accumulate on the Big Three in London. His first instinct was to see if the leak was coming from London. Proving there was a leak might be a completely different task altogether, but he had to start somewhere. Engels, Maeston, and Smith had quite distinguished careers in the Secret Service, and for good reason—they were cautious and smart operators. He didn't expect to see glaring holes in their past but having read the files he had a better understanding of these men and how they plied their trade. If he knew one thing from his time in the intelligence business, every man or woman in the service had a blind side, he just had to look for it.

Dick Engels, the Head of Accounts and Control's top lieutenant now, was the most inconspicuous man you would find in the MI6. He was the puppeteer who was pulling ranks, people, and money for the MI6 operations across the globe. Engels had Control's ears. He was the man tracing the money, deploying it to different stations, laundering it for the scalp hunters (who worked bottom of the pyramid in the echelons of the MI6 structure), its whereabouts, and the efficacy of budgets consumed in the espionage operations. A man of such influence and proximity to money was as good a suspect as one could be; for Henley. He was not born rich but had proper schooling, worked his way to the top, had a stable marriage, and a high functioning work. *His Jaguar was a major inflection point in his persona, Henley thought.* The sudden splurge of wealth could either mean a mid-life crisis or he had just got his hands on new wealth. That was never a good case.

Jim Maeston, the permanent secretary, was the conduit between Control and the Prime Minister. This was a man who built his career playing both sides. A brilliant strategist and statesman, he had garnered a reputation of being the MI6's and State's man Friday, stepping into minefields to handle a sticky situation and coming out unscathed. He played the game the old way—slow yet sure. Henley's problem with him was that he could never make out his true intention—was he serving the MI6 or the man in the highest position? There was a conflict in his allegiance, but something he brilliantly maneuvered and kept a tight lid on. Maeston was the lowest on Simon's list of suspects in London.

Steve Smith, Commander of London station and head of the scalp hunters, was the man with the highest ambition. It was no secret that he wanted Control's job. He himself made it public— pompous and confident. London and Moscow stations were at loggerheads for years. They were both the most important stations for the MI6. It would do Smith a world of good if Moscow and Control were riddled with a mole problem and came down crashing. Smith was a man who would leave no stone unturned to meet his ultimate goal. But was he ambitious enough to hurt the MI6 in the process?

Each man at the top of the Circus had a reason to be the mole, the leak, or the perpetrator. Whether it was a hunch, a conjecture, or a tiny piece of evidence to nail the bastard, Henley knew it would not be easy to prove it. The stack of files could only yield the motivation each one had, but no proof or a link. He had to get beyond the files and dig deeper into their undocumented pasts. He needed to make decisions on facts and information that were beyond these files. He knew just the man for that—Graeme Hicks.

Hicks, Henley's mentor and a good friend, had retired as the Head of Records at the MI6 in 1975. Having left the service a few years ago, Hicks was now living a simple and happy life with his wife—empty nesters, and enjoying the last few laps that life had to offer. Henley picked up the phone and dialed Hick's phone in Islington, North London.

"Old sport, this is Henley."

"Simon! What a pleasant surprise! How was your London trip?"

"Why am I not surprised that you got to know I was in London," Henley said and smiled. There was a reason this man was his mentor. Hicks was the most connected man in London and though retired, still had an ear on the ground when it came to Circus.

"Did Control behave well?" Hicks gave a laugh.

"Control has not slowed down a wee bit, rather getting sharper. I am sorry to disappoint those who are waiting for his downfall."

"Smith must be praying his ass off to see that day come," Hicks said.

"About Smith, I need your help, old sport."

"Tell me, if it's in my power, you shall have it."

"Well, not just Smith, in fact, the Big Three."

"Looking for dirt, are we?" Hicks said.

"Not sure what I am looking for, old sport. I have a problem in Moscow and I need to know if any of the roads lead to Engels, Maeston, or Smith."

"You won't find anything in the files, I can tell you that," Hicks added.

"I realized that, hence this call. I need to lean on your memory and your network of scalp hunters. They are the record keepers of the dirt that remains undocumented after all," Henley said. Hicks was the outgoing head of scalp hunters and head of records before Smith and Engels took over those roles. But they could not replace Hicks' incredible memory and the decades he spent at MI6.

"I will see what I can do, Simon."

"Thanks, old sport. Do you need anything?" Henley asked.

"Nothing. In fact, a small bit if you can. Remember Mike?"

"The scalp hunter from Budapest?"

"Yes. He has been on the sidelines for a while. He has been on the loose for a while and is looking to bring his life back on track."

"Is he still in Budapest?" Simon asked. Mike could possibly be a resource he could use discreetly.

"He is in Vienna these days. Can you give him some stuff to do, probably that pays him off a bit?"

"He is of no use to me in Vienna. Can you have him come down to Moscow?"

"That can be arranged. He will be there by tomorrow," Hicks said. Scalp hunters carried multiple identities to allow them to travel across Europe and Asia.

"Keep it discrete, Hicks. I don't want Smith to catch wind of this," Henley said, and cut the call. Later that night Hicks called and confirmed Mike's arrival in Moscow and the telephone number of his hotel.

The next day.

Simon knew Michael 'Mike' Moore to be street smart and with the right motivations could run a tight ship. But most of all, he knew Mike could keep this from his boss, Steve Smith. Hicks was Mike's boss when he ran the scalp hunters before Smith took over. Moore was in a sticky situation in Prague a few years back and Hicks had called Simon for a quick fix of the problem and get Moore out. He never questioned Hicks for this strange request. Trust him to return the favor someday, Hicks had assured Simon. Today was the day.

Henley ordered a cognac as he waited by the bar across the Moscow Central. Mike, early forties, handsome face, and a penchant for alcohol, was a thorough MI6 scalp hunter. Scalp hunters—those who did the rough job for the agency while the top-tier spies did the counter-intelligence behind a desk were a unique species. These were men on the field, often engaging in risky activities and getting their hands dirty. Mike had the physique and the tenacity to be a damn good scalp hunter. But his temper had often found the wrong end of the stick with his boss—Smith. *Transfer to Vienna was the punishment.*

Henley had a particular job that he wanted Mike to do. Simon wanted to bring Ros into the inner circle of this mole hunt. But, he needed to test her first.

"This is her house address. She leaves for work at 9 am, sharp" Henley said and handed over a piece of paper to Mike. Mike could easily pass for someone in his late twenties. In some ways, he was the cheaper version of Stuart Wright. With a leather jacket, a cravat, and a Rolex, probably something he snicked from Vienna. Mike was all ears.

"Got you, Chief."

"This is a thousand pounds and a key," Henley said and discreetly passed a packet under the table. The bar was busy that evening and hardly anyone would have noticed, if not for Mike's loud ensemble of jacket and a pair of Nikes. *Mike can be a loose wire, but he respects you, use that,* Hicks had said.

Mike quickly took the envelope and hid it in the inner pockets of his jacket. *At least that embarrassing piece of clothing came to some use.* Henley was old school and dressed as such.

"When she leaves, use the spare key to get into her house and drop the package on her desk in the study."

"Yes sir," Mike said and called the server. He ordered a round of cognac for Simon and some salmon rolls for himself. *That was odd,* Simon thought. Mike had not touched alcohol the entire evening.

"Listen carefully, Mike. This is important. Follow her for the next two days. When she leaves from her home all the way to the office. Follow her everywhere, and report back to me in three days."

"You got it," Mike said and waited. He wanted to know what was in this for him—a true scalp hunter that scourges the bottom to find his food.

"And if you get this right, and I get what I want out of this, that thousand pounds is yours," Simon said.

Mike smiled. "Consider it done boss," he said.

"And don't get caught following her, will you," Henley said and left Mike to enjoy his meal.

Henley quickly moved to the next part of his orchestration plan. The package from the priest was due to reach NSP and he could only trust one person to get the contents safely to him—John Marbury.

John Marbury had endured a sleepless night. Henley had ordered him over to NSP to receive a package from the priest. It took him a full twenty-four hours to reach the port. Marbury had to plan a longer route, multiple starts and stops, just to ensure he could drop any counter surveillance behind and 'go black'. He took a bus ride to the nearby bus terminal, doubled back into the city on the train, and got off at Moscow Central. From Moscow Central, he took a rental car and drove 200 miles to reach Kropotkin. From Kropotkin, he walked for three kilometers to reach the Kropotkin bus station, took the last bus at 10 pm, and finally made it to Novorossiysk Sea Ports.

Henley needs to get me a raise for doing this, Marbury thought. He patted his pocket. *I forgot the bloody ID card!* He cursed himself. As ever, Roslyn had prepared his papers. He was supposed to be a cultural attaché of the British Embassy, here to receive a very special artifact from Moroccan royalty. But now he would have to find a new way inside the ports.

A bribe would be the best option, and wouldn't leave a paper trail. He found an audience with the port's assistant manager, Mr. Vladimir, who was now a few thousand Rubles richer and let Marbury inside. For a bit more, he even offered to show Marbury around the port.

"I'll take you up on your offer next time," John said and discreetly moved to Dock Five to wait for *La Casablanca*.

Chapter 7
The Moscow Station

Our doubts are traitors and make us lose the good we might oft win by fearing to attempt.

– William Shakespeare.

Simon Henley was walking frantically across his office. An art aficionado, he had collected many treasures and trophies during his life and had brought them along when he set sail for Moscow. The long conversation earlier in the day with the Big Three in London had thrown him off balance.

They had been in a menacing mood and made no bones of their displeasure. Accounts, agent reporting, and the counter-surveillance materials from Tesla—or lack thereof in recent months —all had been discussed. Moscow Station should have dealt with these 'situations' was the majority verdict. Henley was to blame.

The mole hunt was still kept under wraps from everyone in London except Control, and Henley knew he had to withstand the questioning and the countless debriefs the Big Three demanded about his operations. For them, it was business as usual. Moscow had always been a hot topic—the center of attention and Control's Achilles' heel. If anyone had ambitions to sit on Control's chair, they would have to seize Moscow Station first.

British spies going rogue was not a novelty; it was well documented in the history books that the service had had its fair share of important, high-ranking officials turning traitors and selling secrets to the Germans and Russians. But the service had enjoyed a few good years of peacetime when it came to double agents. They probably dropped their guard, Henley thought. But deep down he knew that the KGB just let them believe that it was peacetime. They were building a solid network of counter-spies and agents, slowly and surely, just enough to fly under the radar. Simon knew this was a problem that had landed at his doorstep, whether he liked it or not.

To have a mole operate right under your nose, and for a while at that, was a failure tantamount to treason in Simon's eyes. It was a systemic failure that led to this. How on earth was his team not informed that those agents were to land in Moscow? Did Control hide that? Or was it an oversight? Every reason seemed unfathomable, yet, espionage had taught him one thing—there are always hidden intentions and agendas at play. But this time, he knew how to play the game. He was not one to play the politics of it, until now. But the time had come. Henley realized that some sacrifices would have to be made. If he were to continue to dig deeper and find the mole, he would have to eventually throw a big name to the dogs to distract them and make them believe that they are safe. He knew just the big name for the occasion. A scapegoat to bear the cross—only till he could land the mole. He had briefed Control on the overarching plan but spared him the specifics. He needed cover if this went south. Patriotism came with its share of scapegoats, especially the higher you go up the ladder.

He had earmarked someone he knew would have the required impact and appease the dogs— Roslyn. The irreplaceable Roslyn was the heart of the operations at Moscow Station. If there was someone big enough who could take the fall, it was her. But he held the cards close to his chest. Trust was the highest card in the deck. When the time comes, he would have to position Ros as the 'doubt'. He knew this was the immoral route to catching the mole. But if he was to operate in silence without alerting the mole, he had to position someone as the center of doubt. That was his best bet—to catch the mole when he felt safe and would be prone to drop his guard and make a mistake. And when the time comes, he knows how to get Ros out of the cages. Until then, she might have to be the decoy.

Henley knew this wasn't the right choice but he didn't have many options. He needed to buy time to find the mole and put it to rest. Besides him, only Marbury knew the plan. And the priest. Before Ros could be the fall guy, he had to make sure that she wasn't the mole herself— that would be an epic failure. Constantin Shelby, his predecessor, was ousted when the London office found his secretary had a checkered communist past. He had quite a laugh, and his mates, at the expense of Shelby and Rosamund. To have his assistant as the mole would bring shame to his entire family—notwithstanding the oblivion he would be sent to. Shelby had been long forgotten and now was serving as the trade officer at the Panama consulate.

It was a beautiful sunny day in Moscow. The cloud cover had lifted, snow had stopped for a while, and the people were out in the streets soaking in the sun. Henley walked past a few kids playing footie. He almost wanted to join the kids and kick the ball, remembering his days at the junior camp at his boyhood club, Arsenal, the second love of his life. The sights lifted him; a big day lay ahead. Our little team grows to three, hopefully, Henley thought. The British Embassy looked grand compared to the nearby buildings but only when you step in, you feel that the building has decayed—symbolic of the state of affairs. He quietly made it to the backside of the building to the designated smoking zone. *Irony,* he thought.

Henley took out his pocket watch, puffed a warm breath onto the acrylic glass dome, and cleaned it with a muslin kerchief he carried all the time. He took out the Cuban gifted by his sons, cut the ends, and lit the cigar. Not that he couldn't smoke inside. Roslyn always took the back entrance. He wanted to see her before she entered the office. Look her straight into the eyes. One look and I would know, Henley thought. Henley could see Roslyn from afar; her slender figure and gait were unmistakable. He threw the cigar and squashed it with his boots.

"You are in early," Roslyn said. She took a cigarette from her purse and looked at the rush of children going to school.

"I miss football."

"I miss my boy," Roslyn said.

"He would have been now, what… thirty-two?" Simon asked.

"Thirty-five"

"Taken too soon, Ros."

"Beautiful day," Roslyn said, and she lit up another cigarette.

"You're on a roll this morning."

"Not as much as you lads. Marbury back yet?"

"Should be back today."

"Since when has Marbury been running off-the-books assignments? We already have enough with Aldridge and Wright running around. Another of Control's whimsies, I suppose?"

"How do you mean?"

"You go off to London, cut short your trip to Turks and Caicos, and come back here. Now Marbury goes off unannounced, what else could it be?"

Simon looked her in the eyes, straight-faced. Had he underestimated her? Her poker face was notorious. Every time they played, Ros took the pot. They stood at the same place for another few minutes and watched people get on with their lives as their own were battling for survival in rough seas. There was an odd silence.

Roslyn turned and looked at Henley. She took out a brown envelope and handed it to Henley.

"What's this?"

"I think you know."

"What did you expect, Ros?"

"Well, some measure of trust."

"You know I do."

"Then why this charade, Henley?" she asked, looking straight into Henley's weary eyes.

"We're under threat," he confessed. "and unlike before, this one has left some dead agents behind."

Roslyn said nothing and continued to look Henley in the eye.

"I wanted to see if you still have the sharpness and the tenacity. I need you at the top of your game if we need to beat this threat. This one will need us to battle beyond the desks. I need those I trust to help me on the field."

The streets had cleared, the sun had gone back to hiding, and a large shadow of the fir tree cast on them. Henley put back his overcoat and gave her a rundown of the events over the past few weeks.

"I suppose John's out there to prove himself as well? Or is he a suspect?" she asked.

"Neither." Simon wasn't prepared to bring her fully into the fold. She had to know enough to help move the operation forward.

"What do you need from me?" Ros asked.

"I need you to sieve through all the case materials, assignments, transcripts, and communications we have on record from Darcy, Wright, and Aldridge," Henley lit another cigarette and felt the nicotine sharpen his focus.

"Make copies of what you find and have it on my desk at the earliest."

"As you say, Henley."

"Strictly for my eyes only, Ros," he said, but he knew he didn't need to. She knew the playbook. Roslyn went into the office, and Henley made a quick phone call to Mike letting him know where to pick up the brown envelope with the cash—his reward.

After the Second World War, espionage changed, especially on the Russian side. Instead of blatant spying and counter-surveillance, which often led to nothing, the KGB started embedding spies into the fabric of Western society. Every Russian Embassy worldwide had turned into a *Rezidentura* with more spies than actual diplomats at work in the guise of diplomats, or political attachés, graced with diplomatic immunity which came in useful if push came to shove.

Moscow Station was built right into the British Embassy in Moscow. A monolithic structure in the heart of Moscow, the embassy building stood as a symbol of the power and presence of the British government. The file room was in stark contrast to the rest of the building, though. The smell was getting on Roslyn's nerves. Roslyn lit up the darkroom. She had brought a pot of freshly roasted coffee to try to mask some of the damp smell, but it wasn't very effective.

She started to browse through the files she had pulled on her colleagues. It was interesting to read them. Spies typically weren't very open about their pasts. She never knew Darcy was at the MI5 London station before making his way through Nairobi and Budapest, and finally to Moscow with the MI6. She'd thought he was a novice; she was wrong to underestimate Darcy. And Marbury had a long winding road to Moscow, too. Wright was Wright; on paper, he looked and felt the part.

She found nothing particularly out of place but highlighted certain portions for Henley to double-check.

Oddly, the stack of files on Keith Aldridge was small. She expected a large dossier, given his fast-track promotions, achievements, and folklore of his talents brewing up in the Circus. Probably because he had moved to the center recently. Ten years in espionage was 'barely getting started'. Most of the files and papers alluded to his work with Tesla over the last five years.

The main task of the Moscow Station was to build an intelligence network deep within the walls of the Kremlin, a bold high-risk high-reward strategy. Before Tesla, Moscow Station had just one significant asset, Mikhail Gordievsky, and had enjoyed a few successes on the other end, closing down KGB agents across Hungary, Poland, and Finland, who were actively feeding the KGB with information.

The Moscow Station had a great asset in Mikhail Gordievsky, codenamed 'Lupin' after the legendary fictional gentleman thief—Arsène Lupin of France. Mikhail had served as an invaluable double agent for over a decade until his exfiltration from Soviet Russia in 1973. The impact Mikhail had with his dissemination of Russia's defense strategy and counter-intelligence information for the Brits on Russia's nuclear prowess and advancements far superseded the money the Brits gave to Mikhail in exchange for his treachery to his country. The MI6 had hoped to land another agent embedded deep within the KGB, *the Soviet Intelligence Agency*, who could continue the work started by Mikhail. But the KGB had tightened up after the Gordievsky debacle. The well had dried up. It was years before they could even have a sniff at another top-tier double agent. But Tesla had changed it all.

Tesla had been on the payroll since 1978, and in the last 5 years, the partnership between Moscow Station and Tesla could be described, at best, as tumultuous. He was invaluable; top-of-the-line quality in his work product, relentless efforts in supplying massive quantities of KGB intelligence, and impeccable workmanship in keeping his identity intact from the KGB hierarchy. Money, oddly, was never discussed nor seemed to inspire him. Henley and the others had a bet on his intentions—money, sex, hatred, all were on the table. Keith, his handler, had a different opinion. *Revenge.*

Roslyn cracked her neck. It had been a long, tense day. Every page she flipped, she expected to find something that wasn't right. She separated the final files into two stacks. One with Aldridge and the debriefing notes of his time in Istanbul before moving to Moscow, and the second stack—his notes on running Tesla. The first stack illustrated why Aldridge found it easy in the espionage business—he was sharp, single-minded, and tenacious.

The stack on Tesla was filled with surveillance run notes, thoughts on Tesla, and how the Moscow Center could further their cause using Tesla's deep-rooted hatred toward his own country, a factual and sweet note about Tesla's wife, Helena, and their kid. It included a brief on a medical emergency for their kid the couple had to endure and found help from the MI5, and the rest were on the financial arrangements and credit notes related to Tesla's operation.

Next to the embassy, the church bells rang loud and clear. Roslyn was happy that the task got done just in time for her to reach home and retire to bed with a glass of wine and her daily soap on the television. She quickly prepared a summary note and index cards, copied the important and noteworthy files, and carefully kept them inside the locker in the boss's chambers.

She felt a huge sigh of relief. None of her boys had anything wrong going on, at least in her eyes. Roslyn walked past the office and empty tables—the rest had left already. She swiftly locked up behind her and scurried back to her apartment.

Chapter 8
Otto and Tesla

Keith Aldridge had been in Moscow Station for four years. He had been a faithful servant of Her Majesty's Secret Service for over a decade, working as a case officer across Europe. But this was his first assignment to the darker side of espionage and clandestine business. Aldridge and his wife, Clarise, had moved to Russia with their one-year-old daughter, Esther, in tow. Aldridge was in Russia in an official capacity as the Chief of Trade Relations between Britain and Russia. An exhaustive and elaborate title for an elite espionage operative.

MI6 needed to replace Gordievsky with another source of covert intelligence, especially on the defense equipment, missile technology, and artillery scan developments that were happening at a rapid pace in Soviet Russia. Moscow Station had been on the lookout for agents within the KGB and GRU. Wright was running an agent in the field who had been valuable, but not the game-changer Control wanted. MI6 profiled Russian operatives with an inclination toward the West for lifestyle, glamor, and enamored by the money that could be on offer. But the efforts of Simon Henley and his crew had borne no tangible results over the last few years. The few nuggets of information they'd extracted were nothing more than 'chicken feed'.

It had been almost five years since they had decommissioned and retired Mikhail. The KGB had restructured internally to ensure a frequent rotation of its agents in the *Rezidentura*. Just as MI6 had put out feelers, made contact, and warmed up potential assets, they would be shipped off to a different location. The revolving door of diplomats was a Russian roulette of a different kind.

In the spring of 1978, MI6 had struck gold by pure happenstance. Budapest Station, which oversaw the covert operations in the Eastern Soviet states, had got wind of a potential defector. They had been receiving packages and drop-offs with notes, newspaper cuttings, and communist manifestos for six months.

Each of the six packages had the same message, coded in different styles and transcripts. But the Budapest Station couldn't break them, so sent them over to Istanbul to their encryption expert; Keith Aldridge. When the code was finally broken, it repeatedly alluded to the same, simple message:

I have information that you would be interested in. I want to speak to Moscow Station.

Moscow Station mobilized, with Henley taking the lead. Swift arrangements were made for a rendezvous. But MI6 in Moscow had a problem. All its case officers were well known to the KGB, and it was complicated to drop the tight surveillance the KGB had on them. If this resource was even half as valuable as Mikhail, then the Moscow Center had to be intelligent and cautious in cultivating and harnessing this prospective double agent. The only way to do this was to bring in a fresh case officer. The obvious choice was Keith Aldridge. Control reassigned him to Moscow to make the first contact.

Viktor Ivanov, who was later codenamed 'Tesla', was a communications expert and electrical engineer who had been working with the KGB for twenty years. The son of a veteran KGB agent, Viktor was drafted into the KGB at a young age. He grew up on the stories of Leninism and the atrocities of the West. At just age ten, he had read the entire communist Manifesto. His young mind was imprinted with the ideologies of communism and its call to unify the working population of Europe to achieve a genuinely liberating socio-economic revolution. It was more gospel than a manifesto for the young Ivanov.

Viktor made big strides early in his KGB career. He had a head start, for his proficiency in English and his capabilities in learning new and advanced communications technology that Russian engineers were building. His background in engineering proved to be a valuable asset. A brief training stint followed, and the higher-ups earmarked their top-performing trainees for more extraordinary things. In 1976, Viktor and his wife, Helena, moved to the *Rezidentura* in Hungary, serving as the Russian attaché for the technology partnership between Russia and Hungary.

Viktor and Helena were enjoying their life in Budapest. Being a Soviet State, Hungary offered all the privileges of being a Russian, yet being closer to the powerful nations in Europe, gave them the modernism and glamor of the Western world. They were living the dream. A beautiful house, the birth of their daughter, and the exciting work that got Viktor promoted at a breathtaking pace were all working out well for the Ivanovs. The upper echelons of the KGB noticed Viktor's rise to the top, and he was swiftly brought into the inner ring of trusted KGB lieutenants with special privileges, access to highly classified information, and the spy network of the KGB across Europe and Latin America. He was sitting on the most extensive intelligence dossier of the KGB operations in Europe.

But the start of 1978 changed everything. A tragic incident changed the course of life that the Ivanovs had envisioned for themselves. Viktor's daughter was diagnosed with a rare, life-threatening condition. Immediate medical attention was needed, and all efforts to go back to Russia for treatment received a backlash from the higher-ups. Viktor was in the middle of a massive operation at his *Rezidentura*. They needed him to continue at all costs. Notwithstanding the sensitive and urgent work that required his presence, with no support from Moscow, Viktor took a leave of absence and secretly took his daughter to Britain for treatment. The British at first delayed the procedure, citing issues in paperwork, but eventually handled the case, with MI5 running the op. Their daughter survived but with lifelong after-effects of the surgery. Once his daughter was out of immediate danger, he flew back to Hungary to resume operations. The Russian intelligence didn't show any remorse for their inaction, nor did they further inquire about his daughter's well-being. *That was the tipping point.*

Over the next few months, Viktor distanced himself from his work. The deeper he delved into the policies and the functioning of the KGB, the more he saw the fallacies in the principles of Soviet Russia that he so dearly upheld. Viktor started taking time off to read about the West, and the damage the ongoing Cold War could have on future generations, and finally, he saw the antagonist he could become if he continued without protest or making a significant impact.

Viktor Ivanov had become a dissident at heart and wanted to correct the future. The values he had fought against, the duplicity and corruption, he saw developing in Moscow. And he was prepared to rebel against the very institution he was part of. He forced a move back to Moscow to work on military technology and signals intelligence, which meant he would have far greater access to the KGB's operations than he had in Budapest.

When Keith Aldridge joined the Moscow Station, there were still doubts whether they had indeed landed a major double agent in Tesla. Henley was wary of the smarts and guile with which the KGB had been operating, and Tesla might well be a Trojan horse. Aldridge knew this was going to be an arduous task—to vet a double agent in the first meet with very little proof to show either way. But he backed himself to figure this out.

Keith Aldridge's first few weeks at Moscow Station were devoted to creating the blueprint for the first contact with Tesla. Breaching the Iron Curtain from within the Soviet Union would be far more demanding than what he had done back in Istanbul. Aldridge used the skills in code preparation and cipher analysis he had honed in Turkey to create a Christmas Greeting Card with a microdot carrying a coded message. Keith hoped that Viktor Ivanov would identify the microdot quickly and then operate the microfilm camera that was carefully concealed within the parcel.

Before he set out for the live drop, Aldridge made one request to Henley: Only he and Henley should know the real name of Viktor Ivanov. No paper trails, and no mention to the other agents at the station. Viktor's identity as Tesla, the double agent, remained a closely guarded secret between Simon and Keith.

Aldridge followed the protocols to go black and sat on the blue pastel bench next to the Lenin statue on the eastern side of Gorky Park. He carried a small brown bag with him that had stashes of microdot blank films for Viktor if he showed up. Aldridge was an hour early, and in an attempt to evade any suspicion from those passing by, he started reading a book.

Aldridge assessed the passersby, hoping to identify Ivanov. He looked at his watch, a gift from his wife, Clarise. 6 pm. As per the coded message, Aldridge would drop his book on the ground, pick it up, dust it, and keep it on his right side.

Within a few moments, an unfamiliar face walked toward Aldridge and sat on the bench next to him, right under the nose of Lenin's statue.

In hushed tones, the two men spoke.

"Hello Viktor, my name is Otto," Keith said and moved an inch closer, continuing to look into his book. Aldridge was not ready to share his real name yet.

"Hello Otto, in this bag you will find your microdot camera. Have your people take a look at the photos that I have taken. That should be enough for you to know my worth," Viktor said and took the bag from under his arms, kept it on the ground, and moved it with his feet next to Aldridge's.

Aldridge was not expecting this. Viktor had come prepared with proof of his value to the British. Now it was up to them to decide if it was chicken feed or of certain value. There was no way they could affirm if he had managed to get the pictures or if he had help from the KGB. Aldridge had to find that at that moment.

"What are we going to see in the pictures?" Aldridge asked as the temperature started to drop rapidly.

"I have taken pictures of the latest signals intelligence files that were prepared for the defense ministry to evaluate as part of the operations in the African peninsula. Right now, there are a few options on the table."

"We wouldn't know which option gets through, would we?"

"Not unless I try and get that for you," Viktor said and took out a pack of cigarettes. He lit a cigarette and offered one to Aldridge. Aldridge accepted. Daylight had almost vanished, and a blanket of darkness had just started taking over.

"What are you expecting in return for your services?" Aldridge asked.

"For now, put the intelligence to good use," Viktor said. There was a heavy gust of wind blowing from the eastern section of the park and a strange bellowing noise took over the park.

Aldridge held strongly to his overcoat, turned a look directly at Viktor, and said, "How would you know if we would put that to good use?"

"I have to trust you with that," Viktor said as he looked toward the eastern section of the park.

"That strange sound you hear—that's the wind hitting the walls and splitting into different air streams," Viktor said.

Aldridge was contemplating the next question and almost didn't hear Tesla's theory behind the loud winds.

"What are you expecting in return for your services?"

"For now, nothing."

"Nothing good comes for free. I have to go back to my masters with an answer," Aldridge pressed him to reply.

"I love my country, Otto. I need to help build its future. Consider this as part of my attempt to change the future of my children, my family, and my country," Viktor said.

Aldridge, at the moment, knew that they had a genuine double agent on their hands. Here was a man ready to do the unthinkable—betray his country with its secrets to its greatest enemy, in an attempt to force the hands of the current regime and hope a new regime brings the change he hopes for his family and his people.

"So be it, Viktor. And I will see to it that your work reaches the most capable hands back home."

"What next?" Viktor asked.

"This very place is our first drop site. There would be many. I will drop a package for you at the same time next week and we will start from there."

"And one more thing, from now on your codename is Tesla. Never sign anything you send our way with your real name," Aldridge said, and slowly got up, picked up the small bag, and headed toward the western gates of Gorky Park.

Viktor Ivanov a.k.a Tesla went the opposite way—straight into the strong headwinds.

Back at the station, Aldridge went straight to Simon Henley's office for a debrief.

"What did you make of him?" Henley said as he stood up and walked past Aldridge and closed the doors. Henley took out two glasses and prepared drinks for them as Aldridge started filling him in.

"He said the right things."

"Things you wanted to hear or he meant those?" Henley asked and handed over a glass of cognac to Aldridge.

"He was quite unlike other agents I have run. He was rather smart, direct, and confident of his abilities."

"Cocky?"

"Not at all, although I could tell this is his first gig doing this," Aldridge said and handed over the package to Henley.

"Is this his ticket to freedom or riches?" Henley said as he inspected the bag and its contents. There was the microdot camera that Aldridge had dropped at his house.

"On the contrary, he expects nothing from us."

"That's never a good thing."

"I knew you would say that. I probed him to understand his reason for doing this, Simon."

"And?"

"I think we have hit a jackpot. His intentions are pure as that white snow outside and strong as this cognac." Aldridge took a big swing at the cognac and said, "He wants to burn them down!"

The two men cheered at the prospect of landing a big-time double agent who, over the next few years, would change the course of the Moscow Station of the MI6.

Between December 1978 and June 1982, Keith 'Otto' Aldridge and Viktor 'Tesla' Ivanov formed a strong partnership. They had successfully evaded the KGB surveillance runs and managed twenty-two dead drops. Tesla and Otto perfected their operations carefully and smartly. The turnaround time and frequency of the drops were incredibly high by any spycraft standards, let alone in Moscow. It was clandestine tradecraft at its finest.

But since the end of June this year, there had been complete radio silence. Tesla had not sent any signals over the past five months. Aldridge and Henley had growing concerns about his well-being amidst speculation within the MI6 that he might have been captured and hung for treason. Henley couldn't help but feel an odd coincidence between the recent problems Control had brought to his attention, and the radio silence from Tesla.

Chapter 9
The Troubled Spies

Stuart Wright, the other case officer, was an antithesis to Keith Aldridge but matched him in ambition, smarts, and the ability to take action under duress. He was born rich and stayed rich through his adulthood. Blessed with good looks and an eidetic memory, and with the family business growing the coffers, he had a clear path to success—Trinity College. He studied economics, political sciences, and Eastern European literature. During the university break, he took up a job at the Herald, shadowing the principal reporter, and learned the trade of hunting for news and stories. The part-time job took him to many countries, including Russia. Within a few months and a few trips behind the Iron Curtain, he had a decent grip on the language and could converse in Russian semi-fluently. Six months later, when he resumed his studies, the secret service came knocking. He was offered to undergo training and join the Panama station under the tutelage of Constantin *(the former Moscow chief who was caught with his pants down with his secretary, who later was found to have connections with the KGB, allegedly)*. Constantin kept harping that he was trapped by the Big Three. Wright continued studying Russian literature, art, and the socio-economic principles of Russia. He had his eyes on the ultimate prize- to run the Moscow Station someday. For now, Panama would do.

Wright joined the Panama station and changed the trajectory of the station. He was flamboyant, sharp, and could talk his way out of any trouble, and he ran his business with flair, guts, and gumption. This was where he found the taste of real espionage as he worked with Constantin and engaged a few dissident Russian agents who were thrown off by the KGB into the oblivion Panama was. But in the seventies, the CIA and the KGB were taking active control of Latin America (thanks to Cuba), and the Brits were being left behind. *This brought Panama back onto the espionage map.* Panama became a hot spot for espionage, and London suddenly took greater interest. Wright was already a force to reckon with in the Panama station and was on a fast track to becoming the station chief. Constantin was at his twilight and recommended Control to hand over the reins to Wright.

Wright was called to London for a debrief and an interview. This was to be his moment. He was poised to become the youngest station chief in the history of the MI6. And then Dick Engels and Jim Maeston walked into his life. Maeston hated the guts of Wright—pompous and self-fulfilling arse was his assessment of Wright. Dick Engels reviewed his files and accounts and found an inconsistency. Wright had a woman problem, and even worse, a gambling problem. But that didn't affect his work and output. Maeston had earmarked his nephew to be at the Panama station and together with Engels he plotted to throw Wright under the bus. A resolution was sent upstairs to the twenty-first floor with credible proof of Wright's accounting incongruencies and a recommendation to bring him back to London and run the file room. Control proposed and Henley threw him a lifeline—Moscow.

November, 1982

John Marbury stood across the street from Henley's house. His return from the ports was no less convoluted than the route he'd taken to get there, especially now he was carrying an intel package, enough to get him killed if caught with it. He spent the entire afternoon trying to lose the scent. He had a tail on him as soon as he entered Moscow. In the years gone by, he had often just driven around aimlessly, just for the heck of it, and to wind up the tailing KGB operatives. Those times had changed. The KGB seemed to have a second wind, a purpose for everything. They had definitely improved their counter-surveillance tactics. *Coincidence*, Marbury wondered, *or is someone feeding them our routes?*

Marbury awaited a signal from Henley. Henley was to do his own walk around, lose his tail, and head back home undetected. A yellow towel on the balcony was the safe signal. Marbury had been waiting patiently from his vantage point. It had been a couple of hours already, and Marbury could feel his knees giving up. His shoulders were sore, and his back was cracking into a million pieces. *I hope he knows I've made it back.* And then he saw a tiny towel being placed on the balcony. From afar, he couldn't make out the color. It looked white. It was a fucking towel, that's what mattered.

"Bloody hell, you took your time," Marbury said, barging into the kitchen. He needed a drink. He threw the package onto the sofa and poured himself a glass of Yamazaki.

Henley opened the package, took the files inside to his study, and started reading. From the sofa, Marbury could see Henley flicking on the table lamp and moving through the pages. As the minutes ticked by, Marbury dozed off.

"Here, have some coffee," Henley said, giving Marbury a gentle push to wake him up.

"Jesus, what time is it?" Marbury said. His head felt heavy, and his body numb.

"Gone midnight," Henley said and kept the file in front of him.

Marbury looked at it, took his coffee, and said, "Any good?"

"It's bloody brilliant!" Simon said and started laughing.

"Easy sport, what's gotten into you?"

"This priest, I must admit. He is a genius."

"Pray and tell," Marbury winked.

"Turner had his engineers mock up a complex machine that will change the face of submarine technology as we know it. It's a piece of tech the Russians have been working on for years, trying to crack—a stealth technology that could keep the sub undetected for much farther and deeper. Each blueprint has a slight difference. One key component and its material differ from the rest," Simon said.

"So, how does this help us with the mole?" Marbury asked. He was still coming to terms with the fact that one of his colleagues could be a double agent for the KGB, and the tiresome travel he endured slowed his faculties.

"All three unique materials require special handling, with a special infrastructure only to be found at three specific warehouses," Henley continued, "One in Hungary, one in India, and one in Blighty."

"I still don't get it," Marbury said.

Henley cleared the table and took three chess pieces out from a drawer.

"Here, the Knight. That's Aldridge. He goes to India with one blueprint," he continued and kept a Bishop next to the Knight. "The Bishop, that's Wright. He leaves for London with the second set of prints." Henley took a sip of the coffee and added a Rook next to the Bishop, "Darcy. He leaves for Budapest with the third blueprint. Once the three are in position, we announce the date and time of the machine to go on trial. Say a couple of weeks from when they land."

"If any of our three lads is a mole, then I expect the blueprint to land with the KGB."

"You sure of that?" Marbury wasn't sure if the plan was watertight.

"Well, that's the working hypothesis," Henley said. He took a pause, thinking through the plan and how it would play out.

"What would you do if you were the KGB handler and got handed a covert intelligence file on new submarine tech?" Henley asked.

"I would take this to the scientists and see if there is any merit in the blueprint."

"Right. And assuming the blueprint has theoretical value for the scientists?"

"I would get a surveillance setup around the warehouse to get a hold of the actual tech or prototype- if there is one. Cut short the time of developing one ourselves," Marbury concluded.

"Exactly," Henley rose up and took a brisk walk inside the apartment. His mind was racing with probabilities and the actions he needed to take to balance them out in their favor. A couple of weeks was cutting it thin. It would require a giant leap of faith that the KGB would receive the documents, value the contents, and force an action in a short span of time.

"And if we are ready with counter-surveillance, we should see some Soviet boys around the warehouses in these locations." Marbury was now seeing the plan work.

"That is the premise of this plan."

"But that's only our lads. What about the Big Three?"

"The priest is sending over three copies to Control, who will share the blueprint with Engels, Smith, and Marston."

"Will they bite?" Marbury was now fully invested in the overarching plan.

"They should. Control will position it as an important technology that is secretly in the works. The files they have will lead to a warehouse right here in Moscow!"

"Well, Sport… That is some plan—wild but I can see it work."

"Luck, John. We need luck."

※

The station was in a state of flux the next morning. Henley had put together an op and had briefings with Darcy and Wright, sending them on missions to Budapest and London. Marbury was busy setting up the protocols for covert comms and drop sites that the Circus used in Budapest, a hot zone for espionage. Henley was still waiting for Aldridge to show up, which was unusual for him to not be at work until late morning. He had spoken to Father Samuel in the early hours of the day and confirmed the plans were underway. Ros was in the embassy section, setting up the paperwork and travel plans for the three agents set to travel.

Aldridge had barely walked into the office when Henley called him into his cabin.

"Took you long this morning?" Henley asked.

"Clarise is unwell," Aldridge said and kept his briefcase on the floor and sat on the couch, his eyes blood red and an unruly mop of hair—signs of a difficult night, a morning routine he was not used to.

"What's with the commotion? And where are Darcy and Wright?" he asked.

"They have been sent on an assignment, already started on their way," Henley said and rummaged through his burgeoning stack of files. He located the blue folder that had the details for Aldridge's assignment.

"Here, this is for you. Take it and have a quick read while Ros sets up your travel docs."

Aldridge flipped through and stopped at the first page itself.

"India?"

"Yes," Henley said, expecting a pushback.

"Father Samuel's station. That should be fun." Aldridge remarked, with a sudden vigor taking over him. Henley was a bit taken aback by the warm acceptance. He had forgotten that Aldridge and Turner had worked together briefly in Istanbul.

"The file details out the specifics of the assignment, but I want you to work on something beyond that," Henley said, "The priest and his deputy will bring you in on a problem we are facing."

"What problem?"

"I need you to comb through all the information they share and see if we can find a pattern."

"Again, what problem?"

"There is a bit there in the files, and the rest I will let the priest tell you that, you don't have much time now. Ros has booked you on the flight tonight. If Clarise needs help, we are here."

"So it's an op inside an op, Simon? Am I reading you correctly?"

"I will let Turner and his deputy bring you in on this. You should get going now, Aldridge."

Keith Aldridge left the office in a state of confusion. Tesla had been off the radar for months, and now this sudden trip to India to monitor a machine trial and a covert op to find a pattern in a problem he was not aware of. The world of Keith Aldridge was fast escalating out of control.

Chapter 10

So It Begins

Keith Aldridge was privy to the upper echelons of British society very early in his childhood. At age five, he had shown great promise at chess and his ability to pick up new languages. His potential exploded when his father secured him a place at Eton, Britain's oldest and most prestigious public school. Eton had long been an incubator for future diplomats, ministers, and spies. At Eton, Aldridge quickly moved from the chessboard to mathematics and cryptography.

Aldridge finished his schooling early and was on a fast-track dual graduate course in Mathematics and Political Science at Trinity College. It was at Cambridge where he found his true calling. The formative years of his youth were spent running from one student club to another, each promulgating ideologies that were taking center stage in Britain. He learned of the capitalist nature of the West and the communist propaganda of the Soviets. He wasn't to be influenced by either but came up with his own set of principles and swore allegiance to his motherland. As his time in Cambridge passed by, his deep hatred for all things Soviet grew and took a firm foothold on what would shape his professional career.

By the time Aldridge graduated from Trinity College, he had built a reputation as a savant. With his pedigree and an eidetic memory, he was recognized as an incredible asset to the Secret Service, and he was fast-tracked through his recruitment into MI5. There, Aldridge ran a wide range of operational work and oversaw their code-breaking efforts. His epicurean relationship with numbers and patterns gave him demi-God status within the ranks, and soon he was spearheading the department. But, as with high-functioning individuals, he soon lost interest in the mundanity of a desk job. The covert action and clandestine operations at MI6 caught his eye. It didn't take much to convince MI6 to give him a shot at being a case officer.

Istanbul station had been a bedrock of international espionage in the Middle East. Owing to its proximity to Arab states and Europe, and fearing being caught in the crosshairs, the Turkish government took a lackadaisical stance on spying activity by other nation-states as long as its own military was not being spied upon. Control took a huge leap of faith in sending a first-time case officer to lead the station in Turkey. It was a baptism by fire.

Spies from all over Europe were present in Istanbul, plying their trade in the august company of the Turkish police as the invisible guardian. Aldridge was allowed to hire a secretary and was soon joined by a highly educated, sophisticated, efficient, and well-groomed secretary to keep his affairs in order and his reports crisp. Clarise, the secretary, would later become his wife.

It wasn't a novelty or taboo to see an office romance between an agent and his secretary. More often than not, it was encouraged to keep relations close to home, rather than expose the service to regular citizens. Having a spouse who understood the travails of the trade augured well for a case officer and, by extension, his superiors. There had been many successful marriages within the intelligence community.

But his whirlwind romance and the free rein he enjoyed at the Istanbul Center had Aldridge losing focus, short of motivation, and losing his grip on the station's operations. Istanbul station was slow-paced, but it was still a hugely important strategic post. Clarise suggested making their relationship official and getting married so that Aldridge could get back in the saddle and regain his focus. They were married in January 1976 at a nondescript hotel that overlooked the Hagia Sophia, and by the end of the year, Clarise was pregnant with their first child.

The following year, Aldridge worked like a beast, running several high-profile agents and missions, and the Circus took note. The event that took center stage was the 'Frogman' mission in the summer of 1977. The Soviet carrier ship, *Serghei*, had been docked along the Turkish coastline on a two-day hiatus awaiting further instructions as to its destination somewhere along the western coast of Africa. The carrier ship was hinted to be carrying the latest in underwater Soviet technology, and the MI6 was keen to know how far the Soviets had come along in stealth technology, if any.

With little resources and no time to execute an elaborate operation, Aldridge hired the best diver in the Bosphorus and trained him to take underwater pictures within a day, promising to have the diver moved to Britain on successful completion of the task. He then had one employee from the British Embassy issued a public circular, declaring an official event, inviting all the employees onto a day-long cruise along the Bosphorus. Aldridge had orchestrated an espionage coup with little help from the Circus, the success of his operation landing him the Moscow job. Mesut, the diver, was on his way to England to start a new life. Aldridge was a man of his word, a rarity in the intelligence business. The exploits led to a happy revelation— the Soviets were far behind the Brits in submarine technology, something that Father Samuel knew and used for the current operation. He knew the KGB would take every chance to steal this piece of technology if the Brits were to show they had it.

"Tea, please. Black with one sugar," Aldridge said as he waited for his baggage at the arrivals of the Madras Airport. Madras, the largest and most populous city in the southern regions of India, had the closest airport to his final destination, Pondicherry—the home of the Indian station of MI6.

"Ten paisa," the tea vendor said and handed over a steaming glass of tea. Aldridge handed a one-rupee note. The vendor looked back at him with a smile that said *that note was worth ten cups.*

The tea was milky, sweet, and strong. The perfect thing to revive him after the long journey. Henley had ordered him to work with India Station on an assignment, scout the location, run surveillance, do the works, and wait for his next order. India Station was too understaffed and under-experienced to run this covert op. But he was more keen to understand the 'other problem' he was to help the Indian station untangle.

The airport was tiny. Just three belts to bring in the baggage for international passengers, but at least ten customs officers to check you through. Aldridge picked up his baggage and came out of the airport. Immediately a dozen porters came running over. He had one bag, but the color of his skin probably invited them, Aldridge was sure. With a gentle smile and a stern grip, he held on to his bag which held the case file.

"Aldridge!" he heard someone shout his name amongst the crowd. Between a sea of porters and passengers, Aldridge saw a familiar face.

"You haven't aged a bit, Father," Aldridge said and shook the priest's hands.

"Flattery doesn't work on me, son," Father Samuel said and asked him to follow. "How's Clarise?" Aldridge and Father Samuel had spent time together back in Istanbul, many moons ago. Something Henley only came to know recently.

"She's fine. She sends her regards," Aldridge said, struggling to drag his suitcase through the cobbled pavements that led to the parking area.

"And the baby?"

"Oh, she's growing up like a charm. All thanks to Clarise, I didn't have much to do."

"We have a long way to go to Pondicherry, lots of time to talk. Have you eaten?"

"I am famished."

"Then I have just the right spot for us to grab some dosas," Father Samuel said and turned toward what seemed like a busy market area.

Madras was unlike anything Aldridge had seen before. It was chaotic, humid, and teeming with life. He felt the energy the minute he stepped outside the airport. From the oncoming rush of travelers to crimson-red-colored uniformed porters, people were on the run. *For their lives,* Aldridge thought. He was wrong. It was a run for opportunity, dreams, success, money, and fame.

He followed Father Samuel through a maze of roadside hawker stalls, auto-rickshaws, and hundreds of families gathering around a large merry-go-round. There was laughter, cries of little kids prodding along with their families, fish sellers touting their catch of the day, and then the most amazing and inviting smell hit his nose. *I hope those are dosas*, Aldridge thought.

He took out his suit coat, folded it, stashed it between his armpits, and carried his suitcase through the steps to enter the restaurant—*Saravana Bhavan,* the neon-lit signboard said. The priest and Aldridge took a seat by the window. The huge ceiling fans brought him some respite from the humid weather. The priest placed the order to a bright and springly waiter with a large smile that seemed permanently etched on his face.

Aldridge felt a strange wave of happiness sweeping through this city. It almost seemed like a constant undertone that made up the social fabric of this place. Strange, he thought. Or maybe, Moscow made people cold inside their hearts.

"Someone joining us?" Aldridge enquired.

"What do you mean?" Father Samuel said, feigning offense.

"Didn't you just order three of everything?" Aldridge asked.

"You catch on quick," Father Samuel said, impressed.

"That would be me," saying so a tall, dark, and ruggedly handsome man took a seat and sat next to Aldridge.

"Aldridge, meet Neil Alvares. He calls the shots in this part of the world."

"Neil Alvares,' he proffered his hand. "Did you meet anyone familiar on the flight?" Alvares asked.

"I didn't. How long have you been working with him?" Aldridge asked, looking squarely at Alvares. Only a seasoned operative would open with such a question. Alvares was no novice.

"Long enough to know you both met in Istanbul five years back and that he beat you at chess," Alvares retorted with a hint of a smile.

"Ha! I thought priests weren't allowed to lie!"

"If you gents have finished, let's have some food, shall we?" Father Samuel said as the server brought in a tray full of dosas and little steel tumblers of filter coffee.

An hour flew past, and Neil Alvares and Keith Aldridge exchanged a few words about families and their general lives in India and Russia. But being career spies, soon the discussion moved to serious topics. Aldridge quickly shared everything he knew on the trip he undertook and then posed the first serious question to the agents from the Indian station.

"Henley said there is a problem I am supposed to help you guys with. The files he gave me doesn't give away much besides a few missing agents. Nothing new, aint it?"

"This time it's different Aldridge. Alvares, you want to share the details?" the priest said as Aldridge took a sip of the steaming hot cuppa.

"Not the right place for that. Let's head back to the station and I will run the debrief," Alvares said and got up to pay at the counter.

The walk back to the airport parking felt slow and long. The streets were still bustling and didn't feel like slowing down soon.

"So this is your famed Jeep, the one you wrote in your letters," Aldridge said as he took the rear seat.

"Yes, though now, I let Alvares take the wheel."

"And he says I run the show here," Alvares said with a gentle dig at his boss.

"Get comfortable," Alvares said as he turned on the ignition, "We have a bumpy few hours ahead."

"Hope you are talking about the roads," Aldridge said, trying to locate the seat belt. There wasn't one.

Welcome to India, he thought, and so it begins.

Chapter 11

In Plain Sight

Alvares was a skillful driver, navigating the treacherous roads that led to Pondicherry, and keeping them on time to reach the Indian station before sunrise. They had been on the road for more than two hours, and with an hour more to go, he needed to stop for a quick break. He parked the Jeep next to a coffee shop and brought in three filter coffees.

"Here, try our famous filter kaapi," Alvares said and handed a small tin cup with steaming hot coffee with a large froth that covered the top of the cup.

"I am surprised I never heard about you…and thanks for the kaapi," Aldridge said and settled down on the pavement next to the tiny coffee shop. It was pitch dark, and without a moon, the Jeep headlights provided a bit of light. The pavement was laden with stones and stuck together using cement, making way for a makeshift seating area for the coffee lovers along the highway between Madras and Pondicherry.

"Well, then, a job well done, I suppose," Alvares said, although feeling slightly offended that the number two at the Indian station was not that well known.

"I am sure others have, but never came to my desk."

"Let's correct that history this time, shall we?" Father Samuel said. It was at his request that Henley had sent over Aldridge to India. He needed Aldridge and Alvares to work together and build a partnership.

"Have the Americans set up a station in India yet?" Aldridge asked, coming to terms that India was becoming an important region in the world of espionage and was sure the Germans, Americans, and Russians would start following soon.

"From what we know, they are active in Delhi and Bombay, but we haven't heard of an outpost yet. But I wouldn't be surprised if they select a location like we did—away from the metros and closer to the ports," Alvares said. Father Samuel nodded in agreement.

"I could almost bet my next month's paycheck that the Russians have set up a satellite unit in Goa," Alvares proclaimed and went over to the coffee shop and paid the bill.

"So, Father, I never asked this before—how come India, and how come Pondicherry?" Aldridge asked.

"Careful what you wish for!" Alvares said as he shifted the Jeep into top gear.

"I didn't start outright in Pondicherry. Back in the late sixties, I was commissioned to India by the Archdiocese in England to preside over the church's mission to India," Father Samuel began the story, still remembering it like it was yesterday.

"I was first stationed in Calcutta. Our church was hosting a special envoy of folks from back home, and that's when I met the big boss."

"Control?"

"You bet. He barely waited a day before pitching me the job."

"He can be convincing," Alvares said, remembering his first meeting with Control when he visited the safe house and audited the Indian station's operations.

"Control wanted a safe house away from Europe… more so a safe country where we could send agents who needed a new assignment or a place to hide," Father Samuel said.

"What better place than a country with a billion people and little-known espionage activity," Alvares added, "but over the years we've grown beyond that. We run complex projects, bring over exfiltrated agents from the Asian and African side of our business, and run a strong communication center to deliver critical intel to Europe and Asia."

"And now the big guns from Moscow are seeking your help," Aldridge quipped.

"Wait till you meet Shakuntala," Alvares said.

"Who's Shakuntala?" Aldridge asked.

"Glad you asked, Shakuntala is not a person. It's a bloody train!" Alvares continued, "Well, this is where it gets interesting. The Indian Government does not own Shakuntala Railways. It is privately owned by a British company called Killick-Nixon. It was an era of private railroad companies in 1910 when Shakuntala Railways was founded by a British firm called Killick-Nixon. The private firm floated the Central Province Railway Company (CPRC), a joint venture with the British colonial government in India, to lay railway tracks to transport cotton from around the Nagpur region and finally to Manchester in England."

"How come this is still run privately?"

"Shakuntala Railway is still owned by CPRC, presumably because the government of the day forgot to nationalize it, and Killick-Nixon, a British firm, still owns CRPC. Even though Killick-Nixon has since moved from British to Indian hands, it still leaves us with a privately run train running on Indian railway tracks."

"Interestingly, the trains running on these tracks are the only ones in the country where the guards double up as ticket clerks, as there is no railway staff at most stations on the two routes!" Father Samuel added to the story.

The long drive to Pondicherry brought Keith Aldridge into the inner workings of the Indian station.

Father Samuel had carefully intertwined himself into Indian society and built profound relationships to further his interests and those of his employers back in Britain. As a man of religion and a spy for his country, the moral ambiguity of being a spy and a priest at the same time was a tough one. Lying was an art and a requirement to be a spy, and as a priest, in his day job, who doesn't condone lying and trickery, it must be an incredibly tough job to balance the two, Aldridghe thought as the Jeep sped through the forest and heading into what seemed like dawn.

Alvares continued briefing Aldridge on the station's remit. Over the years, he and the priest had provided a transition and a meaningful hiatus for decommissioned agents, preparing them for a normal life back in Britain. Having served years in a foreign country, these agents would spend a few months, sometimes a couple of years, in India until their return as regular British citizens who were prepared to stitch back into society.

The Indian station managed these assets' transition, well-being, and happiness, with safety being the paramount aim. Some newly trained academy graduates would also come to the Indian station to prepare for a new identity and background. This elaborate ruse would ensure they were 'clean' before embarking on their assignments in a new country, with the Indian identity to support the start of their espionage activities.

The Shakuntala Express was actually a safe house that served as a hideout for MI6 agents and handlers to go black before they moved to foreign shores. Alvares, with the help of a few 'brown envelopes', had placed the 'travelers' as Visiting Signals Engineers, Quality Control Managers, and Mechanical Engineers. Shakuntala gave them a perfect facade for the reason for their stay in India, however short or long.

It also served as a perfect starting point for recruits, who would gain valuable experience and training while in India. With its status as private railway transportation and British ownership, the Shakuntala Express gave Father Samuel the perfect smokescreen to build a safe house and training ground for these 'travelers'.

Agents who were decommissioned would join as quality control managers or visiting research faculty of a farcical university, which barely required any intervention or expertise. For decades, the train ran on the same track, between the same stations. These agents, often emotionally troubled, depressed, and overly suspicious of everyone and everything, would find India's quiet and easy life suitable to acclimate to a sense of normalcy, slowly able to develop some level of trust.

A spy would never completely trust anyone, not even their spouses, for they were designed to lie, to act in complete opposition to what their mouth says. And to be an average functioning individual in a society, a bit of trust goes a long way. India was not on the radar of international espionage, unlike Istanbul, Cairo, Lebanon, Hong Kong, and Vientianne, some of the most active locations in Asia and the Middle East.

Neil Alvares had this entire operation running like clockwork. All the agents were barracked at Nagpur, a strategic location not just for its proximity to the railway line but also because it was a couple of hours away from the military cantonment of the Signals and Corps division in the Indian Military. MCTE, the infantry division of the Military, developed communications technology. *The Indian station had developed a key asset there; Porom Singh.*

Singh was a division leader at MCTE or the School of Signals. MCTE was known as the School of Signals till 1967 and later became a full-fledged Infantry School. It is the alma mater of the Corps of Signals. It conducts courses related to the infantry for men and officers of the various regiments of the Indian Army. Singh worked as a trainer at the Infantry School, specializing in guerrilla warfare.

Listening to secret airwaves, receiving and transmitting coded messages, and decrypting messages sent by enemy operatives were the second and essential part of the function that the Indian center was carrying out for MI6 in India.

The early days of Father Samuel as a spy were in Calcutta. He had been looking to recruit able assets and scouting for a location. Calcutta was not the ideal location for setting up the base for the Indian station. Calcutta was developing into a metropolitan at a breakneck speed, foreign investments from China had seen many foreign settlers, and an ongoing opium crisis had the youth in frenzy; the city was too tricky for his taste. Father Samuel needed a low-key, discreet place, and Pondicherry fit the bill. With help from the headquarters, the priest joined the Sacra De Coeur as Chief Chaplain.

He was almost going to leave Calcutta with nothing to show for it, until the last week of his stay. The mutiny of North-East Indians in Calcutta in the summer of 1968 brought Porom Singh to the doorstep of the church. The rebels marched to the Victoria Memorial to voice their dissent toward the North East Indians. The non-violent movement had turned into a massacre.

Without prejudice or any outward intention to develop an asset in Singh, Father Samuel and his church assistants helped Singh, his rebel compatriots, and their families stay a few nights at the church. During those tough nights, the church had helped the rebels, and Singh found himself in debt to Father Samuel.

It wasn't until Father Samuel reached Pondicherry and started working at Sacra De Coeur that he began turning Singh into an asset. Father Samuel found his weakness during their umpteen telegram conversations and started exploiting Singh. Father Samuel pushed his agenda further when he realized Singh's position at the infantry training school.

Over the years between 1969 and 1982, Singh and Father Samuel formed a formidable partnership to create a surveillance bubble that would allow Father Samuel to begin the second function for MI6. Singh used surveillance and radio technology at the School of Signals to create a listening post designed to intercept and interpret messages on behalf of MI6.

Singh continued to receive financial aid for his rebels in return for his discreet services. They had not given up on the cause, and a mutiny that would last years, couldn't go on without resources and money. *MI6's Indian station solved the latter problem.*

As the operation grew stronger, Singh and Father Samuel created a series of interceptions and secret radio waves, which Father Samuel could access from his little room in the parsonage. Pondicherry's secret radio would give him the messages relayed from MI6 headquarters in London to Moscow and elsewhere; he could listen and intercept messages from the International MI6 stations.

"Some asset you have in Singh," Keith Aldridge said, totally blown away by the extent of operations happening in India, hidden in plain sight.

"*Had*," Neil Alvares said, "He died last year."

Chapter 12
Sleight of Hand

"It could be a while before I'm back," he said and took out a file from his satchel and handed it over to her. A tall, lanky, and bespectacled man with long flocks of hair, he looked younger for his age. She was a beautiful mature woman who knew how to get what she wanted—not just by her looks with those red locks of hair, slender body, and dove-shaped eyes, but for her intelligence and the experience of running a double agent.

"This is some really good material," she said, and got up from the bed, her curves and the silhouette of her body shone against the daylight. He loved her, and it only grew stronger over the years, against all odds.

He gazed through the windows at the sprawling cityscapes in front of him. Not much had changed over the years. He checked his watch. A few more hours before he sets sail. He looked at the file again; this was an important piece of information that he had to safeguard and keep with her, till he knew it was the right time to hand it to the right people. She had been his handler for years; probably, MI6 would never consider a woman to be his conduit to his ultimate masters. Their egos will lead to their downfall, he thought.

This time, he would prove his might, that he was the best source of British intelligence they could ever dream of. Over the last few years, he had given them the surveillance routes, important military documents, and the names of the top dogs of MI6 across the world, including those in hot zones such as Moscow, Budapest, Nairobi, and Panama. Find out about any Russians working for them, they said. How could he tell them that the names were always top secret and maybe above his pay grade? He sent a few their way—those at the bottom of the pyramid. Turned out they were triple agents the KGB hired. They wanted real double agents from the KGB working for the MI6, or even the CIA. He had his eyes set on the big prize—rise to the top of the Circus. A few good years and the right moves, and he would be there, he promised her. If only I could land the top prize; Tesla. But the Moscow Center was running a tight ship on Tesla.

"Where are you going? You never told me."

"It's best if you don't know, for your safety."

"And, what do you want me to do with this file," she asked as she stepped out of the bathroom, her perfect figure still wet with droplets of water trickling down her body. Not many could guess her age, and that she was a mother herself.

"For now, just hold tight. I will tell you when I receive further information on this, without the next details, this file won't make the impact it should," he said, pulled her from the waist, and kissed her.

"Be safe, will you?" she said.

"I am untouchable, love," he said. I am at the top of my game, he told himself. He took the original file and packed his satchel, leaving the copy behind for his lady, his love, and his handler from the KGB.

Chapter 13
The Big Three

Henley had been through the files Ros had marked up and had spent the last two days going through every sequence of events, past and present, laying the puzzle in every way possible, to find the missing piece. But his men at the Moscow Station had turned out clean, at least on paper.

Henley pulled out the satchel that Moore dropped at his house last night. It was a debrief from Hicks as promised, he had gone down the memory lane and prepared information on the Big Three—stuff that one would not find in the registry of records. This was what he was looking for. He opened the red file and went through the notes.

Dick Engels: Engels has played the game quietly and securely. He has the Control's ears and provides him with the insights and information to keep the CIA from knocking at our doors for every single ball dropped. Not many know this, but Engels is who Control leans to when it comes to managing the joint CIA-MI6 operations. Engels decides what information flows from MI6 to the CIA and vice versa. If Control has a blind spot, then this is it. Engels has a free run at managing the CIA relationship. If the CIA ever decides to put a top man inside the MI6 on their payroll, it would be Engels. Although I doubt he is at the center of your problem as of now. CIA wouldn't dare to disturb this relation, not for now.

Jim Maeston: The inside walls of the MI6 top floors are looking at Maeston as the true successor to Control. He has the political might and has often shielded Control from the politics of running a government agency often at the crossroads with

10 Downing Street. He is the fly on the wall of every conversation that happens in the corridor of the PM's office and Control's desk. He has enormous power but doesn't show it, not yet. Long before his political career began and his entry to the top floors at Century House, Maeston worked as the editor for the Herald—a very short stint. Maeston was the one who picked up the dirt on the previous head of MI5 and blew it open on the front page. It got him the traction and attention and Control's good grace. He is a sitting time bomb, probably biding his time for the right moment, if he ever chooses to wreak havoc. He is a friend you never want but would need to sit at the top of the Circus.

Steve Smith: Control's prodigal son. Everyone knows Smith has got an eye on Control's chair. But has anyone wondered why his influence keeps growing at the center? Smith leads the London station and the scalp hunters, and his portfolio and power keep growing. The question is not why his power is increasing despite his fallacies; the question is how is he insulated from all of this. It's because Control protects him. Now the question is: what does he have on Control that he is forced to keep Smith at the top?

This dossier from Hicks had left Henley in a quandary. The plot was only getting murkier. He had underestimated the Big Three. These were powerful men and hustling them would not be easy. He would have to tread carefully if he were to point a finger at them as the mole.

Ros had also pulled up Henley and Father Samuel's files for review as well. Henley wasn't surprised. It was tongue-in-cheek to have his own work being scrutinized. Even in such intense and trying situations, Roslyn's meticulous nature and her need to protect those she worked with won through.

Simon Henley stood up from his desk and scanned the collection of bottles on his shelves before pulling out a bottle of full-bodied Vinho Verde from the hills of northern Portugal. It was a house favorite, one that they usually opened at the end of a successful mission. Henley hoped it would bring him not just cheer but some luck with it, too.

Henley sat down by the fire, feeling the heat from the embers, and felt his eyes droop. Sleep was a privilege in this game, especially when the stakes were running high. He opened a new bag of logs and threw a few into the fire. The cracking of the woods gave him the fillip to stay awake. He opened Father Samuel's file.

For someone who had been in MI6 for so long, there was not much to be read about Father Samuel; at least in the files cleared for Henley to read. Even Darcy, a tech expert, had a more extensive dossier. Over the next couple of hours, helped by the eclectic mix of wine and Miles Davis' Jazz playing in the background, Henley combed through every bit of information on Father Samuel.

At long last, he knew a tad bit more than he knew of the priest previously. He saved the best for the closing—MI6 boss's notes on the priest. It was customary for all Station Chiefs to receive letters, debriefing them on the other station heads and a general laundry list of contacts in the other cities with MI6 presence.

He read through Control's note:

Father Samuel, an exemplary operative and a devout Man of God, has essayed both roles with elan and composure. It takes an outstanding professional to balance the angels of his true calling and the demons of the work his country asks of him.

When Father Samuel offered his services we all had a merry laugh at the thought of a priest becoming a spy. In hindsight, that was the genius of his recruitment—his ability to pull off the role of a priest while operating as a spy. He is razor-sharp, focused, empathetic, and calculative. When you take these assets and put them under a priest's cloak, you cannot help but think of him as a man destined for greatness in this business of espionage.

The reasons he offered his services to MI6 have long been a mystery but I believe I have some insight. I asked him if he believed in the devil one late night, and he told me a story of his time in Rwanda. The Militia ruled the land and had an iron grip on every village they could force their way into. One village, led by a charismatic leader, Kelechi, had put up a brave fight. The head of the Militia ordered his men to give Kelechi a slow death to teach a lesson to his followers but the chief's men became enamored by Kelechi and suggested they might shoot him instead and give him a quick death. Intrigued, the Militia chief met Kelechi and spent hours talking to him in his house. After which, he dragged him into the open and skinned him alive in front of his people.

"So, to answer your question, Control," he said. "Yes, I have seen the devil, and he walks amongst us."

Henley got the chills. He half-expected to hear a wolf howl in the distance. Then something struck him.

Some nerves on the old priest, Henley thought, *to offer his services to the secret service*. But might it be a sleight of hand? The greatest trick the devil ever pulled was to convince people he didn't exist. But what were the priest's motivations? Maybe it was the wine talking. Henley felt his eyes droop again. The night was running out, daylight was approaching.

※

Roslyn was the first to report the next morning. To her surprise, she found Henley pacing across the wooden floorboards of his office. She'd had a sleepless night and had an eerie feeling that something was going to go wrong the following morning. Her hunches and premonitions were famous amongst the Moscow Five. For once, she thought, she got to be wrong. Henley looked the best she'd seen him in weeks. *A positive sign,* she thought.

Roslyn cleared her desk and brought out the small table clock she had carried that morning. For all her smarts and wit, she was thoroughly superstitious. Her grandfather's clock, passed down by her late father, had been her symbol of luck and comfort over the years.

She barely noticed John Marbury come into the office—the others had been put on overseas assignments. A man of routine, he poured himself a cup of tea and bit into a sandwich from Anatoly's.

As Marbury made his way to his office, Henley called out of nowhere.

"John, we've work to do," Henley shouted out of nowhere.

"Long night, was it?" Marbury said and handed over a cup of tea.

"Eventful."

"When is it not, you have made it your life's mission it seems."

"So the lads are in position."

"What's next?"

"Before we move, we need to engage London."

"Why?"

"I need to know if the files that went their way had any effect."

"And how do we find that out."

"Wait and watch," Henley said, "Ros, do we have London on a secure line?"

"Line one!" she shouted.

"Gents, this is Moscow. Can I confirm who's in the room there?" Henley spoke into the telephone.

After a brief pause, Henley and Marbury heard a crackle, "Control here. Maeston, Smith, and Engels are with me."

"This may come as a bit of a shock, so brace yourselves," Henley said, "We are onto something that could have a huge impact on our submarine tech. You have got the files, I presume."

"I read the files. I'm not as shocked as you seem to believe," Smith, the London station head said.

"Why are we suddenly so interested in the submarine tech?" Engels chipped in.

"Wrong question, Engels," Henley said.

"Why has the brief been so secretive and not come from the Minister's table?" Maeston asked.

"Now, that's the right question," Henley said.

"Henley, let's not play games here. Your point, please," Control asserted, making the rest feel that this was a shocking bit of revelation, although he knew the plan all along.

"Without question, this stays in the room, do I have your assurances?"

After a slight pause, Henley heard three affirmations.

"You have the room and its secrecy, Henley, go ahead," Control instructed.

"Titanium. That's the bit that we are looking for in our new submarine frontier," Henley said. "It is lighter, tougher, and works better undersea."

"How much better?" Smith was now engaged.

"More than we could ever imagine."

"Titanium is not a new metal, we have looked into it before. It's too expensive to scale up." Maeston retorted.

"It seems a workshop in Moscow has found a way around that particular problem. We were thinking we might nab a few samples for our boys to study," Henley said.

The files sent to London had a different story than those from the Moscow Station. The top three were made to believe that the Russians had developed a superior metal that could help the Brits. Henley and Marbury had located a dysfunctional warehouse on the outskirts of Moscow and relayed the address as part of the files. Surveillance was in place to detect any movements there, and Mike was at the helm of that surveillance, laying low, ready to report.

"Why are we being told this? Not the first time you are running an op in Moscow," Smith said.

"You're right, but I wouldn't dare run an op this size without the blessings of London," Henley played to their egos.

"What's the potential damage if this goes south?" Control played along. He sensed Henley was up to something out of the playbook they discussed previously, though he couldn't quite see what was the underlying play here.

"I'm putting my best team onto this. If things go south, they'll be completely blown, possibly in grave danger of a loss of life. I will need immediate exfil. No expense spared," Henley said.

"Thank you, Henley," said Control. "We will discuss and send you our position on this soon."

"Thanks, all. We can't sit on this for long."

Marbury cut the call and looked at Henley. That should ruffle some feathers.

Chapter 14
Missing in Action

In 1976, Father Samuel took a detour and stopped at Bodrum, Turkey, during his annual visits to London. He was looking forward to meeting a particular individual—an enigmatic code breaker, a fast-rising rock star case officer in the MI6 ranks. Keith Aldridge, then station chief at the Istanbul station, was equally stoked to meet Father Samuel, a former code breaker, case officer, and priest who single-handedly managed the MI6's transit home in India.

The four weeks that Father Samuel and Keith Aldridge spent together laid the foundations of what was to become the handbook of signals intelligence and code transmission for all case officers and agents run by MI5 and MI6. But, even then, Keith had a bigger vision. He envisaged a larger espionage community built amongst spies of multiple national agencies. Under a cloud of smoke and in the search for the end of a bottomless mug of Turkish wine, Father Samuel taught Aldridge everything he knew about being a case officer and a spy, and the younger man went away with a treasure trove of knowledge, the most significant skill being: *patience*.

One afternoon, while completing a review of the proposed MI6 handbook, Father Samuel and Keith Aldridge took a break from heavy cryptological work and found solace in the afternoon sun. Bodrum was spectacular that afternoon. The hotel, *Stella Continental,* perched on the southern tip of the marina, overlooking the magnificent Bodrum castle, was the place of retreat.

The Aegean blue sea, the vast expanse of the southern Turkish bay, and the shimmering facade of the castle had the two spies spellbound.

"When you don the robe of a priest, do you completely and utterly become a Man of God?" Aldridge asked.

"What do you think, Aldridge?" Father Samuel had long mastered deflecting a question with another question.

"Probably when you started, you didn't…." Aldridge kept staring at the castle, contemplating if America was his correct calling. He had a new wife and a newfound pressure to start a family. There was an offer on the table from the MI6 to take an assignment to the US and co-run the espionage operations in the South American belt with the CIA. The offer was tempting and the pay was better. Clarise would love the States and possibly they could plan their first kid and start a family together. But something held him back. He liked the work he was doing in Europe and wanted a 'meatier' role than playing second fiddle to the CIA.

"Being a spy doesn't mean you serve Britain as your only master. A man is allowed his transgressions when carefully chosen," Father Samuel said and snapped his fingers to bring Aldridge back from his daydream.

"At what point do you know you've served your country enough?" Aldridge turned his head and squarely asked the priest.

Father Samuel didn't have a clever reply this time. Deep inside, he knew he had never considered retiring. He had heard stories of career spies driving themselves to utter madness. Civilian life could never fill the immense void.

Retiring without a plan was not Father Samuel's style. As the sun started slowly setting into the backdrop of the majestic coast of Bodrum, Father Samuel realized he had to put a plan in place.

"Have you considered working behind the Iron Curtain?"

"I will be honest. I have. But that seems a bridge too far for someone at my stage of the career."

"You will be surprised to know that people your age have made it to Moscow, but…"

"But…"

"Moscow is a beast, Aldridge. It swallows you, chews you up, and spits you back in pieces. It takes resilience to survive there."

"Have you never considered leaving the Indian post?"

"India is far more complex than many give it credit."

"Just because it's not a traditional outpost?"

"More than that, many in our business just don't know what we actually do… someday I hope, for the right reasons, you visit our station."

"Someday Father, someday…" Aldridge said and stared at the horizon as the sun slowly faded into the depths of the ocean.

Pondicherry

November 1982,

"This serves as our comms room," Alvares said as he gave Aldridge a quick tour of the facilities they had built right inside the parsonage.

"The church never found out?" Aldridge asked, impressed yet concerned.

"He manages a good Chinese wall between the church and the station," Alvares said. Aldridge stared at the glass-walled cupboard with stacks full of files, ready to fall out at a moment's notice or might just be held up enough to keep it in shape. *Schrodinger's cat all again,* Aldridge thought.

Aldridge slowly turned the key and nudged the doors of the cupboard. He opened the door, and barring a few files that succumbed to gravity, the rest stayed in place. He carefully took out a bunch of files and laid them on the table.

"These date back ten years," Neil said. "You looking for something specific?"

"Yes, I am looking for something recent," Keith said.

"That top drawer is the one you're looking for."

"May I?" Aldridge asked.

"By all means. Father Samuel said to give you a free run."

"When is he back?" Aldridge asked. He was still waiting on the full debrief from Alvares and the priest on the MIA agents—the larger part of his remit on this trip to India, supposedly.

"The Sunday mass finishes at ten and then he runs the accounts with the trustee."

Aldridge looked at his watch. *A couple of hours before the priest was back.* But there was something he needed to check. One of the reasons he quickly accepted the Indian assignment was to check on someone who was positioned in India; it had been months since he last heard of the person. Between the baby and the Tesla radio silence, he almost forgot to check in on this person earlier, something Aldridge was terribly ashamed about. He had an idea of the secret project that Henley wanted him to work on. The MIA agents that were logged in the file had him thinking of that close colleague and friend with whom he had lost contact in the last few months.

"Do you know where the files on the recent agents that were stationed in India are kept?"

"Looking for anyone in particular?" Alvares asked.

"Vince Gilligan," Aldridge said.

Alvares rummaged through the files until he found a red file marked MIA.

"Here," Alvares said and handed over the file. Aldridge went to the priest's desk and opened the file. Alvares joined him. The two men looked like long-lost brothers, if not for the color of their skin, working in tandem as if they had been doing this together for years.

"Kate Miller, that name sounds familiar," Aldridge said. Alvares took a step back as if a large piece of stone hit his chest.

"You Okay?"

"Yes, just remembered something," Alvares lied. That name was not just a memory; it went deeper than that for him.

"Gilligan's not here," Keith Aldridge said as he reached the back end of the file. He stood up and walked toward the window and stared outside. Something was amiss. He knew he was missing something. He was sure that Gilligan was being commissioned to India and his name should have surfaced in the files.

Alvares went back foraging into the cupboard of files.

"Aldridge, here!" he said, showing Aldridge a file that had INCOMING written in bold on the cover page, "It mentions Gilligan and his legend along with the details for his next cover."

"Where's his file on his time in here?" Aldridge asked as he felt hopeful.

"That's the thing," Alvares said. "He never made it to India."

Alvares didn't understand why Aldridge was so invested in Gilligan.

Aldridge kept both files side by side. The timelines made little sense.

"See here," he said as he flipped through the files. "Three agents came to India in the last couple of years; all of them missing in action."

"Technically, only one is MIA… Miller," Alvares said, his face turning slightly pale when saying her name.

"What about the other two?"

"They spent their time here and then in Shakuntala and then left as per the directive."

"Then why the hell do we have their names under missing in action?"

"That is the million-pound question," Alvares said.

"MI6 agents have gone missing, and London never cared to look further? That, my friend, is the million-pound question."

"What question?" Father Samuel said as he walked into his office. He slowly removed the laces of his shoes, hung his robe on the walls, and sat down at his office chair. He browsed through the two sets of files in front of him.

"I am guessing you already know," Aldridge said. Alvares kept quiet. He knew half the story— that the mission for which Aldridge was sent to India was fake and designed to trap a rogue agent. It was the other half he was after, and so was Keith, he presumed.

"Why do you think you are here, Aldridge?" Father Samuel asked.

"To scout for a workshop with some precious machine materials…and a special op that you want me to run in tandem with Alvares."

"That's a smokescreen," Father Samuel said,

"For what?"

"For you to be here without raising a suspicion."

"And do what?"

"To find what happened to the missing agents, Alvares cannot do it alone. I have to run the business as usual."

"Why is London not following up on this?"

"We are understaffed here, and since the agents went missing from or to the Indian station with a final stop at Moscow, it's our problem now," Father Samuel said. He could not afford to let either of the agents know of the mole hunt, yet.

"Why did you and Henley think I would take this up?" Aldridge asked.

"Because Vince Gilligan is your best friend."

"How on God's earth..." Aldridge said and before he could complete the priest banged the desk and looked directly at Aldridge.

"It doesn't matter how I know. If there is someone who has a good enough reason to drive this forward, it's you. If not for the service, do it for your friend," Father Samuel said, cognizant of the fact that Aldridge was not here on the official manhunt for the missing agents. For once, he had to play on Aldridge's emotions.

There was a sharp silence in the room. Aldridge sat down, hand on his forehead, trying to understand his position here. The information had come like a bunch of raging bulls running toward him. His best friend was missing in action, possibly captured, tortured, or worse—dead.

"And what about the op that Henley sent me here for?" he asked.

"Don't worry about it, I have that covered," Alvares said. He had known the fake plan all along. He was the one who had gone to the safe house to work with the engineers in devising the fake submarine tech.

"And not just Gilligan, we need to trace what happened to all of them. We have reason to believe that Kate Miller is still out there somewhere," Father Samuel concluded. Alvares could feel the shivers. Every single day that passed, he worried for her. Was she captured? Was she being interrogated by enemy forces? Was she already dead?

"I'll pull the files," Alvares said and went back to the file room. He now had Aldridge to double up on the efforts.

Father Samuel could understand what Aldridge was going through.

"Do you need a minute alone?" he asked Aldridge.

"Gilligan sent me a message a few months back saying he was being brought into the Moscow Station with a stop in India for a few months before. Clarise and I were so happy to hear that," Aldridge said, flashes of his best friend coming before his eyes. "And now I am supposed to find out if he is even alive?"

Neil Alvares came back with a stack of files.

"Before we begin, do we have any reason to believe they have defected?" Neil Alvares said, throwing the room into jeopardy.

Keith Aldridge said nothing. He knew Gilligan the friend, but not the spy. Anything was possible.

"And why are we focusing on just Gilligan and Miller? There are two other agents, MIA," Alvares asked.

"Pete Rush and George Barkley are dead. Confirmed by London," Father Samuel said and waited for the other two to come to terms with this information. A minute later, the priest broke the silence in the room.

The dynamics had just changed. Two dead and two missing. There was a lot to factor in.

"I have to talk to Control and Henley now..." Father Samuel said and rose from his chair. Alvares and Aldridge were already going through the files. They didn't hear him ask the question. The priest understood the answer to their silence.

Alvares started drawing out a timeline of events. Aldridge started going through the files of all the agents who had landed in India in the last five years. If they could go back far enough, they might find a pattern.

"Gilligan never made it to India. But Miller did," Aldridge said, "How much do you know about her?" he asked.

"Not much," Alvares lied and excused himself to have a smoke. He had known Kate Miller very well. So much that he had loved her. And one day, she just went missing. For the last few months, Alvares was running his own investigation to trace her whereabouts within his time and resources.

"Well, you must know something," Aldridge joined him outside. It was a statement, not a question. The skies had turned a shade of crimson as the evening drew closer.

"Care for one?" Alvares said and lit a cigarette. Keith took the offering. "So, Gilligan was your friend,"

"He still is."

"Good. So, we both agree to assume that he is still alive."

"Same for Miller," Aldridge said.

"That's a dead end," Alvares said. He had already spent several months trying to figure out where and why she had disappeared. He had made peace with the idea that she was dead. It was the only explanation.

"Funny that I'm the one looking out for him. He was the smarter one, often bailing me out at Eton," Aldridge was somber and trying not to get invested emotionally. If he were to do his job, he had to keep his emotions at bay. "This July, he would have turned 36, same as me." Aldridge choked back a tear.

"We dropped the ball," Alvares said, "Protocol requires us to be in close contact with London till the agent reaches our station, settled, and put up at Shakuntala."

Suddenly, Alvares ran back into the parsonage. Aldridge threw the cigarette and ran behind him.

"What happened?"

Alvares threw a couple of files down in front of him. "Check the dates on the top page."

"1979, Jan to Dec," Aldridge said,

He rushed to the priest's office table, lit the lamp, and opened the pages in the file.

"Which month did Barkley leave for Shakuntala?" Alvares asked as he started writing.

Aldridge opened the file that Father Samuel had given them, "It says July 1979."

Alvares wrote the date against George Barkley.

"Now check for Pete Rush. I can bet all the money in my bank that it's July or August."

Aldridge quickly moved through the pages and looked at Alvares, shocked. "July 1980."

"What about Kate Miller, let me check," Aldridge said.

"No need. She left for Shakuntala last year, June," and wrote Kate Miller - July 1981. "And your friend, Vince, was to be with us in July 1982."

"What the hell happened at Shakuntala those couple of months every year?" Aldridge asked.

"Isn't it obvious?" Alvares said, "Someone has been meticulously trying to cover their tracks."

They spent the next hour tracing the time in India for every agent that had landed in India in the last ten years. The pattern started somewhere between 1977 and 1979. Before 1977, every agent who came to the Indian station had started his new assignment at the right location, with the right cover story.

Something changed in 1978.

"This is my old man, Martin," Alvares introduced Aldridge to his grandfather as they partook in some food at Martin's Bakery.

"Find him a girl to marry, will you?" Martin said and handed a cup of freshly brewed coffee to Father Samuel. "At his age, I already had a kid half his age," Martin said, "I'll be back with some food."

As some freshly made curd rice and papadums got served, Alvares and Aldridge apprised the priest of their findings. Father Samuel heard through the entire narrative.

"Clearly, there is only one way to find out if your theory holds any water."

"Which is?"

"You both have to go to Shakuntala, and run a deep investigation."

He was right. If there was some anomaly, it was at Shakuntala.

Chapter 15
The Safe House

December 1ˢᵗ, 1982

Bombay International Airport

"A thousand kilometers!" Aldridge said, "And you call that close by?"

"This is India, we are a big country," Alvares shrugged, then laughed.

Bombay airport was the closest to Nagpur—a small, peppy city, fondly dubbed the Oxford of the East by its residents, nestled right in the center of India that also happened to house Shakuntala. It was known for two things: spicy food and sweet oranges.

Bombay Airport looked like a massive theater in action as people bustled around, all with different roles to play. For a curious onlooker, it was India on a plate. A high-class and chic crowd stayed on one side with their expensive bags and jewelry and walked through the first-class line and then there was this huge line of much simpler, presumably middle-class—working people running to find the furthest point in the queue for the economy cabin line. In the backdrop were hundreds of people running helter-skelter to find their boarding gates, kids crying, parents yelling, and best of all—a calm and poised janitor, cleaning the floor with a dancelike motion, almost like the conductor of this theater.

The passport control queue was the least of Aldridge's problems. His trip to India had taken a different turn altogether. What was to be a simple scouting exercise for a materials workshop was now a full-blown operation.

Father Samuel had agreed to inform Henley of the change in plans. He didn't buy this bullshit from the priest for a second. For sure the priest and Henley knew of these missing agents and wanted him and Alvares to trace the missing agents. Why was no action taken before that was the question troubling him? And, it took them two dead agents to trigger the hunt? Why were Darcy and Wright sent out of Moscow? Were they running similar covert operations elsewhere? But the biggest question that bothered him was: Were Henley and the priest considering if this was an inside job?

A beautiful dove-eyed woman approached him. "Sir, do you hold a diplomatic passport?"

For a moment, he stood stunned. She was breathtaking.

"Y…yes," he fumbled his way through to say something legible.

"Please follow me, sir."

With a million thoughts running through his head, Aldridge had forgotten he was supposed to be the attaché for the British government and would get priority access through the airport.

Neil Alvares stood behind the immigration desk as Keith Aldridge made his way through.

"Oh, forgot to mention something…"

"What?"

"Beware of Indian girls, they can be hypnotic!"

"Strap up and get comfortable, this is going to take a while," Alvares said as he turned on the engine and drove the car out of the airport parking into the bustling city of Bombay.

It had been two days since Alvares and Aldridge had made it to the safe house. It was less of a safe house and more of a residential quarter. The actual spies from the British side worked alongside the regular employees of the rail network, some British, but mostly Indians. It seemed like a perfect break to Keith Aldridge—country air, great views, and crucially outside the KGB hot zones. *I wouldn't mind being here myself.*

They couldn't just barge in and demand information. Careful planning was needed, along with a little luck. The groundwork had already been laid by Father Samuel—Alvares and Aldridge were here under the guise of running an audit.

"Where do we begin?" Aldridge asked as he stared at a large pile of files.

"I think the railway operation is kosher, but no harm checking," Alvares said, having spent a few days running the rule on the operation when he came looking for Kate Miller, "I'll engage Astle from operations to go through some of the stuff as well." Daniel Astle, a former scalp hunter, was now a permanent feature and the warden of the residential facilities for the agents.

"Well, then sport…I will go through the finance audits, requisitions, and money trail if any." Aldridge said and split the files between him and Neil.

"Look at the accounts for anything unusual during the months of July and August over the last five years."

"Long shot."

"Let's start from there and see what we find out."

"Are you hopeful?"

"If there is something here to be found, we will find it."

"Hope these guys are not taking the mickey out of us," Aldridge said, as he neatly arranged the stack of fifteen files submitted by the guys from Accounts.

"I'm fairly sure they're following orders," Alvares said as he grappled with his own deck of files from the lads in comms.

"Beer?"

"That should help."

They spent the entire night sequencing the events around George Barkley, Pete Rush, Kate Miller, and Vince Gilligan. July and August for the last five years revealed nothing out of the ordinary. A few state visits from MI6, notably Engels and Smith, and a few from Father Samuel, none of which screamed suspicion to them.

Aldridge had fallen asleep at some point, but Alvares had continued to comb the files. He rose and rushed toward the kitchen and put a pot of water on to boil. As the call for the early-morning prayers rang out from the nearby mosque, Alvares felt a second wind. They had obviously missed something. He knew deep in his heart that the answer lay in those files. He felt a sudden rush of adrenaline alongside a sudden epiphany.

March, last year

Neil Alvares was visiting the safe house for his general operational overview and processes. Dan, the scalp hunter and now the head of facilities at Shakuntala dropped a note on Neil's table at the safe house. Could you make the trip to Bombay-incoming agent, Kate Miller? Need to personally escort her to Pondy—the note from Pondicherry station said.

Her, he thought, a female agent for the first time to the Indian station. Not a semi-retired 50-year-old secretary making her way to an early retirement in India, Alvares hoped.

He hated last-minute switch in plans. He was in Nagpur on a personal trip with a bit of work— a marriage to attend. His best friend, Albert was to be married in three days. But the priest had his ways. Alvares, a thorough professional, kept aside his personal plans and set off for Bombay. This better be worth it, he had some explanations to do to his best friend for not making it to the wedding, despite being in the city.

The train to Bombay was a tumultuous one. He was tired, angry, and unpleasant—not his usual self. A creature of habit, he liked to meticulously plan his days and weeks. To be an effective spy is to always be ready for the unknown, the priest would say. After ten years of working alongside them, the priest never failed to throw in a piece of advice now and then. Neil Alvares was effectively as good a spy as one could be in India, in some parts to the tutelage of the priest.

He bought two tickets to Pondicherry as he waited for Kate at Bombay airport. He wanted to get done with this detour as quickly as possible. *I could still make it.* He quickly made a mental math of the time he would need to drop her off at Pondicherry and make it back to Nagpur via Bombay. *If and only if the priest doesn't ask him to babysit the new guest for a few days.*

The flight from London Heathrow had already landed an hour back. He stood with a sign that read 'Kate' as he saw a flurry of passengers walking past him. Not a soul came even close to looking for him. He had a flight to Madras leaving in an hour. *Another fifteen minutes, or else we lose that flight.*

Neil walked over to the coffee shop to get some food. He had barely eaten in the last few hours. A young foreign national came to the shop and ordered tea. Short stature, long auburn hair, and a round beautiful face with flawless skin. *Tourist; why couldn't spies be this pretty,* he thought.

She stood right next to him, sipping into her hot cup of tea, and looked at the passengers walking past the exit doors. *Probably she is here to receive her husband or boyfriend,* he thought. She smelled great—of violets and lilies. It calmed him. He couldn't help but let out a smile. He was smitten—love at first sight as Rajesh Khanna, the Bollywood hero and icon would say.

Time to move, she isn't here or worse, I missed her. She is a spy, how difficult would it be for her to reach Pondicherry, he thought *and turned around, kept the placard on the billing counter, and opened his wallet to pay.*

"How much?" he asked the shop vendor.

"1 rupee," the vendor said.

"Make it two. Her tea is on me," he said to the vendor in Hindi, handed him a two rupee note, and moved.

"I am famished, won't you buy me some idlis to go with the tea?" the lady touched him on the arms and said.

"Excuse me?" Alvares said, a bit shocked.

"I heard the Indian station took good care of its visitors?" She said and gave out the most beautiful laugh he had heard in his life.

Neil Alvares blushed. It was Kate Miller—not fifty or a retiree as he presumed, but a young, pretty, and a spy with a dash of humor. His idea of British spies changed over that instant. Rajesh Khanna was right.

The gentleman he was, he bought her some steaming idlis. As she ate, they caught up on a few things. She asked, and he answered. His life in India, his family, and his time at the Indian station. He told her it was a last-minute plan for him to escort her instead of the priest.

"My lucky day," she said. She had him on tenterhooks. He then helped her with the bags and told her about the marriage he was to attend, hence the quick changeover to the next flight.

"Take me," she said.

"Take you where?" he asked.

"To the wedding."

"Are you sure?"

"As long as you promise to be my date and not leave me hanging at the wedding," she said and asked him to cancel the flight to Madras. Father Samuel, a priest taught him everything he was to know about espionage and British spies. Obviously, British women were never his forte, Alvares thought and laughed.

Neil Alvares went back into the office and began cross-checking both stacks of files against the timeline—his from operations and Aldridge's from finance and the money trail.

"What time is it?" Aldridge said as the daylight hit him through the curtains.

Alvares was frantically writing on a piece of paper. Aldridge went into the kitchen, made himself a cup of coffee, and went over to Alvares to see what he was doing.

At first glance it made little sense, he had scribbled his timeline from operations against Aldridge's from the accounts audit. But then it suddenly made sense. He was now cutting across both departments for the timeline and tracking the movements of the agents during their time in Nagpur.

"There it is!" Alvares said and stopped writing and took a deep breath.

"That is inspiring!" Aldridge said as he reached the same conclusion.

Every year, during English summers, the safe house would undergo a massive overhaul. Their communications technology would be refreshed or sometimes replaced as the engineers deemed fit. The stack of files from finance recorded the costs of the change in tech. But when checked against the stack of files from operations, a pattern emerged. Every time the technology was changed, the agents' files were changed with a new destination. By design or by intent, every time the tech overhauled, the agent's destination changed.

"Barkley was destined for Vientiane and then to Moscow before the overhaul, and then post-overhaul, he was assigned to Budapest," Alvares said as he continued to go deeper.

Aldridge ruffled through the files of George Rush and found a similarity, "Here, Rush was to continue in Nagpur for another six months before heading to Istanbul and then Moscow. And then a sudden assignment to Budapest with immediate notice."

"Both reportedly dead a few months later."

"Here, Gilligan was to reach India via Budapest. Accounts have credited a few thousand pounds to his bank in Budapest for the onward journey," Alvares shouted as Aldridge browsed through the files.

"That means he never made it past Budapest," Aldridge said.

"What the hell happened in Budapest?" Alvares asked.

"The bigger question is: who changed their assignments to Budapest?"

"Someone managed to change the codes when the tech was overhauled?"

"Likely," Alvares said.

"So, London Operations still thinks Barkley was to go to Panama and Rush to Istanbul."

"And, they think Gilligan made it to India before he vanished," Aldridge had a firm look on his face.

"And what about Miller?" Aldridge asked Alvares, he long had this nagging feeling that Alvares was hiding something. Alvares's eyes were brimming with tears.

Aldridge was silent. He had been there before, falling for someone and then having to leave unannounced. He had been on the other side though, he was the one who had to leave every time.

"So, you fell for her," Aldridge said, "I had this suspicion whenever Kate's name came about."

Alvares said nothing; silence was golden. He fell in love with her that very instant when she asked him to take her to the wedding. Three days at the wedding—there was food, alcohol, dancing, music, and the works. She took part in all the rituals and ceremonies as any invitee at the wedding would. She was a natural people pleaser. No doubt, by the end of the wedding, she was the toast of the town. Everyone loved her. Neil Alvares did a bit more than everyone else. The romance continued in Pondicherry. Between work, assignments, and all the ad hoc work that came his way, Alvares always found time for Kate. Within two months, she was moved to Shakuntala, yet he visited her at every opportunity. But as with any long-distance relationship, he started feeling the distance as she spent time at Shakuntala. And then one day, Astle from operations sent a note: Kate is missing since 14:00 on July 23rd, 1981. *His world came crashing down.*

"We spent an amazing summer together, and that's it," Alvares said, trying to downplay the extent of his relationship.

"Like me, now you too have some skin in the game," Aldridge said. This had to be kept under wraps; Control would not want to know that two of his agents were running personal agendas. *The two agreed to not speak of this with a third person in the room.*

"Right, then," Aldridge continued, trying to avoid the awkwardness. "Back to Budapest, then. How do we play it?"

"All roads lead to Budapest, nothing more to check in Shakuntala…unless we get lucky and find out who made those changes to the files."

"The only way is to find the logs of the changes that were made during those months. If we are lucky, we will have a name."

Chapter 16
The Plot Thickens

Dan Astle and the engineers had circled around the table with a stack full of files, next to which lay a single piece of paper with the months in question neatly written. Astle, a veteran servant of the intelligence agency, had been a stellar scalp hunter and worked under Hicks across London and Budapest stations. When the change of guard happened between Hicks and Smith, Astle decided to step back. He disapproved of Smith and his ways and preferred to leave the service and retire early. But Control prevailed and urged him to stay back in the service. Astle longed for a quieter and less exhilarating life; having served for decades, he wanted solitude. But Control was not letting go of one of his most able men on the field. His experience far outweighed the slowness of his age. Control found the perfect answer: running operations at the Indian station, specifically its safe house.

"I need to know what happened in these months. Who made the changes, and more importantly who asked for those changes?" Astle was driving the investigation full throttle.

"We'll have this for you by tomorrow," one engineer said.

"You have six hours," Astle commanded. The engineers respected Astle; not for his title, but for his body of work and understanding of the business they were in.

"You reckon they'll find anything?" Aldridge said as he lit a cigarette. He and Alvares were standing outside the building. Rains were on the cards; the clouds had swallowed up the sun as a train halted on the tracks right opposite the building.

"If there is anything to find here, Astle is the guy. See that train, that's Shakuntala," Alvares pointed out to the train—a brilliant red with stripes of blue running across the coaches.

"How far does it go?"

"To a local station close to Bombay," Alvares said as a gust of wind blew across the building.

"Wonder if any of our guys ever went the whole way? Might be fun. I'd love to, if not for this mess," Aldridge asked.

Alvares' jaw tightened, his fist clenched as if something hit him on the chest. "What did you just say?"

"That I would love to travel on that train."

"Not that, before…"

"Wonder if any of our guys took this train ride…why?"

"I never checked if she ever took that train the day she went missing!" Alvares said and ran toward the Killick-Nixon building. Aldridge flicked the butt of his cigarette and went back to the engineers. It was a long shot. But the Killick-Nixon guys, who ran the train operations, were suckers for records. If they did their jobs, he should find out.

It had been a long day, and there was a lot to process. The two agents had brought back their findings to their room.

"This doesn't look good," Aldridge said as he went through the reports. "London approved the system changes, but…"

"But?" Alvares asked, fumbling through his own stacks of ticket sheets.

"Come, look here," Aldridge said. "July 13th, Barkley was to go to Panama. 1123 is the code for Panama. And here, August 1st, the code has been changed to 1111."

"1111 is Budapest," Alvares felt his stomach churn.

"And same for Rush. Code changed to 1111 on July 29th."

"So, who changed those codes?"

"That's the problem. They don't know. They just assume the codes are re-entered by London, once all the system updates are done."

They had reached a dead end. All they could prove was the codes were changed. Who and how—that was the real question, and they had no answers to that.

"Any luck with Kate?" Aldridge asked.

"Nothing in the ticketing records. But the clerk said he remembered *Memsaab* (madam) asking for directions to Bombay from the last station where Shakuntala stops."

Two possible leads. Two explanations, but not enough. That was the state of play.

"It's time we call them," Alvares suggested. Astle helped set up a secure line to Moscow and Pondicherry, and within an hour, they had Henley and Turner on the line.

"How is it that we are only tracing Miller now?" Henley raised his voice.

"We did. Off the books and to some extent," Father Samuel responded.

"There was no official investigation?"

"There was. For the first month of her disappearance, Maeston came down with a few from the ministry and handed over the investigation to the local police. They recorded it as a missing persons case," Alvares added.

"That's convenient. We left a female agent out on her own, not knowing what she might be going through!" Henley sounded frustrated.

"I will relay this back to Control. He has some explanations to do here," Father Samuel said, fully knowing that Control would bat this off as an oversight or a shortage of resources. Turner and Henley knew that a lot of these challenges lay on Control's feet and that their boss was losing it. No wonder the vultures—the Big Three—were circling around, looking to pick on the dead meat.

"And the codes... any explanations here?" Aldridge said, trying to steer the conversation forward.

Henley took a deep pause. He and the priest knew this was a major event and could easily be the mole playing his game. But they would need evidence of this being a human intervention and not the tech going kaput. Neither was prepared to tell Alvares and Aldridge of the mole hunt, yet.

"I will speak to Control and see if we can pull the files that relate to the tech overhaul every year and see if we can make any connection to someone..."

"Hang on a minute!" Alvares shouted.

"Now what?" Henley asked

"If these agents were to travel to Budapest after the codes were changed, wouldn't the Budapest Station receive a welcome package?"

"You are right. They would have received the legends, cover stories, personals, and travel plans," Father Samuel said.

"Assuming the change of codes reached the operations team in London and they did their jobs to prepare their arrivals in Budapest?" Aldridge was not sure if the change in codes would have been picked up.

"Well. It's worth checking. Aldridge and Alvares, I believe you both should head out to Budapest and run the investigation in person. I think we all agree that the trail leads to Budapest."

"Hopefully, the trail leads to Miller and Gilligan," Father Samuel added.

Chapter 17
Post Hoc Ergo Propter Hoc

December, 1982

Moscow

Mike Moore was a thousand pounds richer.

Tailing Roslyn was easy. A thousand pounds was enough to last him a year in Moscow without so much as breaking a sweat. *Fuck Smith*, he thought. Their tussle was well-recognized in the corridors of the London station.

It was the easiest money he'd ever made. There was a catch, of course; Henley was not the one to have the shorter end of a deal.

He had been staking the Moscow office from morning to afternoon and then setting up in Gorky Park from 5 pm to 8 pm. *I don't care what you do beyond those hours, but I want you on this every day*. Henley had been clear. Mike had asked how long he would need to do it, but Henley had just walked away.

Whatever, it put him one step closer to his goal. Prague. It's where Linda was, with their son Roxy. He had convinced himself that if he had the money, he could leave this fucking shit hole and find his way back to them.

It had been two weeks since he'd been patrolling the peripheries of Moscow Station during the day and Gorky Park in the evenings. He was a man of his word.

Gorky Park was his favorite spot in Moscow, which wasn't so hard considering how much of a shit hole the rest of it was to him. But the winters made the park turn white, cold, and soulless.

His hands were trembling, but it wasn't the cold. It had been three weeks since he'd had a drink. *I am doing this for Roxy,* he told himself and shoved his hands deep into his pockets. He stood under the usual birch tree, the perfect vantage point that overlooked the blue benches next to the lake that Henley had asked him to watch. His best guess was that he was waiting for a drop. *I hope I didn't miss it.* But Henley hadn't pulled him off the assignment, so he must have still been needed.

He opened his box of cold turkey sandwiches. Still, thirty minutes to go before he could leave. The full moon gave him a good view of the benches. And the reflection splashing off of the lakes was a nice touch. And then something made him take notice. There was someone slowly walking toward the benches. Tall and lanky, the figure moved toward the bench and sat. Mike looked at his watch: 7:45 pm.

Mike didn't move an inch. The visitor sat for ten minutes and then in a swift action stooped low and placed something under the bench. A few minutes later, he stood up, looked around, and slowly made his way out of the area. Mike stayed hidden for a few minutes to see if anyone else approached, but when no one appeared, Mike headed to the benches. Mike, a career-hardened operator, was wary of the games those at the top of the ladder played. He already had a few near misses, thanks to Smith and his plans to make Mike a scapegoat when an operation went awry. Naturally, he was suspicious that Henley would do the same. He was being paid exorbitant money for this and that was his only motivation to work on this task. He trusted Hicks and Hicks trusted Henley. That meant Henley sat above Smith on the scale of trust.

The bench was as clean as a whistle. No markings, no codes, nothing. He looked around to check if anyone was watching, stooped low, and moved his hands under the bench.

There it was—a small box stuck under the bench. He left it there and headed back to the birch tree to wait.

An hour passed by uneventfully. An elderly couple with their dog walked past. His watch showed nine o'clock. This is when he eventually realized this was a dead drop, and he was the designated agent to pick it up. Why didn't Henley just tell him the exact day and time? *Not my business*, he thought and went back to the bench before heading off to Henley's apartment.

"What are you doing here at this ungodly hour?" Henley said as he pulled Mike inside the front door of his house.

"This couldn't wait," Mike said and rushed to the kitchen to grab some water.

"Tell me you aren't drunk or in trouble?"

Mike ignored him and went to the kitchen to make himself some coffee. The cold and the run he made from the park had him exhausted. As the water boiled, Mike relayed the events of the last couple of hours.

"You're sure you weren't followed here?"

"Positive," Mike said and handed the small box to Henley.

Henley looked at the box. A small brown box with an inscription on the top. One look at the inscription and he understood who had sent it. He got up and went to his study, leaving the box on the coffee table. If this was from who he thought it was, then he needed more eyes and ears when he opened it. He picked up the phone and called John Marbury. Marbury reached the residence within the hour.

"*Post Hoc Ergo Propter Hoc*," Marbury read it out loud, "What in the devil is that?"

"It's Latin," Henley said, pouring himself another cognac. He offered the bottle to Mike, who shook his head. "Means *after this, therefore, because of this*."

"Right," Marbury reached out to get his fill of the drink. "But what does *that* mean?"

"It's a logical fallacy that occurs when someone assumes that one event caused another simply because it happened before the second. But that's not important—it's just a code phrase the case officers use. What's important is the handwriting."

Mike and Marbury leaned in closer.

"It's Tesla," Henley said as his jaws clenched.

There was silence in the room.

"Mike, go to the back room and close the door, please," Henley instructed and Mike dutifully moved off.

"It doesn't make sense. Why would Tesla approach *Mike* of all people? And what was he doing at the park in the first place?" Marbury asked.

"Marbury, take it easy," Henley said when he heard the door shut. "I asked him to be there."

"But why?"

"To keep an eye out. Aldridge and the lads are not here. We are short of eyes. I needed someone to be on the lookout if Tesla were to reach out."

"But Tesla hasn't contacted us in months and now he suddenly appears out of the blue. Convenient timing, don't you think?" Marbury said.

"You could be right, or maybe he just found the opportunity for the drop only now?"

"Still. Just when we cast a net to catch the mole…I just cannot see this as a coincidence," Marbury was adamant.

"We don't know what he wants," Henley said and opened the box. There was a single piece of paper with a scribbled note:

Mayday. Meet urgently. Gorky Park. East entrance. 12/12, 10.30 pm. Bring L-pill.

Henley and Marbury looked worried. This was not good. The writing was unmistakably Tesla's. The question was whether he'd written the note under duress. Did the KGB already have him and were preparing for an ambush? And the worst of all was his request for an L-pill. *An L-pill was a poison pill that spies and undercover agents requested if they feared getting caught.* Tesla had written the request verbatim and not in code, which meant he had to write the note with some urgency.

"What do you think, John?" Henley asked, many a time he leaned on his best friend for guidance or a nudge in the right direction, "Do you think the KGB have him?"

"We can't take this lightly. The L-pill is something he and Aldridge would have talked about in the past," Marbury said. "And that makes me think that the KGB doesn't have him, yet."

"But he fears for his life?" Henley asked.

"Presumably. That should be our working theory."

"I still can't understand the timing of this," Marbury said. "We're about to trigger the final step of your plan with the priest and Tesla suddenly reaches out?"

Henley was pacing the hall.

"What could he possibly want?" Henley said, "If it was money, we could get it ready. Is his daughter sick again?"

"I think he wants out," Marbury said.

"Exfiltration?" Henley was almost considering the same.

"I can bet all the money in my account."

"Let's say he does. Do we want him out?"

Tesla was their golden goose. The mole hunt Henley and Father Samuel had set up was not just to catch the mole; they also wanted to protect Tesla. More importantly, to protect the valuable information he provided. As much as they wanted to protect his life, they wanted to use him as well for as long as possible.

"We owe him that. He's not asked for money or anything in return in all these years."

"Are we sure London would agree?"

"What is the difference between us and the KGB if we leave him out in the cold?" Henley had made up his mind by now. If Tesla wanted out, he would get it, and Moscow Station would do everything possible to keep him safe.

For the next hour, Henley and Marbury considered all outcomes. Every which way, this was going to be a tough ask. They would need all hands on deck. Especially since Aldridge was his handler. He managed Tesla single-handedly. Henley couldn't risk spooking Tesla by sending a new face to run the exfil. *They needed Keith Aldridge back in Moscow.*

"I hope you know that we have to stall the mole hunt," Marbury said. "Bring our boys back to run this."

"I'd considered that. But before we do, I need to speak to the priest." He turned to the back of the apartment. "Mike, could you come out, please?"

The latch on the door handle clicked, and Mike walked into the hallway.

"Stay here until we're back," he ordered and left with Marbury. "Don't do anything until you hear from me again." Mike nodded and stared at the bottle of cognac.

Henley could feel the rug slipping under his feet as the events of the past few weeks seemed to have run past him. The Moscow Station chief was finding it difficult to keep a hold of the events. Something's got to give, he thought. The ever-evolving premise of laying down the gauntlet and passing on the baton to the next station chief kept wringing around him like a noose, but he wasn't ready to leave his legacy unfinished. He was too proud and hard-knuckled to bow down to the pressure of the new way espionage was being played by the spy community.

Simon Henley had been in these situations before, his authority being questioned by the powers that be and sometimes, his team. But, he always prevailed and kept his reputation intact and the Moscow Center of the MI6 protected; at all costs. This time, though, the enemy was both within and outside.

Modern espionage demanded fast, decisive, build-as-you-fly moves whilst the traditional dance of spies was slow burning; letting the pot simmer and making a move when the time was right. Henley was stuck in transition, finding it hard to determine whether they should rely on the old and proven methods or go with the modern terms of engagement. It was made doubly difficult not knowing on which side the enemy fell. Which rules of the game were they playing with? The old or new?

He knew the call with the priest had to happen tonight, no more time to be lost. Marbury signaled him that the line was hot. Marbury had his ways around the system—one thing Darcy taught him. *Young blood and their workarounds,* he thought.

Chapter 18
Spanner in the Works

Thirty Minutes to Midnight.

A few thousand miles away, Father Samuel had just finished a late dinner and retired to his study. He stowed away his Bible and took out the files that Alvares had kept in his office. His greatest asset was his ability to balance his angels and demons. He diligently ran his duties at the church and rarely let the espionage side of him derail his duties. But when the shutters were down and the candles extinguished at the church, his alter ego took center stage. Father Samuel read through the files, combing through every single detail at hand on Miller and Gilligan.

For half a year, Neil ran his own investigation into the disappearance of Kate Miller. Father Samuel at first suspected that he was running covert operations without his knowledge, but when Astle from Shakuntala started informing him of Alvares' persistent questions about Kate, he realized that she meant more to Alvares than just a colleague. He didn't deter Alvares from this investigation as long as Alvares was running the official ops and duties and kept the personal agenda separate from the call of duty. But, that is where he realized the folly of his decisions—the decision to not support Alvares' investigation officially. Only if he had given Alvares the opportunity to open up to him and ask for help, together, they could have arrived at the same conclusion as he and Aldridge did last night regarding Kate and her disappearance much earlier. Probably his inexperience of loving a woman deserted his thinking.

Alvares and Aldridge should be back to Pondicherry by tomorrow and soon set sail for Budapest, he thought. But there was something that kept nagging him—how far up the value chain would the mole have to be—to affect the code change and completely misdirect everyone else at the same time? What authority would one need to run a covert op of this scale without alerting someone? Was the mole acting out of self-interest, or was the KGB behind this mole? The actions of the mole were still not clear to him. The key to finding the mole was to find his or her motivations. *The raison d'être.*

With the premise that someone in a position to affect this scale of espionage had to be the mole, he got to work—preparing his list of suspects. He took out his pocket notebook and put down the names that would fit the bill—Smith, Engels, Maeston, and Henley. Control was the only one he knew was not the mole himself. Henley was the far right, out-of-the-box option. But what would Henley gain from this? Was he honey-trapped by the KGB? Was he in their debt for something he did in the past? With the Big Three, the ambition to become the Controller of the MI6 was a big enough reason to put them on the list. But Control trusted Henley and by extension, he had to give some weight to that trust. And there were the rest from the Moscow Station. He didn't know them by any stretch and had to consider them as possible suspects. But hopefully, the fake plan they put together might lead them somewhere, he thought.

And then he almost wanted to include Keith Aldridge on the list but stopped. Over the last week, Aldridge had shown no intention to stall the investigation. Rather, he was driving it. It would be crazy to consider Aldridge as the mole. But years of espionage and the kind of men he had worked with, anything was possible. At this point, there was only one person he knew was completely clean: Neil Alvares. Henley and

Aldridge, a distant second. Father Samuel spent the next few minutes working through the files to find any evidence that could be traced back to the mole. He heard the stray dogs bark in the distance, and then a silence engulfed his room.

The phone on his desk rang, disturbing the silence.

"Sacra Coeur, Pondicherry," he said into the receiver.

"Hello, Father. This is Father Pierre from Sacra Coeur Paris, do you have a moment?" the voice on the other end said.

"Of course. It's good to hear from you. How can I help?" Father Samuel said, startled at the call at this hour of the night. He could sense this was not a call related to the church.

"I have a friend who needs to confess to you, and only you. Can you hear him out?"

"No one is denied in this church. Please, patch them through."

Father Samuel then knew someone had gone through a lot of trouble to keep this call off the records.

"Hello Father, this is your old friend from the North. Can we talk?"

"You were in my thoughts Henley; how can I help?" Father Samuel was comfortable naming him, considering this was a secure line.

"We have a big spanner in the works and I need you to weigh in," Henley said with an air of lightness, finding comfort in a confidant.

"I trust the line is secure?" Father Samuel asked, not fully aware of Henley's position.

"We have a code Blue," Henley said with a heavy voice, straight from the book co-authored between Father Samuel and Aldridge.

"I sense this is going to be a long conversation?" Father Samuel asked, leaning back in his chair.

Henley recounted the situation and waited for the priest's response.

"The timing of this is something I believe you have considered?" Father Samuel asked.

"I took that into account, but I have to consider the request in isolation, outside the mole problem. What if Tesla is in real trouble?"

"With the mole problem we have, you cannot run the exfiltration in isolation," Father Samuel said.

"That's why I called you," Henley said.

"First order of business, Henley, who are we assembling to run the exfil?"

"For an operation of this scale, if we are to go ahead, I need all hands on deck."

"Even if any of them could be the mole?"

"I have no other option. I need them here, regardless of how much I trust them. Specially Aldridge, he is Tesla's handler."

"I understand the situation. There is someone who is not part of our mole problem, who can babysit this."

"Who?"

"Alvares. I think he should join the operation."

"There is value in that, can you make arrangements?"

"Consider it done," Father Samuel said, as he stared at the list of suspects he had. He struck down Aldridge and Henley's names. The situation had completely changed and for him, the list was getting narrower.

"We were so close, Father, I could sense we were going to catch the mole with the recent discoveries."

"That plan is now down the drain. The mole hunt will have to wait."

"But why can't we do both at the same time?" Father Samuel said.

"What do you mean?" said Henley.

"Why can't we run the exfil and hunt for the mole at the same time?"

"Do we have something in the playbook to do this?" Henley asked, feeling encouraged.

"There isn't, but I may have an idea to stitch two different plays together," Father Samuel said and took a deep pause.

"Misdirection, that's what we need," Father Samuel said as his sound reached a higher pitch.

"You will tell me more when you have a plan?"

"Stay put, Henley. With a little faith, I think we could make this work," the priest said and hung up the phone. He set about working on a plan that could work in light of the new challenge they were facing. But this time, he was going to need something that he never employed in his work as a spy *faith*. For his plan to work, he and Henley would have to place an incredible amount of faith in Alvares and Aldridge.

Chapter 19
Bon Voyage

The man wiped the dust and fingerprints off his spectacles, lit a cigarette, and shadow-boxed around his apartment with no shirt on. He had called her, and she was to call back shortly. There is a surprise gift waiting for you on the other side, she said.

"You have done excellent work...the Chief Directorate sends his regards," *the voice on the other line said.*

"Happy to hear that," *he said with a sense of pride in his work. He was trying to guess the person behind the voice.*

"Is there anything we can do for you?"

"I'm okay... for now," *he said.*

"Good. We are quite interested in finding out the further details of the technology."

"I am working on it."

"It will be better if we can find something soon," *the voice on the other end tried to assert itself.* "Our agent will deposit the money in your account, as always."

"For what? I believe you already paid for the last time."

"Consider it an advance. Also, the chief would like some intel on the Viennese operations. Your work on the Budapest outpost has helped greatly," *the voice said and hung up.*

Carrot and stick, he thought. He knew what he had signed up for, and now he had to see it through. There was no coming back. So far, he had trodden the line carefully, making sure he left no trail of breadcrumbs behind. This was the first time someone from the leadership had spoken to him and not his handler. He was on the fast track to becoming the highest-placed double agent for the

KGB in the history of British secret surveillance. A few more years and I will sit at the top of Circus, he thought.

"Darling, how did it go?" she had called back.

"Who was he?"

"That was the General Directorate. He directly reports to the Chief Directorate," she said, as a sudden crash of plates surrounded her space.

"Are you calling from your home?" he asked.

"Sorry about that, it's my kid," she said.

"Someday I want to meet her," he said. She had taken over his thoughts, his work, and essentially his life. This was not just about money. It was to please her, to show her he could be the man she deserves. She had a family, but that didn't stop him from wanting to meet her, have passionate sex, and talk about emotions, life, family, and what they could build together. Working together was the start of the relationship—being together and living together was his ultimate ambition.

Indian Station,

Pondicherry.

Alvares and Aldridge had come so close to figuring out what had happened at Shakuntala, only to hit a brick wall. And just when they made plans to further their search, Father Samuel broke the news regarding Tesla and his request to defect.

"Who received the dead drop from Tesla?" Aldridge asked.

"The wire from Moscow spared the details."

"Then, how do they know it was from Tesla?" Aldridge was the only one who had met Tesla. He looked at Alvares. The two had the same intuition. Had the same entity broken through the codes and figured out the real name of the Moscow Station's precious double agent?

"Give your station chief some credit, I am sure he would know," Father Samuel said.

"And what happens to the operation that he sent me here for?" Aldridge asked, visibly upset.

"Let me take care of that," Alvares said, trying to play along the fake plan.

"That won't be necessary," Father Samuel looked up to Alvares, put his glasses on the desk, and rose. "You are leaving for Moscow with Aldridge. Do you have your English passport?"

Alvares didn't ask why. "I do," he said.

"Good. I've booked your flights to leave from Delhi tomorrow at ten in the morning."

There was unfinished business in India. They both sensed the foul play but they needed more time and resources. Tesla was his priority; Aldridge understood that.

༄

Delhi International Airport

Neil Alvares flipped through his passport—Dev Patel. He was a British national for now—a world-traveling businessman-son of a migrant Gujarati family, with visit stamps of South Africa, Kenya, Germany, Brazil, the United States of America, and a few more across South America. He felt a multitude of emotions: fear, excitement, loneliness, and above all redemption. This was the payback for years of his running the MI6 station in Pondicherry, looking for his Sikander, to put a marker on what he wanted to do with his life. He looked at himself in the mirror on the adjacent walls of the waiting area in the airport. He looked sharp, dressed perfectly in a navy blue suit, black shoes, and a brown leather suitcase. Aldridge was in the shopping area, probably buying stuff for his daughter and Mrs. Aldridge.

He felt a sense of gratitude to Martin. He had taken every single penny saved to get him the suit stitched a couple of years back. He didn't need to. Neil earned twice the amount that Martin made in the bakery in a month. He owed his career to Father Samuel, for seeing something in him and giving him the wings to fly more than a decade back, the briefcase, the priest's gift to Alvares, a poignant reminder of it. The shoes were a gift from Kate. The gift from her came with a promise to travel the world together. Yet, here he sat, alone as she left off without as much leaving a note behind to explain her actions. He looked over at the clock and saw there were still a few minutes left to board the flight. He knew he had to make one final phone call before he set sail.

"Martin, it's me," Alvares said, his voice heavy, his heart heavier.

"Have you reached Delhi?"

"I have, and tell you what, the airport looks amazing. Nothing like the last time."

"It's a blessing that you can see the world," Martin sounded ecstatic about his grandson.

"I wish you could join me," Alvares said, looking at the watch. He had a minute more worth of money to continue the long-distance phone call.

"You very well know I cannot leave the bakery alone; Khan will not manage it by himself. And this work with the British press you have is too important for you to take care of me while you are working."

The British press has invited him to cover the preparations for the upcoming cricket World Cup next year, and they have invited journalists from the participating nations, including India, *amongst those taking part. This cover story worked well for his friends and family, and importantly for Martin. Neil Alvares was a journalist in his day job at the Deccan Herald newspaper—*

the chief editor, a devout catholic, had returned a favor to Father Samuel. Neil Alvares made it to the news office once a week for namesake.

"I promise you that I will take you to England to watch the World Cup. I don't know how, but I will."

"It's fine, beta *(son in Hindi)*. Pondicherry is big enough for me. And then I have a massive business empire to run…" Martin laughed out loud into the phone.

"Take good care of yourself, will you?"

"I will. And you take care of the hot air hostess for me!" Martin said and gave out a long laugh.

Alvares kept the receiver and took a deep breath. He was truly blessed to have Martin in his life. The void left behind by his parents was filled by Martin. Something he never thanked him enough for. For the first time in his life, he felt alone, amidst a sea of people around him. He was now longing for affection, his mid-thirties was upon him and about time most Indian men would have settled down with a wife and kid.

The intercom announced the start of the boarding for the Air India flight from Delhi to Moscow. The boarding went through smoothly and safely. Thank God for the lax officials, he thought. Not a question was asked. The immigration officer didn't even look at him and just stamped his passport and let him board. Alvares took his seat next to the window and saw the runway speed past him as the airplane took flight. Aldridge was seated next to him, writing stuff onto his diary, anxious for what surprises awaited them in Moscow.

༺༻

Sheremetyevo International Airport, Moscow, Russia.

"We cannot be seen together from here on in," Aldridge said and immediately distanced himself from Alvares. "I will see you outside, come straight to parking lot two."

The flight had landed in the dead of night. Neil Alvares wound the Omega Calatrava on his wrist; a parting gift from his father. It had meant a lot to his father, and he made sure to take good care of it. He set the time to 2 am. Alvares was aware of KGB surveillance in the airport— a brown skin, British national in Moscow would stick out like a sore thumb. He needed a cover, someone who would help him slide past immigration without much fanfare and to the parking lot.

In the distance, he saw a group of saree-clad women walking toward him. He instantly recognized the smiling face of Zoya, the beautiful flight attendant who had served him several cups of coffee on the flight.

"Ms. Zoya!" Alvares shouted toward the group of flight attendants, hoping to catch her attention.

Mild surprise crossed her face as she broke away from her colleagues and walked toward him. *That walk is going to kill me*, Alvares thought, mesmerized by the sway of her hips as she came toward him.

"Care for some coffee, Ms. Zoya?" Alvares asked.

"Mr. Patel, didn't I serve you enough on the flight?" she said with a hint of a smile.

"But that was not Russian coffee. Can I get you one, as a small thank you for making the awfully long flight bearable?"

"Bearable? I thought you had a splendid time chatting with my colleagues?"

"Oh no, that was me asking them for you. But apparently, you got busy with some Mr. Popov and his kids."

She laughed. "Mr. Popov was a chatterbox, alright! Thanks for the offer, but I have to rush."

"At least let me get you something for the road ahead," he signaled the vendor and asked him to pack a cookie and a coffee quickly. Alvares was in his element—his suave demeanor rubbing onto Zoya.

"Are you from Delhi, Ms. Zoya?"

"Hyderabad. And Zoya is fine, you can drop the Ms."

"I am from..." Alvares hesitated for a second and said, "London, but my parents used to be in Pondicherry before they moved to England." Alvares rued the fact that he had just given up a part of his true identity.

Alvares paid and picked up the brown parcel and the steaming cup of coffee and handed them over to Zoya. "Can I walk along with you?"

"Be my guest, Mr. Patel."

"Dev, please," he said and fell in behind Zoya finding it hard to match the brisk pace that flight attendants were used to.

"So... Dev, what brings you away to this cold country?"

"Just business. Do you travel often to Moscow?"

"More than I'd like. I prefer the warmer side of Europe."

"Well, London is sometimes warm in July. I'd be happy to show you around."

"Yeah, right!" Zoya laughed out loud. Her laugh echoed and lingered in Alvares' ears far longer than he thought it would. *That laugh will kill me.* A few more minutes and he would be out of the immigration. He continued to engage Zoya along the queue.

"Would it be alright if I took down your number?" he asked.

"That's a stretch, Dev."

"Well then, tell me where can I find you, if I wanted to take you for dinner?"

"Why do you think I would want to have dinner with you?"

"At least let me try to change your mind?" Alvares said, looking over his shoulder. His senses were tightened as he continued moving up the queue alongside her.

"Well, if you really do want..then find out where the hostesses from Air India are going to stay."

"Challenge accepted," he said and moved toward the immigration counter.

He got the entry stamp and waited at the back of the immigration counters for Zoya to join.

"Expect to hear from me soon, Zoya," he said and shook her hand. She gave a smile and picked up her luggage.

"I will take your leave here," Zoya said as she pointed to the parking signboards. "Maybe we will bump into each other again. Take care, Dev."

Chapter 20
Circle of Trust

Henley had been playing second fiddle until now; he could feel that. He knew the priest was running the show from afar, although his intentions weren't to challenge Henley's authority; rather, Henley was seeking him out, and the plans and ideas came from him. Henley had never been in this situation since his early days in the service. He had always been the man of action, the one calling the shots and steering his department forward. Henley knew he needed a course correction; he had been slipping away for the last several months. The mole would have left enough breadcrumbs. Had Henley been looking, he would have found some traces and run an op even before Control came calling or left a trail of dead or missing agents. This thought kept him awake through the night, as he tossed and turned in the bed of his plush apartment. If this was to be his last dance, then he was going to go out with a bang. Henley felt an adrenaline rush—something he hadn't for a while.

By the early hours of December 14th, Henley knew the first order of business was to make sure he was running a tight operation on Tesla. Anyone from the station could be the mole. He had already placed a bit of trust and hope on John Marbury and Roslyn not being the mole. He now needed to place a bit of trust in Aldridge as well. It was time to bring him into the inner circle a bit, if not completely. At his command, Ros had sent wires to Stuart Wright and Charles Darcy summoning them back to the station. He would need an all-hands-on-deck operation if they were to run the Tesla operation, and regardless of his level of trust, he had to bring everyone back.

Henley was aware that there could still be a covert operation hidden inside the Tesla operation. He would need to lean on the priest to come up with the plan while he mobilizes his team to focus on Tesla. But, beyond the Moscow Five, he had a couple of jokers in his deck of cards. Two men, if used carefully, could help him move his operations on the fly if the situation needed it. Mike Moore and the deputy station head from India—Neil Alvares. Henley had a strong feeling that they were going to be key if he was to succeed in bringing Tesla out and catching the mole.

Moscow, the next day. Mosfilm Studio.

Aldridge and Henley discretely tip-toed toward their designated seats. Henley was not built for such crowded places. He stepped on a foot or two, inciting an angry exchange of words. As he moved to his seat, the projector cast his shadow onto the screens, a few angry Russians voicing their displeasure.

"You sure this was the best place we could meet?" Henley asked, almost ready to head back.

"This is absolutely perfect, trust me," Aldridge assured a visibly uncomfortable Henley.

"If you say so," Henley said as the screen lit up and the opening credits rolled in.

"Did the Indian agent make it?"

"Alvares, yes. He's staying put at the quarters, next to Roslyn's street."

"Any good?" Alvares asked. He wanted to hear Aldridge's assessment of the new agent in their ranks.

"Very. And by George, those guys at the Indian station know how to run shop," Aldridge said. Henley was feeling even more confident of the move of getting Alvares to help them out. The joker was now out from the deck and on the table. Simon still had one joker hidden in the deck—Mike.

With the winters in Moscow going full scale and the weather unforgiving, the spies had met at Mosfilm Studio, right under the noses of the unsuspecting Russians. With the concerns over their usual spots being spied upon, Henley felt they needed a change of scene. He asked Aldridge to choose a random location—somewhere they would not be expected to be. Mosfilm was a legendary theater and movie venue and was a popular choice of entertainment for an everyday Muscovite. *Lenin in Paris*, a docudrama based on the four years Lenin spent in Paris, was running during the matinee show.

Amongst a house full of fur coats, mufflers, and a heavy smoke-filled audience, the two career spies sat, probably making the most significant covert plans of their career thus far.

Henley, frustrated and tattered because of the sub-zero windstorms sweeping across the city, initially welcomed the idea of meeting up at a cinema. Some change of place. His idea of a theater was of the Royal British Society, with comfortable chairs, a delectable array of food, drinks, and close friends. But the Mosfilm theater was unlike any he had seen.

The theater was too purple for his liking and the velvet textured seats gave an uneasy feeling in the groin. The people around were loud, the colors bright, and the cinema outrageous—all antonyms for what cinema stood for in his mind. The screen was impressive, though.

"A fine spot to talk shop," Aldridge said. He always wanted to have a covert meeting right in the middle of the locals. The adrenaline was pumping through his veins.

"Yeah, right. I can barely hear you, so I am sure the others can't!" Henley retorted.

The movie was slow-paced and the music, ecstatic. Lenin and his communist propaganda were on show, but a lot more tempered with bits of comedy. Subtle, Henley thought.

"The meet with Tesla, have you thought out a plan?"

"I have. It will not be straightforward. As you said, we have to expect an ambush or some sort of counter-surveillance."

"I think the puppet play could work," Henley said.

"Not heard of it."

"If you pull it off, it's brilliant and works like a charm. Marbury would know the details of the play," Henley was now into his elements. "You'll need a body along. The puppet play only works with two in tandem."

The two spies went out during the interval. Fresh snow had fallen over the movie's first half. It was a sea of white with an array of colorful silhouettes of men, women, and children walking the streets.

Aldridge lit two cigarettes and gave one to Henley.

"We never spoke about the last operation, Simon," Keith knew when to address his boss personally.

"We just have to put a pin in that for now."

"I would imagine Tesla's request would need any other plans to be on hold," Aldridge said but still wanted to push his boss a bit more.

"What was the last op about? The India Station was more vested in the missing agent's case than the operation I was sent to work on."

Henley rubbed his hands to fight the cold that was getting through his gloves. He didn't say anything and waited for Aldridge to complete his thought.

"It was almost as if the trip to India was a test or a reason to keep me away from Moscow. Which one was it, Simon?" he asked.

"It was not just you who went on a mission. Darcy and Wright left, too."

"And are they back as well?"

"Sure. They did."

Aldridge was now getting more interested in his boss's cryptic responses.

"But you never debriefed us when we switched the operation to Tesla exfil?"

Henley took a long puff and stood looking far into the corner of the road. His weary shoulders seemed heavy.

"We have reason to believe that the stuff you uncovered in India could be part of a larger problem."

"You believe that those agents are not the only casualty and that there have been more?"

"It goes beyond that. We could be looking at our entire operation getting blown up."

"You mean leaks?" Aldridge said to stop his boss from beating around the bush. A leak worked, but he was looking for that word. A mole.

"It goes beyond conventional leaks. This looks like an insider job, someone deep in the Circus. We haven't been able to put the finger on it, or the level of damage already done" Henley said. Carefully, he kept out the part that the London bosses and the rest of the Moscow Station were suspects.

"What made you believe so?"

"There have been situations where you or the others have gone on surveillance runs, dead drops, where we saw activity springing in at the last minute from the KGB. We clear the routes every time, but just by a small margin."

"And we had these routes covered well and easy before?"

"Yes. That's not it. They seem to know every single agent coming in and out of the country. Sometimes, before we do."

"How come we are only realizing this now?"

"The dead agents triggered a search for similarities elsewhere," Henley said.

"Do you think they already know about Alvares?"

"I hope not. India Station flies under the radar."

"Earlier this year, when Wright met his agent, I remember he had a tough time," Keith added. He started counting the pieces together from his memory.

"Not just Wright. Last summer, when you had a drop-off with Tesla, I had you tailed discreetly. Before Tesla could pick up the package, your shadow picked it up. The KGB was on your tail all along."

Aldridge stood shocked. Not because the drop didn't go as planned, but because his boss had him tailed.

"And then we had the biggest surprise of all. Our papers on the Panama project made it to the Russians. Word for word."

"How did you come to know?"

"That's above your pay grade, Aldridge."

Aldridge could reason with that.

"Well, then let me do my bit and give you a full debrief on what we found in India, probably you could connect the dots better than we could," Aldridge said and started giving him a detailed brief on what they uncovered in India and perhaps they have a couple of strong leads that lead straight to the Budapest Station.

Aldridge felt the Budapest Station was the center of their problems and leaks. But Henley knew this was the work of the KGB-led mole.

"Can I ask you something, Henley?" Aldridge said and looked directly into Simon's eyes, straight from the shoulder, "Henley, no messing about," Aldridge continued.

"We have a mole problem, don't we?" Aldridge asked.

"You may be right to think so," Simon said, put on his overcoat, left the theater premises, and headed home.

Henley felt a strange vein of relief. He had just managed to bring a key player into his inner circle of trust halfway through, enough to trust him to run the Tesla operation without risking the other part of his plan.

Chapter 21
The Request

Moscow Station,

Dec 14th

The Moscow Station was at full capacity. Stuart Wright and Charles Darcy were back, and Neil Alvares had set up on the spare desk. His time at Moscow was off to a better-than-expected start, thanks to Roslyn, who eased him in. The Moscow Station was nothing like India. The scale of operations was much larger.

"Did he tell you why he called us back in the middle of an op?" Darcy asked Wright, who was still in his traveling suit. Along with Aldridge, Darcy, and Wright were rushed back to the Moscow Station.

"Look at my face, Darcy," Wright said, "Does it look like I have an idea?" Wright in his usual nonchalant attitude to matters that didn't concern his agent. He only had two objectives as a case officer: first, to bring the best out of his agents in the KGB, and second, to keep them alive and safe as long as possible to make them work toward his first objective.

There was a briefing due at eleven hundred hours.

"Marbury... tell me this is important, else I could do with some sleep," Wright said as he stretched his legs onto the billiards table that served as the conference point when the team needed to group in for a chat. "By the way, who's the new guy?"

Marbury wasn't sure how to respond to that. He had only met Alvares last night over a dinner at Roslyn's apartment, serving as a makeshift war room when needed. Henley and

Aldridge were there, and the discussion was mostly about Tesla and how to go about the operation. They talked about everything but forgot how to introduce Alvares to the other lads. *More so, the reason he was here.*

"Henley should be here any moment. You can ask him directly." Marbury deferred the question to his boss.

"Wow, we are a cheerful lot today, aren't we?" Wright said and went back to his desk. He had stuff to do—far more important.

Aldridge walked in minutes later. He hung his raincoat on the coat stand and went straight to his desk.

"And?" Wright asked as Aldridge took a seat and quickly took out his notepad and started writing.

"What?" Alright asked, a lot running through his mind.

"Nothing. Thought you would know what the heck is happening around here," Wright said as Aldridge opened his briefcase and pulled out a couple of files.

Aldridge started writing on his notepad, totally ignoring Stuart Wright.

"Everyone; my office, ten minutes!" Henley shouted as he entered through the main door, dripping wet, and headed straight through to his office.

Roslyn and Darcy took the couch. Aldridge stood next to the door and Marbury sat on the chairs in front of Henley's desk. Alvares walked in with a cup of coffee, placed it on Henley's desk, and then took a spot next to Aldridge.

"Someone's sucking up already," Darcy whispered to Roslyn. Roslyn gave a stern stare back; this was not the time to run personal agendas.

Henley took out his pack of cigarettes, lit one, and then passed the box to Marbury. He did the same and passed the pack of cigarettes around.

"You all must be wondering why we had to halt our operation," Henley said as he took a deep drag on his cigarette. "That's because we got a package from Tesla with a request to meet up, urgently."

"Damn you, Aldridge, I asked you if you knew what's happening here. You could have just said you had a drop from Tesla," Wright said, looking to invoke a reaction from Aldridge. He had always been envious of Aldridge running Tesla. Wright's guy, Dmitri "Eddie" Petrovic's output was completely dwarfed by Tesla over the last few years. Control dubbed Tesla as the 'million-pound spy'. Although he and Aldridge were colleagues, they had their own little gamesmanship going around. At every possible opportunity, they would try to win over the other in every possible way, while staying within the decorum and fair play that Henley expected from the Moscow Five.

"Steady on," Henley said. "Aldridge wasn't here."

"Then who got the package?" Darcy asked.

"Not important. We have established it came from Tesla," Henley gave the note to John to pass it around, "This takes precedence over everything else."

"No wonder we were called in quick," Darcy said.

John Marbury rose and took center stage, "Listen up. We need a plan. We cannot take the usual routes; we expect that the KGB is on this. Don't want you lot to be ambushed. Aldridge, Wright, can I ask you both to work on the Puppet Playbook? Alvares, you're with Ros. We need to trace all the previous dead drop routes we have used in the past and come up with a new route to the location."

"Where will the live drop be?" Darcy asked.

Marbury gave him a stare, "You know better than to ask. It's way above your pay grade, son."

Of the twenty-two drops Tesla and Aldridge had made over the past four years, only one had been live. They'd met in person only once in the last five years. A live drop required careful planning, counter surveillance of the highest order, and dummy routes to throw the enemy off the scent. They both had to go utterly black before they could meet under extreme counter-surveillance this time around.

Keith Aldridge moved across the room and stood in front of the windows as a light shower of snow started settling up on the windowsill. His conversation with Henley weighed up his thinking and planning. This meeting with Tesla would have to be arranged perfectly. Any mistake and he would lose his agent forever. With the threat of a mole, they would need to be smarter and braver. He would need a smokescreen to evade a KGB trail that was sure to follow him right outside the embassy gates.

The planning had moved onto the billiards table. Ros had always been the brains behind running live drops and identifying new routes and dead letter boxes. Although a secretary by title, she was no less an agent than the others. In fact, the rest regarded her as the oil that smoothened the machinery that Moscow Station was. She knew where the bodies were buried, which outpost had the best value to Moscow Center's operation, which briefings were to reach Control's desk, and when. Above all, she could guess, almost always, what Henley was going to do in a situation. She was his mind reader, and that put her in a position of strength among her peers, although she never misused it for her own career advancement. She started as a secretary and thirty years later, remained a secretary.

Keith Aldridge walked into a busy table of agents putting together a series of maps, drop routes, and plays used in the past.

"Aldridge, about time. I am assuming you know exactly where to meet him at Gorky Park?" Roslyn said as she prepared notes.

"Yes, ma'am," Aldridge said, responding to her authority in the matter.

"Here, I have the last five routes you took for the dead drops around Gorky Park," she said and passed on a file to Aldridge and Wright. Spanning across 300 acres, Gorky Park was an active site for the spies to operate right in the middle of the city.

Wright took the file and started going through the pages when Aldridge asked him to stop as Ros was not done yet. She had come back with another file.

"Go through this playbook and find the puppet play. Run the schematics of the play and see which route from the past will work best for the play," she said.

"Ros?" Aldridge said and moved closer and whispered in her ears. *I need a giant smokescreen right out of the gates.* She understood what he wanted; she had already planned for it.

Aldridge and Wright set to work. Ros went to the comms room to find Darcy and Marbury. They were to prepare the data from surveillance on the KGB hot zones and submit the latest information that the team could use before they live drop.

Last, she went to Alvares.

"You and I are going to work on this stuff together," she said and showed him an invitation letter.

"This is an invite from the Ambassador for a Christmas ball which he is hosting tomorrow?" Alvares asked.

"Exactly, and we are going to use that as a smokescreen to ship Aldridge and Wright out of the embassy."

Alvares looked at the invite. If the official parties were any similar to the ones they hosted in India, then by definition there would be a lot of regular employees, their families, and dignitaries. It should be relatively easy to get them out of such a big party. But Moscow was never easy. Ros's first piece of advice: always assume they are around.

"Our biggest challenge on the night would be to evade a few of the Russian dignitaries."

"There would be Russians in the party?"

"You bet, son. This is Moscow and this is a party for diplomats first,"

"Wouldn't that just put the place into a high-alert zone?" Moscow was a different gravy, he came to realize.

"It would. But that also means, once we have the boys out of this place, they would expect less traffic on the road."

"By traffic, you mean surveillance."

"Exactly that."

"Just making sure I am not leaving anything to assume," Alvares said, quickly catching on the proceedings at Moscow Station.

Ros and Alvares worked on a few ideas. None held its ground. The classical 'waiter switch' looked like the best option thus far. But, Alvares was adamant they could do better. He liked to be *avant-gardian* in the way he did business. Ros had the veto to the plan they would take to Henley, but she let him indulge in a bit of creativity.

"From the team we have here, do the KGB track each and every one of them?" he asked.

"They have us on the books sure, but not like they are on us every day all the time"

"And when they do, they think everyone is a case officer running a double agent?"

"That would be hard to tell. But for sure, they keep a close eye on Henley, Aldridge, and Wright."

"And less on Marbury and Darcy?" he asked, knowing that case officers were the prized assets for every intelligence agency, lesser so the techies.

"Possibly, where are you going with this?" Ros asked.

Neil Alvares took a pause and paced around the room. The Tesla meet would at least take 4 to 5 hours, including the time to go black and to be back at the party. It would be impossible to have both the case officers missing from a party. He took out his personal notebook and quickly put together a sequence of events. Ros looked carefully, partly admiring his thinking and partly his audacity to throw a plan that was edgy.

"Here, do you think this would work?" Alvares said and passed on a note with a brief outline of his plan.

"If we choreograph it properly. And a bit of makeup!" Ros said as she ran through the notes.

"From afar, Marbury can easily pass off for Wright and Darcy for Aldridge."

"And if we get them moving around in crowds, that should keep our guests guessing enough to miss the count."

"Well, you think Henley would approve this plan?"

"Leave that to me," Ros said and left. The plan was brave, even preposterous to think of. But if they could pull it off, it would give just enough time and cover for the Tesla meet-up.

By evening, the group met to put the final touches to the planning. Aldridge and Wright had worked out a route that was longer than usual but gave them enough key positions along the route to make a switch if needed and make it to Gorky Park in time. Wright would stay back in the car while Keith met with Tesla at a location only the two would know.

"That's a bloody good plan, sport!" Marbury commended Alvares and passed the operational plan to Henley who sat next to him along the corner pocket of the billiards table.

"All looks good. But, Wrighty, you will stay back. Alvares, can you work with Aldridge on the drop?

"Happy to," Alvares kept his composure as the adrenaline rush took over. He was hoping to be in on the action on the streets.

"But boss, we need an experienced agent to help with this," Wright said.

"He has been in the service longer than you Wright!" Henley said with a stern look on his face.

"And we could do with some fresh legs and eyes on this operation." Only Marbury understood the switch. Henley wanted to make sure there was no jeopardy. He had played his first joker in the deck.

"This is Moscow mate, blood-sucking agents at every mile" Wright softly said to Alvares and left the room.

Chapter 22
The Game's Afoot

The Next Day, December 11th, 1981. The day of the live drop.

The embassy was decked with a festive fervor for the grand ball and Christmas party organized for all the staffers, MI6 agents included. Today, they were all just embassy staff. Roslyn knew this was the perfect cover. The timing was just right. Too good to be true and the Moscow Station contemplated if this was a setup—spies were trained to look for extremes and the tiniest of details. Darcy had argued that Tesla purposefully picked the day of the Christmas ball. But the Christmas party was their best bet to organize a Tesla meet-up right under the noses of the KGB. The agents met for a quick debrief in the morning and then left to prepare and get ready for the event and the operation thereafter.

Ros had put on an ensemble—a beautiful red gown and crimson red stilettos to match. She had not dressed up in ages and today she went for it—a chance to enjoy a bit of dress up and have fun before the day becomes hectic and tense. The men had done their bit and dressed up in sharp suits and tuxes. By late afternoon, the guests had already filled up the large visiting section turned ballroom for the day. Visiting dignitaries, state officials from friendly embassies, and a few Russian delegates had started making their way to the bar and enjoying the live music and finger food. Keith and Clarise Aldridge were mingling with fellow colleagues and guests and keeping things casual and moving. Stuart Wright was his usual pompous self and was entertaining a few single ladies, regaling them with his travel stories, adventures, and chance meetings with celebrities. Charles Darcy was having a friendly argument with the visiting state secretary from Britain on the technology upgrades they would need to keep pace with the other agencies, especially the CIA. John Marbury was a bit reclusive. He knew the stakes were high for the day, and he was tasked with the big 'switch' that was to commence a bit later in the evening.

Henley was busy welcoming the senior staff and dignitaries when he spotted a familiar face. A short, stocky man in his mid-fifties with perfectly kempt hair had just entered the ballroom. That was Andrey Chekhov, Henley's counterpart in the KGB, but, carried the official title of Director General of Soviet Science and Technology Mission. Henley knew if there was a mole from his team, then it was Andrey Chekhov running the rule over his agent. Chekhov was a many of mystery. He was calm, calculative, and had a charm-offensive style that could disarm someone easily. He was the antidote of what a KGB spy should be, and that made him the most difficult opponent Henley had ever faced in his career. Chekhov was the reason the KGB was having a second wind in their tails; they were now flying, making strategic changes to their operations that had the MI6 running around chasing their town tails. Henley was preparing for this showdown. A chance to test the waters, a chance to see if he could ruffle the famed KGB operative and see if he slips.

Henley took a glass of whiskey and walked up to his fabled opponent, who was busy having a chat with the General Counsel of the Swedish Embassy. Chekhov saw Henley joining the conversation and took the first shot.

"Some party Mr. Henley. So good to see some of the friendly faces." That was a veiled dig. The Swedish gentleman saw an opportunity and took his leave.

"Mr. Director, kind of you to attend our little party. Have you been treated well?"

"Your people have been extremely kind, thank you."

"What's new in the world of science and technology mission?" Henley probed.

"I wish I could tell you that, but then I will have to kill you!" Chekhov laughed at the top of his voice. The room heard his laugh, but Henley saw an anxiety. Henley had touched a nerve. There.

"Even if you tell me, I wouldn't understand a thing. I was in London a few weeks back and they were admiring the fast advances Soviet is doing in defense military science," Henley said, continuing to shadow box with his opposite number.

Chekhov knew this was a trap. He couldn't confirm nor deny it. Either way, he would weaken his position.

"I am sure someone from London will definitely ask someone in the Soviet Science and Technology mission about it. I wouldn't like that, but you and me, Mr. Henley, we know better, don't we?" That was a veiled threat—a classic Chekhov move.

"I agree Mr. Director. Always better to wear velvet gloves when hitting someone on the face in our line of work, isn't it?" Henley knew better than to end the conversation there and walked away from the director. This was a personal bit of triumph.

At about 5 pm, Ros made a signal to Aldridge, who in turn passed on the signal to Marbury. He quietly left the scene of the party and headed to his apartment situated in the staff quarters just adjacent to the embassy's main building. They had exactly 30 minutes to put the plan into action. Between 5:00 and 5:30, there was to be a show with magic, fire breathing, and other daredevil acts.

"How are you, Clarise? Been a while since we had the pleasure of hosting you at the embassy?" Marbury greeted in a loud voice. *There were ongoing concerns that the Russians had bugged the apartments.*

"Care for a drink, Aldridge?" Marbury asked Aldridge as he walked alongside his wife Clarise

"Of course, the evening has just started… nothing like a bourbon to start your afternoon!"

"Not for me, unfortunately. I have to leave and check the machine shop for new supplies." Marbury shouted.

"That's a bummer. We will be here all evening, will save you a shepherd's pie," Clarise said.

"Did I hear bourbon?" shouted Alvares as he entered the room, Darcy closely walking behind him. Aldridge winked back at Alvares as he poured him some bourbon. Once they realized the pleasantries were exchanged loudly, they got to work.

Aldridge and Darcy were of the same build. A bit of makeup and a change of clothes were needed to bring the semblance. The plan was to switch him and Darcy and Alvares with Marbury. Techies for Case officers—that was the play. Clarise and Ros helped with the makeup to match the two men as closely as possible to the other two. From afar, with the swap done, it would have been tough to spot the difference between the two men, especially at night.

"Darcy, shall we get going?" Marbury said and started walking toward the main door of the apartment. But it was Alvares who left with Aldridge while Charles Darcy and John Marbury waited with bated breath for a long evening that was to unfold. The point of the identity transfer was to leave the embassy without arousing a lot of suspicions. The KGB ignored the British Embassy tech guys when they left the premises. They had followed the tech guys quite a few times, ending in a drab chase. *Moscow Station believed the KGB concluded this was a regular feature and warranted little attention every time.*

Alvares and Aldridge got into the green MZMA 'Moskvwitch' station wagon parked right outside the building. The windows were tinted dark to the degree the Russian Road traffic laws allowed. As they began the drive outside the embassy, Aldridge made a small signal, pointing at his chest, to indicate he was carrying the L-pill. The two had an anxious look about them but maintained a calm demeanor, for soon, they would have a vehicle in hot pursuit.

Alvares was at the wheel of the green station wagon as Aldridge navigated. They had prepared themselves for a long evening, as dropping the surveillance by the KGB officers could often take five to six hours, depending on the agent's status. John Marbury and Charles Darcy, the technical team at the embassy, would often leave the embassy premises and head to the city to buy inventory, fix supplies, and do other technical work required for the British embassy. Over the years, the KGB, seemingly, had decided to lax its surveillance on the tech guys.

"What if Tesla doesn't make it?" Alvares said, eagerly looking at Aldridge, hoping for a positive confirmation.

"If the note is from him, he'll be there," Aldridge sounded assured. "But that's the big 'if'—we still can't be sure it's him."

"That's reassuring..." Alvares couldn't avoid the sarcasm. He wasn't pleased with the odds of them making it out safe at the end of this evening. "Talk about a baptism of fire!"

"We all respond to the call of duty, don't we?" Aldridge was trying his best to instill some passion and confidence in his partner, and himself.

"We drive straight to the electronics shop the lads generally go to. Once we are there, go into the store, buy the regular stuff such as batteries and wires, and come back while I wait in the car. Spend about ten minutes in the shop, don't rush back nor take too much time," Aldridge gave the instructions while constantly checking the rearview mirrors on his side.

"You know we have a black wagon on our tail, don't you," Alvares said, looking at the rearview mirror on his side. Both Alvares and Aldridge knew that this was a hot pursuit, and it would take some doing, to lose the surveillance.

As was the plan, Alvares took the service road, slowed down, and stopped by the electronics store. He got down and stooped to tie his shoelaces, trying to spot the man on the wheels of the black station wagon. The moonless night didn't help and he walked into the store to grab the supplies.

Alvares brought back the supplies from the electronics store, opened the boot, and threw the supplies in. He casually turned, inspected his surroundings, and could still see the black wagon parked at the corner of the street.

"The black car is still on us, waiting for our next move," Alvares said and started the engines, revved up and ready to go.

"We stay on course with the plan. Next up, we go to the other end of the city, take the highway," Aldridge said and directed Alvares to the exit to the highway.

The two rode the highway for close to an hour with traffic and the black station wagon keeping them company. Aldridge kept checking his Cartier. He had another three hours, and hopefully, enough time to drop the surveillance, go black and reach Gorky Park. Alvares made a mental map of the route as they drove around the city streets.

By 8 pm, Alvares and Aldridge had been on the road for almost three hours and had now stopped at a pub, two kilometers off the highway. They had spent the last one-hour drinking beer and patiently waiting for the black wagon to leave them.

"About time, this is our most important move. Hopefully, this works," Aldridge said and asked Alvares to leave, slow and cautiously. *Earlier in the day, John Marbury had a life-size dummy hidden in the middle section of the wagon.* The plan was to have Aldridge stay back at the pub; Alvares quietly goes back into the car, keeps the dummy next to him, and hopes that the surveillance misses the switch in the dim moonless night light and the tinted windows of the station wagon.

Aldridge quietly moved from the center of the pub and sat at the barstool that overlooked the parking lot. He could see Alvares skillfully walking behind the other parked cars and making his way into the green station wagon unnoticed. There was a blind spot from the position the car following them had taken. Time stood still as he waited for Alvares to complete the switch and put the dummy in his place. Alvares started the car, waited for 30 seconds, and slowly maneuvered out of the parking lot. The black van that had been following them all day started the pursuit. *The plan had worked. They had been able to drop the hot surveillance, at least for Keith Aldridge. They both hoped that the KGB members in the party wouldn't figure out that two of the MI6 agents were missing.*

The final leg of dropping the surveillance was on Aldridge. He now had to track back into the city, double-check if there was additional surveillance, and finally make it to Gorky Park. Aldridge left the pub, took the tram from the station next to the pub, and rode to the farthest end of the city's local train line. He was now two hours away from Gorky Park. From the last station, he took the bus that was to drive him back to the city center, and from there walked the last three kilometers to Gorky Park. He had to time it correctly and go utterly black before the live drop.

The game was afoot.

Chapter 23
The Face Off

Gorky Park, 11 pm

Keith Aldridge was seated on the same blue bench under the statue as he had for the first live drop he'd made with Tesla years back. Aldridge was a seasoned campaigner in the world of running counter agents. But even for him, tonight was a big test. Tesla was by far the most important, productive, and riskiest double agent he had run in his career, and tonight was going to be a defining moment of this partnership. He had a fairly good idea about what Tesla was going to request. But the service had taught him one thing: always be prepared to expect the unexpected.

As the moonless sky darkened, he saw a silhouette walking toward him slowly but surely.

"Hello, Otto," Tesla said using Aldridge's codename. It had been four years since Aldridge and Ivanov had met each other, but Aldridge instantly recognized the other man's rich, baritone voice. Without that, Aldridge might not have recognized him.

"You look weak."

"I have seen better days," Viktor said and sat next to Aldridge, staring at the empty lake ahead of them.

"We have not heard from you in a while. The package you sent had us worried. How can I help you, my friend?" Aldridge asked, one eye carefully canvassing the area.

Viktor leaned forward, adjusted his spectacles, and spoke. "I need to defect. I know this is not part of the timeline we agreed on Otto, but..."

"But?" Keith asked, leaning backward and moving a bit toward Viktor as a gush of wind made his voice less audible.

"The last few months I have had this feeling that someone is looking for me."

"What made you think so?" Aldridge asked—the thought of the traitor, the mole weighing up in his mind.

"My secretary, who has been by my side for many years was suddenly reassigned to another officer and the new one seems a bit off."

"Can it be just that you are getting adjusted to her?"

"No, Otto. The first two months I thought she was just being good at her job—taking detailed notes, verifying every meeting I was taking, tracking my time in the office, and outside…"

"What changed?"

"Then last month, I realized she had been going through my desk while I was away. I was suspecting the same and I started keeping a small contraption device—a clip that changes position with the slightest movement around."

"The device worked, it seems."

"It did. Besides her, no one has the keys to my office."

"And you have reason to believe she is acting on the orders of someone higher up the KGB?"

"It cannot be an official inquiry, else I would not have made it to this meeting. Someone is running an off-the-books investigation on me," Viktor said, breathing heavily. Aldridge could feel the anxiety creeping up on his agent.

"I understand. I will make it happen for you. How long do we have to plan this?"

"Immediately after Christmas, I am ready to make the move."

"Understood. To be clear, it will be you and your wife?" Aldridge said, hoping the answer would be a no.

"Yes," Viktor said, his eyes weary and a face full of concern for his future.

"I will do a dead drop with the plan in two days from now. The plan will have all the details."

"Thank you, Otto," Viktor said and looked straight into Aldridge's eyes and asked, "Do you have the pill?"

He hesitated for a moment as he reached into the inner pocket of his overcoat. But, he knew Viktor to be a man of tremendous willpower and mental strength, else he wouldn't be working as a double agent under such duress. Aldridge realized he could trust Viktor to not use the pill till the situation demanded it. Aldridge took out the pill from his pocket and handed it over to Viktor. Even for an experienced and ruthless spy, this wasn't easy.

"Along with the pill, there is a note. We need you to run one last assignment and deliver it before we begin the defection plan. Do you think you could manage that?" Aldridge said, having added this to his plan last minute. He knew Tesla could offer some insights into the Budapest Rezidentura and help understand the mystery around Miller and Gilligan. He was not prepared for that lead to get buried completely.

"I will do my best. Thank you, Otto," Viktor said and handed a small file to Aldridge, "There are some interesting bits here, thought you should take a look."

Aldridge took the file and checked the surroundings, slowly rose, and started walking. As he walked away from the bench, he looked back at Viktor one last time.

This was the biggest moment of his career. For five years he had run the biggest double agent in MI6 history, and now he was to run the biggest exfiltration MI6 had ever seen.

It would be a long journey back to the station.

※

After he dropped off Aldridge, someone else had picked up Alvares' scent. He had been on the road for over two hours, driving through the city, at a steady pace, in order to not raise any suspicion. He stopped at the gas station, made a refill, grabbed a sandwich, and continued driving on the highway. If I stay here any longer, then the guys back at the embassy would start a search, Alvares thought. I have to drop the tail, he realized. He kept a steady pace and opened the map of Moscow city. Thankfully, he had picked up a city guide at the petrol station. It had a detailed map of the transportation networks in the city. Wright was right, he thought. This wasn't India. Moscow was faster and riskier. He'd been on edge since he'd got here.

He looked at the map, one eye on the road and one eye on the map, trying to figure out his best course of action. If he took the next exit and circled back to the other side of the highway, he could hit the pedals and make a dash for the Central Bus Terminus. *The terminus would be crowded at all times; easier to lose the tail,* he thought. The tail still followed him onto the other side of the highway.

Alvares steered the green station wagon into the Central Moscow Bus Terminus. Thankfully, it was rush hour. Probably, people were making a move out of Moscow before Christmas. The black Landa was still in hot pursuit. He waited. The guy in the car waited. Patience, that's what you need to take the next big step in your career, he remembered Father Samuel's advice. He heeded the advice, waited an extra fifteen minutes, and then quietly stepped out of his car. Alvares stooped low and passed through the row of cars in front of his, making his way to the back entrance of the building. Alvares saw the man step down from his car and look through the barrage of cars in the parking lot. The lights in the parking lot, for a moment, shone onto the person's face. Alvares couldn't ID the person properly, but he got a decent measure of the man.

This was his chance. He made a dash for the bus terminal, hoping to intersperse amidst the rush of passengers. Hundreds of people had gathered inside the terminus, looking for bus timings, and running toward their designated buses. There was utter pandemonium. Perfect, Alvares thought and discreetly moved behind the phone booth.

There was no way he could take the van back to the office. He was sure whoever was following him would have checked inside the van by now and seen the dummy. Thankfully, he had removed the papers that lay inside the car and carried them with him, tucked inside his jacket.

Alvares opened the city tour book and searched for alternate transportation routes. He flipped through the bus schedules. There were a few long-winded options he could take to get back to the embassy. But Alvares was worried his absence for such long hours would start a manhunt by his colleagues. He reached the section that detailed the metro rail network.

That's it, he thought, *If I walk to the metro, I could then reach the closest metro to the office and walk down to the office.*

Alvares checked his surroundings. The exit door to his left was the closest. But it was brightly lit and least crowded. The man would easily spot him leaving the exit. The door on the distant right was his best option. That was the crowded exit, and he felt confident to slip past amongst the rush of people. Alvares swiftly moved toward the general store inside the terminus and bought a hat. That should shield his face a bit, he thought.

Alvares swiftly joined the outbound passengers and slowly walked along with the crowd to the exit. But suddenly a hand stopped him right at the gates. He turned around and saw a security guard—a tall, imposing figure.

"Please step aside," the guard asked in broken English. Alvares' skin color had made it obvious to the security guard. He kept his composure and slowly took out the bunch of papers he had taken from the car and showed his embassy papers. Satisfied, the security guard stepped aside and asked him to leave.

Alvares felt relieved but soon he realized the face-off with the security guard had put him in the limelight. As he walked outside the terminus he felt a familiar figure on his heels, following him. Alvares slowly walked toward the main crossing of the road and waited for the lights to turn green. He checked over his shoulder and saw the man a few feet behind—his face still dark under the moonless sky. Within a few seconds, the light would turn green and he could make a dash across the street, Alvares thought. But so could the man following him, Alvares considered.

Alvares looked at the people standing next to him. An older woman stood behind him with a heavy piece of luggage. As soon as the lights turned green, he took a step back, joined the old woman, and offered his assistance to help with the luggage. She was happy to take the offer, and Alvares asked her to wait for the next green signal so he could pull the luggage slowly across the main street. He and the older woman stepped by, while the rest of the crowd pushed forward quickly along with the man following.

With no option to stay back, the man had to continue his walk and brushed past Alvares. At that moment, his face gleamed under the street lights, and Alvares could take a quick look. As soon as the man reached the other end of the street, he turned around and waited for Alvares' turn to move.

At that moment, Alvares dropped the luggage and made a dash to the far corner of the street. He ran for a good few minutes and swiftly took cover behind a phone booth. The street was empty, far from the main street where he had left his tail. He scanned the area for a few minutes. The man was nowhere to be seen.

He was now confident that the walk to the metro would be clean.

He had taken one good glance at the person following him. Medium height, stocky with one unmistakable feature—a long scar under his left eye that ran all the way to the tip of his mouth.

A couple of hours later, he had made it back to the Moscow Station. It was almost empty inside the embassy—regular diplomats, employees, and their families had left for the evening. He spotted Keith Aldridge among the few who had stayed back and gave him a signal.

"What took you so long?" Aldridge asked.

"I had company after I dropped you off."

"So, Henley was right, things are getting serious."

"Good start to my time here in Moscow," Alvares said and opened a can of beer. The adrenaline was still pumping through his veins.

"Any chance you could spot them?"

"Him. One guy."

"That's odd. They always hunt in pairs. How did he look?" Aldridge asked.

"Average Joe, but yeah, he had this scar that ran across his face. Poor bastard!" Alvares said and left Aldridge to grab a bite.

Keith Aldridge bit his tongue, trying not to quell the odd feeling in his stomach. He knew someone with that description. What the hell was Mike from scalp hunters doing in Moscow? And more importantly, why was he following them?

Chapter 24
Hook, Line, and Sinker

The woman got up from the bed, put on her silk robe, tied her short golden hair into a small pony, and looked back at him. He was asleep. It was way past midnight. This was the first time they had spent more than twenty-four hours together. She walked into the kitchenette in their hotel room and poured some water into the kettle for a boil. He was her prized asset; it took her a while to turn him into a double agent, longer than she thought.

The regular tactics didn't work on him—money, titles, promise of a hero's welcome, and a life thereafter in Russia. He said no to everything. Then the bosses told her to use her charm, her body, and her passion to turn him. She did, reluctantly at first, but soon she started enjoying the passionate sex, the pillow talk, and hearing his ambitions as they smoked cigarettes together. The honeypot tactic worked. But it was now having an effect on her too. Maybe I am falling in love, she thought. But she had a family of her own, her career, and the vengeance that she was to extract. She controlled her emotions; there was a bigger state of play and she was running the most important pawn on the board.

The clock chimed two in the morning. It was pitch dark outside and she could see the faint street lights in the farthest corner of the street. A gush of cold wind swept through the windows and into the room. She made two cups of coffee, went to the bedside, and slowly gave him a kiss on the lips to wake him up.

"What time is it?" he asked and slowly rose and rested his head against the headboard of the bed.

"Two in the night. About time, I head back, Milaya."

He took the cup of tea and silently sipped the tea. Unlike him, she thought.

"You seem worried darling," she said stroking his long, black hair as he lay naked next to her.

"There's something happening at Moscow Station… but I cannot put my finger on it."

"You always find a way," she said.

"Did you hand over the file?" he said, holding his thought.

"I did. Just as you asked."

"And?"

"I think the General was very happy to see the progress we have made."

"Anything specific?"

"You know him. He doesn't show his cards. But if anything, I know he has big plans for you," she said and poured him some more tea.

"He better does. I can do more for him, but I have hit a wall."

"What wall?" she asked. She had mastered spoken and written English but had yet to master the nuances and subtlety of idioms and phrases.

"I'm worried someone has started looking into me."

"You are smart, Milaya, I know you will find a way to clear your tracks."

"This time it seems different. If it goes on I might have to ask you for some help."

"Tell me, Milaya," she said and took his hand, draped it around her shoulders and lit a cigarette.

"I may need to kill someone," he said and handed over a thin red file to her. "Keep this safe with you. I will call you when the time comes to action this."

Small, seemingly trivial events may ultimately result in something with much larger consequences.

– Edward Lorenz

Keith Aldridge felt an unusual calm. His younger self would fret around trying to find someone to bring him some sanity. He didn't know if he was ready to pull off the Tesla extraction. His thoughts ran amuck, but the look on the faces of his wife and child brought him back down to earth. The life he wanted to build around them made him a stronger person and, by extension, a stronger spy.

Clarise was in the kitchen running between the stovetop and the coffee machine, working to get the breakfast ready. Aldridge walked over to her and warmly embraced her. She knew what it meant to be the wife of a spy. She knew firsthand the risks and the incredibly difficult choices her husband had to make.

"What's troubling you, darling?" she asked.

"Nothing that I can't handle." Aldridge kept a tight lid on the matter. Although she was in the service, she was not an active member. There was only as much he could tell her without compromising his position in the Circus.

"Whatever it is, you'll manage. Just don't do anything silly. Remember, we have a daughter to raise."

"I can promise you one thing: I will always come back home for you and Emily," Aldridge said and went to the living room. He took the morning newspaper—a routine he maintained to keep his language skills sharp.

There was a loud knock at the door. Clarisse opened the door. It was Alvares; he had arrived with a box of patisseries and a bouquet of flowers.

"This is for you, Mrs. Aldridge," he said.

"Isn't that lovely, and just call me Clarise? Mrs. Aldridge makes me sound so old," she said, taking the flowers and placing them in a vase in the middle of the breakfast table.

"Some party last night, I hear," Alvares said, taking a seat at the table.

"You didn't miss a lot. Just the usual drama and trying to escape bores who've had too much champers."

"I heard Wright was quite the entertainer?" Alvares said as Clarise poured him some coffee.

"When is he not...?" Aldridge said, coming back into the kitchen. He planted a kiss on Clarise's cheek.

"Quite a charmer he is. But quite odd that he left shortly after you both did," Clarise said and started setting up the breakfast spread.

"Mind if I steal him for a few minutes, love?" Aldridge said and asked Alvares to join him in the study.

"Should we be concerned that Wright left the embassy?" Alvares said as Aldridge locked the door behind them.

"I thought as much. Worth discreetly checking with Ros if she knows a thing or two."

"Let me do that. Keeps it vague enough coming from me," Alvares said.

"How are you holding up?" Aldridge asked Alvares. "That was quite a shock to the system yesterday."

"Not too bad. Nice family, by the way," Alvares said, taking in the wall full of pictures of Aldridge, Clarise, and their daughter.

"Could be you someday, if you're lucky," Aldridge said without thinking. With the whole situation around Miller, he realized this could make Alvares uncomfortable.

"Someday, yes. What is our play now?" Alvares said, changing the subject quickly.

"I know Henley. He'll want to know a bit more from Tesla."

"About what?"

"If he's really still on our side. I'm certain he'll make a play to find something out."

"Father Samuel would have done the same," Alvares said.

"When I handed him the pill yesterday, I also slid in a note asking something."

"About?"

"The details of the KGB Rezidentura in Budapest."

Alvares was awed by Aldridge's doggedness. If they could get hold of the key people in Budapest, they could very well have a starting point to find out what happened to Miller and Gilligan in Hungary.

"And if he gives us that, it will also show that he's pretty much still on our side."

"That's my hope. Play along when the guys at the office think of a way to test him."

"Reckon they would do that," Neil asked.

"I bet all the money in my bank. These are hard-knuckled spies, my friend. Nothing is left to chance, ever." Aldridge said and then the two career spies enjoyed a normal breakfast and a dogged drive to work.

Moscow Station,

December 18th, 1982,

Aldridge headed straight into the file room when he got to the office, stowed the file he received from Tesla the previous evening, and headed back to the billiards room. He added a note for Roslyn to log it in, after the debrief.

"All go to plan?" Darcy asked and opened up a cold bottle of Ziguli and handed it over to Aldridge who had just walked into the office. There was some leftover food from last night and Roslyn had them heated and sent over for the team along with beers.

"It did. Alvares was great," Aldridge said as he saw Alvares walking into the office.

"And?" Henley had appeared from his office.

"He wants out, confirmed," Aldridge said and took a pause. "Soon."

The silence in the room was deafening. Henley looked at Marbury—they had a real situation on their hands.

"Do we know why?" Roslyn asked.

"Difficult to say. We spoke briefly. He doesn't look his usual self," Aldridge continued guzzling down the rest of his beer. Aldridge knew more than that, but he wanted to keep the reason to himself. He couldn't pull off the exfil by himself. Any slight hints of a weak double agent would always mean one thing—burn notice. Back in 78, the Nairobi station had left one of their double agents in the cold when they realized he had become an emotional wreck and could jeopardize the exfil. The Nairobi station found a way to let him get trapped without as much leaving a trace. Tesla had his own fears—valid and reasonable. But, Keith wasn't prepared to tell the team that his fears were linked to the actions of a secretary.

"Well, the first order of business is to figure out if he's been compromised," Henley instructed.

"So, we drop some of South London's finest chicken feed and see if they nibble," Wright chipped in casually. A man of high taste and often questionable conscience, Wright wasn't known for his tact.

"That would be one way to go about it," Aldridge responded. "He wants exfil on Boxing Day. That gives us a week."

The group mulled over the other options and the repercussions of each. MI6 had a strict protocol to weigh each counter-surveillance option and merit it against the most adverse outcomes.

"Do we share the plan and mix some chicken feed with it?" Wright leaned in. *His idea, his rules,* he thought.

"I don't think that would give us an answer if he's compromised or not. What if he is already turned by the KGB?" said Darcy, trying to put together the coding machine. They would need approval from the Circus before they could do anything.

Roslyn was quiet. Like Marbury and Henley, she played the game the old way. She had the patience and the smarts to hear through the clutter and make a decisive judgment at the end.

Neil Alvares went back to his desk for his passport and the notes he had prepared on Kate Miller. He had to be ready, just in case.

"Let's ask him for another piece of information when we deliver the plan of action. Something risky," Alvares floated an idea. Keith couldn't help his smirk. Just as they'd planned.

Marbury leaned in and asked, "What would that suggest?"

"If he's compromised, he'll have no trouble getting information to us. If he hesitates, or if he can't do it, we'll know he's still clean."

Henley looked impressed. He turned to Ros, but she was already addressing the room.

"Well, then, Darcy, get to work; we have a message to send to London. Next contact between Tesla and Aldridge to happen in 2 days from now, right Aldridge?"

Keith shook his head in affirmation.

"And let's pray all the dominoes fall in the right places!" Marbury said as the group dissembled.

The group looked spirited, Henley thought as he watched his agents working through the plan. He felt confident that they could see the plan through to the end but the threat of the traitor still troubled him. He couldn't just let his team walk into an ambush. And this was no simple drop-and-go. If Tesla cleared their test of faith, then they had the obligation to exfiltrate him. Besides him and Aldridge, no one knew the real identity but there were enough breadcrumbs lying in the file room if one wanted to make a meal out of it. And every file in that room had a copy in London.

"Roslyn, can I steal you for a moment?" Henley took Ros by her arms to the sofa.

She was busy working on the inquest Henley had asked her to prepare on the stalled operation in India. Engels had made sure that Circus had the details.

"What's bothering you?" she asked and sat next to him on the sofa.

"Drop the inquest. I need you to run a specific check on the files."

"I already checked everything on the lads."

"It's not the lads. It's Tesla."

"You suspect the KGB has him?"

"I'm confident he's not turned. But I want to be absolutely sure that there's no way we have his name or his identity on records."

"How far back do I go?" she asked.

"Since the start," Henley said.

"Fine, but you're making the coffee," Roslyn said and immediately headed to the file room. This could take days. She had a day to get this sorted.

Chapter 25
Wheels in Motion

Simon Henley was waiting for the priest. Father Samuel had been the architect of their plans. But they'd made no concession for how to extract Tesla without subduing the traitor. Simon had a decision to make if the situation worsened. There was every chance he would lose an agent or Tesla, or worse, both. When the time came to make a choice, Henley knew he would have to protect his legacy. Burning Tesla would have to be his last resort, but he knew he had to make the play—save his legacy and Tesla, both. *Tonight, I have to speak to the priest,* he decided.

"Aldridge, don't you have an op to run?" Henley asked, not looking up from the files on his desk, as Aldridge walked in.

"That can wait a moment. I have something important to talk to you about, care to step out?"

It was a beautiful evening. The sun had shone on the city after a long week of snowfall, melting it away to reveal the canopy of trees that surrounded Moscow Station. For how long, was the question? Simon Henley had grown to love the city. Despite the intense line of work, he still found time to understand the culture, the people, and the city. His political and personal ideologies were polar opposites to what the city stood for, but he couldn't put aside the strength of its literature, culture, and, by some measure, some good people he met along the way. Aldridge was still a long way off from where Henley was when it came to accepting the city for what it was. Aldridge never warmed up to Moscow.

There were a few embassy colleagues around as they walked toward the embassy garden. A path had been built to help the employees find some space to walk, work out, and even have an outdoor lunch. Aldridge found an empty bench for the two to speak in secrecy.

"What is Mike Moore doing in Russia?" he asked, straight-faced.

"How did you figure it out?"

"The last drop with Tesla. Alvares was tailed," he said, "He dropped the tail, but not before he got a good look at the person."

"Are you sure that was Moore?" Henley asked, shocked. His instructions to Moore had been clear. To drop all work, till he reached out for further instructions.

"Definitely him. So, again; what was Moore doing following us? Was it you or one of the London arses who put him on us?"

"I honestly don't have a fucking clue," Henley said and then relayed why he'd hired Moore.

"He's gone rogue," Aldridge said, "and we need to get hold of him and find out why is he hot for us."

This was bad, Henley thought. It would look like Henley was the one making Moore run an off-the-books covert op. All roads would lead to Henley. Was someone setting him up?

❦

Pondicherry, that night.

The radio suddenly sputtered to life, spewing out a series of numbers and words that made little sense to the untrained ear.

Father Samuel quickly grabbed a notepad and started to make notes.

C 1 12 3A Tesla 26 E

He went to fetch his copy of the King James Bible.

The message read: "Moscow Station (1) to call Indian station (12) at 3:00 hours. Tesla exfil on 26th."

Father Samuel rushed to the file and comms room. He had an hour to prepare for the call. Henley had pushed the timeline. 26th was barely 6 days away; it would take a massive operational feat to achieve an exfil in such a short space.

Right at the cuckoo's calling from the grandfather clock that was hung in Father Samuel's office, the telephone rang.

"Turner, Henley here. Thanks for taking the call on short notice."

"Did I get the codes correct, Henley? Exfil right after Christmas?"

"Right," Henley said, knowing this would have come unexpectedly.

"Your agent is in grave danger, I presume?"

"Aldridge met him and concurs."

"He is a smart handler, I would trust him to read the situation correctly."

"We clearly cannot run the exfil with a traitor in the ranks," Henley said, sounding exasperated.

"Where's the operation at right now?"

"We are working on an exfil plan-routes, surveillance, dropboxes, the works. I have requisitioned a full exfil package from London."

"We have to assume the mole knows the plan is in play, Henley."

"That's my worry, Father. I fear I am sending my guys straight into an ambush."

"I have been working on our problem, Henley. Listen carefully," the priest said and paused for a moment to gather his thoughts. Henley waited on the other line, anxious.

"We need a misdirection. We have to lead the mole in a different direction, while we run the exfil."

"How?"

"Do you trust Aldridge enough to run the exfil alone?"

"He is Tesla's handler, and until now, he has given me no reason to think otherwise."

"Then that's where we start. We team him and Alvares together to run the exfil off the books."

"Aldridge is a sucker and a tight ass when it comes to protocol. I doubt he will run this off the books, especially with a high-profile double agent."

"We don't tell them it's off the books. We force their hand." Father Samuel said and over the next few minutes, he detailed out the plan.

"Do you think they will take the bait?"

"If Aldridge doesn't, Alvares will. He will push Aldridge to take the plunge. But we will need a babysitter for them, in case they need more hands. But we can't let them know there is a babysitter."

"I know someone who will do that," Henley said as he visualized the overall plan. He knew just the right guy to babysit Alvares and Aldridge discreetly.

"We need the dominoes to fall perfectly for this, Father. It's a big leap of faith," Henley said.

"Control will be the first domino. I will write to him to get this started."

"You know we will have to burn a few bodies in this plan, don't you?" Henley said.

"I know. That's why I am coming to Moscow. Hold tight, my friend."

This was serious. Extracting a double agent cleanly was no easy feat. They had done it before, and they would do it again, but it would need smarts, guile, and a whole lot of luck. He had already prepared for the plan to work. Now, to start with a request to Control. The hardest part would be convincing the boss that this was the only way to take stock and be one step ahead of the mole.

Father Samuel carefully opened the bottles of Paris Green, Acetone, and Amyl Alcohol that he had carried along the bumpy and torturous roads of Vellore, all the way to Pondicherry. He carefully mixed the chemicals in the right proportion like a skilled sommelier and let them breathe. Combined, they smelled of potpourri.

He poured the chemicals into a small glass bottle. It was all about timing and proportions. The old hand had done this umpteen times but age had got the better of him. The tremors in his hand hinted at the onset of a tough next few years, but he was focused.

As the chemicals mutated into a transparent liquid, Father Samuel reconsidered his decision. The last communique between him and Control had lacked the usual clarity and concision. Control wanted to increase the scope of operations at the Indian station. However, the priest was not prepared to onboard a larger remit without clearing his future. About time, he thought. This communication had to be done the old-school way. He couldn't risk anyone knowing the main purpose behind the letter.

He took out the wooden box he carried in his knapsack. It was a Japanese puzzle box, a *Himitsu-Bako*, which could only be opened by moving the sliding pieces of its surfaces. Control was the only person other than Father Samuel who knew the combination. This was old school- tongue in cheek.

He laid the box carefully onto the small wooden table in his office. The chemicals on the paper had settled down and were now crystal clear. Using the secret ink, he penned a letter for Control:

The wheels are in motion to extract the package. Station X reports this has to be done on Boxing Day. With the other problem we have, this could end up being a suicide mission. The only way out of this would be to misdirect the adversaries to a different package—the one Wright shepherds. We need to make his sheep look like being untethered. I trust you to make the arrangements while the actual package extraction runs in the background.

P.S. It's about time that I plan my retirement. Weak knees. My deputy, Alvares, is the right man for the job. He has been in the service for a decade and is much smarter than we were at his age. He has all the minerals to be our next man in India. I have sent him to Moscow to assist the ops there and show his worth in the trenches. I will travel to Moscow to further the cause. This will be my last dance.

He put the note inside the box and packaged it. It would be taken onboard Shakuntala, later finding its way on an air courier from Bombay to London MI6 headquarters. For curious hands, it would look like a gift for Control.

Chapter 26
SpyGames

5 days to Christmas.

It had been two weeks since Neil Alvares arrived on the front line of the Cold War. He had seen enough action in these weeks that would otherwise last him months in India. Moscow and the business of espionage here were on a different scale. Father Samuel had radioed him last night about his plans to be at the Moscow Station. This could mean only one thing—the exfiltration of Tesla and the findings at Shakuntala are connected.

Of the Moscow Five, Roslyn was Alvares' babysitter, tasked to bring him up to speed on the operations at Moscow. But that lasted a few days; Alvares was a fast learner. Ros didn't need to babysit, rather was planning key ops and strategies alongside him and the rest of the team. He had just taken to the role like a duck taking to the water, she had joked to Marbury. Alvares was the fastest to reach Simon's circle of appreciation; a rarity and an oddity by equal measure. There was something about Alvares.

But despite the countless meetings, planning sessions, and administrative work he had been assigned, Roslyn showed him that there was life for these spies outside the walls of the station. Every morning—except for yesterday, when she had been fully immersed in the file room, running an errand for Henley—Roslyn and Alvares had breakfast together. It was a moment of solace. Her apartment was a few minutes' walk from his quarters.

"Merry Christmas, Neil," Ros kissed him on the cheek and ushered him in. She took his overcoat and hung it on the door and went back into the kitchen.

"Something smells great," Alvares said, taking a seat at the table. Fresh coffee, croissants, and some potato salad were already laid out on the table.

"That would be the potato curry I have been trying to nail down for a while," she shouted from the kitchen.

"Isn't it a bit too early in the morning for a curry?" he asked, stepping into the kitchen to see if he could help her. He enjoyed this morning routine with Ros. He saw her as an elder sister—a feeling Indians were emotional about, but a far-reaching thought for some Brits. But Ros was built differently too. She echoed his feelings and saw him as an older version of her deceased son.

"Eat up as much as you can, you don't know how the next few days are going to be," she said and took out the curry and a loaf of bread to go along with it.

"I'm not complaining," he laughed and thanked her for taking this massive effort early in the morning.

"Oh, don't bother. I have been up all night, couldn't sleep."

"What's troubling you?" Alvares asked as he dipped the bread in the curry and took a bite. It reminded him of home, the bakery, and, most of all, Martin.

"Maybe not the best time to talk about it. Let's eat," she said and joined him at the table.

They spoke at length. About families, friends, India, and Roslyn's past assignments that took her to Istanbul, Budapest, and Vientiane. They found a shared love for food. Pho, rice paper rolls, kebabs, and the scrumptious papaya salad from Laos made the rounds of their discussion on the breakfast table.

"When were you in Budapest?" he asked. Kate was still on his mind.

"Oh, it feels like a lifetime since I was in Hungary. About seven years back, I reckon, why?"

"Nothing. I might know a friend who is there, but haven't been able to get in touch in a while," Alvares tried not to mention Kate.

"I can help. Peter Vaughan, the station chief, is a good friend."

"I will count on that," Alvares said and went into the kitchen to bring the coffee.

"You never told me about your son," he asked, unaware of the difficult spot he had put her in.

Roslyn's face changed. Alvares reminded her of her son since the time he arrived. *Daniel would have been the same age.*

"His name's Daniel. He passed away in a train wreck a few years ago. He was a lovely boy—a big heart and a big smile," Ros said and picked up the dishes and walked into the kitchen, trying hard to stop the tears from rolling down her cheeks.

Alvares sat silently, giving her the time to get back.

"I miss him mostly during this period. Christmas was our thing. He would take a break from work and visit me wherever I was," she said and walked to the bedroom and came back with a photo album.

"Here: this was in Vientiane. A small Christmas market was set up in the capital and we found this photographer who traded photos for food from the market," she said and flipped through the photo album. Daniel was a tall, handsome man who had unmistakable features like his mother.

"Well, this New Year's Eve, hopefully with the charade ongoing has finished, why don't we go and get some photos together," he said and gave her a hug.

"That would be lovely, Neil."

"I have to get going. Aldridge and I have a drop to work on."

"Tomorrow, after the drop, meet me at the cafe across the street from here. There's something I want to share with you," Ros said.

"What is it?"

"I have a hunch about something, but I'm not sure yet," she said.

"Good or bad?" Alvares asked.

"If I'm right, then it's terrible. Don't worry, once you lads leave for the drop, I'll be double-checking everything."

"Is that what kept you awake?"

She nodded. She had also sent a note to London to confirm a couple of things. As soon as she got the intelligence files she would be able to put the pieces together. Something just wasn't right.

"You should get going," she said.

※

There was a mad rush at Moscow Station as they prepared for tomorrow's drop.

Darcy and Marbury were preparing the microfilm and getting the subminiature camera ready. Ironically, it had been developed by the KGB. The Arsenal factory in Kyiv produced the civilian camera, Kyiv Vega. They also happened to offer an identical camera disguised as a cigarette packet that the KGB used. The camera's working principle was copied from the Minox subminiature camera, which had been used extensively on all sides during the Second World War.

Darcy and Marbury had reverse-engineered a Kyiv Vega, developing a more advanced mechanism designed to snap higher-resolution photos. Tesla was a chain smoker, and having a cigarette pack camera would seem natural and explicable in high-security rooms. The mechanism was simple and smart. Moving a cigarette up prepped the camera, and pushing it back down took a photo. There was space left for real cigarettes so that Tesla could take out a cigarette without raising suspicion.

Aldridge was to don the coding hat again. He waited patiently in Henley's office for the chief to come in and go through the debrief. He walked in a few minutes later.

"Ros confirms the plan is a go," Henley said, promptly took a seat, lit his Marlboro cigarette, and looked keenly at Aldridge.

"And you're taking Wrighty along," Simon said to a surprised Keith; he expected Alvares to join him for the drop. It was a risk, but Henley needed the most experienced of his agents to handle this. He also needed Alvares for a job he had planned for later.

"We have the message ready to be coded," Aldridge replied and then continued. "This is delicate, Henley. I would have preferred to go alone…"

"Wrighty can be a bastard but he's a bloody good spy. You will need him."

Aldridge hesitated, wanting to say more. For all the autonomy he afforded his officers, Henley still called the shots.

"Fair enough. But he stays outside the perimeter," Aldridge said. He wanted to keep Tesla's identity a complete secret right until the day of his exfiltration.

Henley nodded, acquiescing to his ace handler's request.

"What's the message we are sending?"

Keith laid out the piece of paper with the decoded message on Henley's desk.

First stop India. Then safe house in Bodrum. Then England.
Keep essentials only.
Plan for six months.
Final assignment: Need photos of the new Soviet attaché for Budapest.
We leave on the 26th.

"What's the play with the attaché request?" Henley asked, worried if they were biting more than they could chew. They were already preparing for his exfiltration.

Aldridge wanted as much information on the Budapest KGB setup. He was still hopeful of finding answers to Gilligan's time in Budapest. So would Alvares. Alvares had a working theory that Kate had landed in Budapest as well.

"Remember the dead end we had with the Indian investigation. All roads lead to Budapest."

"Well then, go full in. Ask for as much information as we can on Budapest—drop sites, handlers, the works."

"If you say so," Aldridge smiled. Henley was truly back in his old form.

"Great. John gave you the cigarette pack?" Henley felt confident his troops could get the job done.

"Got it, boss," Aldridge said, tapping his right chest. "We are ready to go."

Two live drops in a week was a risk. But they couldn't have chosen a better day than Boxing Day for the exfiltration. However much the KGB thought of itself as a well-oiled machine, Christmas always threw them into a state of laxity, with elaborate and extended stupors of drinking and debauchery. Aldridge thought it best to use this to their advantage.

Aldridge went back to his workstation, coded another line into the note, and prepared the final package for the drop. One last live drop before the exfiltration to convince Tesla of something he didn't mention to anyone at the station: *He wanted to exfil Tesla alone, without the family.*

Keith left the office and headed straight to the Moscow Philharmonic Center. This was one of the few dead drop sites he used to communicate with Tesla. He needed to let Tesla know of the meeting the day after at Gorky Park. He hoped

Tesla would remember to check in on the drop sites every day. The timing was of the essence.

❦

As soon as Henley saw Keith and the rest leave the office, he called Alvares at his residence, instructing him to meet.

Capital club,

Same day, 7 pm

"Find a table in the corner and order a couple of drinks," Henley said to Alvares and went into the crowds of people dancing to the music at the Capital Club.

The Capital Club was the place to be if you were young, free-spirited, and enjoyed the company of women. Neil Alvares was in a discombobulated state; he didn't understand the reason he was at the Capital Club. Why was Henley asking him to be at a nightclub when he could have gone with Aldridge for the Tesla drop? Why Wright instead?

He scanned the crowd of fashionable twenty-somethings. He could just about blend into the crowd, but Henley would stand out like a sore thumb. As the music grew louder and the lights dimmed, Alvares felt a hand tucking into his waist.

"Can I join?" a tall, beautiful blonde asked.

"Not tonight," he said, trying to maintain his composure. "But let me buy you a drink." He walked with her to the bar and ordered three vodkas. She kissed him on the cheek, took her drink, and left. He walked back to the table and waited for Henley to reappear. Moscow suits me, he thought.

Simon Henley reemerged from the crowd after about twenty minutes, heading toward the table with another man who Alvares vaguely recognized. As they approached the table, Alvares suddenly stood up. He remembered the face clear as day.

"Mike, this is Neil Alvares. He's on secondment here in Moscow," Henley said, taking a seat.

Mike Moore sat next to Alvares. He knotted a brow; he was sure he recognized him but wasn't sure where from.

Alvares didn't quite get the play here. What was Henley doing with an enemy agent?

"Boss, how did you know I was here?" Mike asked, keenly looking at Alvares.

"Your old boss, Hicks, told me this is where I would find you at odd hours," Henley said and drank his cognac.

"If you say so," Mike said. He kept looking at Alvares, clearly trying to place him.

"Have we met before?" Mike asked.

"Indeed, you have, Mike," Henley interjected before Alvares could respond. "And that is why we are here."

Henley moved closer to Mike and whispered into his ear. Mike looked shaken for a second. He reached into the inside pocket of his jacket, took out an envelope, and threw it on the table. "That can't be true. I received orders from you to follow the agents leaving the Christmas party… and I've the money to prove it."

Henley kept quiet, contemplating something.

Henley opened the envelope, looked at the stack of notes, and said, "I always gave you pounds, not Rubles, Mike."

Mike's shock was evident. Someone had set him off on a tail, making him assume it came directly from Henley.

"So, the question is…who put you on this job," Henley said and then turned toward Alvares.

"More so, how were they going to extract the information back from Mike," Neil asked.

"No clue, boss. That stack just lying on my bedside table in the hotel room like always," he said.

"Was there a note?" Henley asked.

"There was. It just said, follow protocol as before for the Moscow Station agents leaving the Christmas party," Mike said and handed over a typewritten letter to Henley and Alvares. Henley kept it inside his pocket.

Alvares had his own theory; he had seen this before, just weeks back, when he and Aldridge almost had the enemy in their hands, only to face a dead end.

"Who else knows you're in town?" Alvares asked.

"Well… Henley, Control… and payroll in London," he said, looking at Henley earnestly. Someone had just played him.

"Someone just played you, mate," Alvares said, those words coming out like a dagger toward Mike.

"This is a shit storm, boss, and you have me caught right in the middle of it!" Mike said with a thunderous rasp.

"Moore, sit down and hold yourself. This is not a scalp-hunting business," Henley said. "Just thought you were better than to be played like this."

"Well then, who put me on this? Does this have to do with the drop site I sat on the last time? The Tesla business?" Mike said as he remembered the word Tesla distinctly.

"Nothing you should be concerned about, for now, Mike," Henley said as he clenched his teeth.

Simon Henley was in a quandary. Who could have put Mike on the task? Could it be London? It didn't make sense for London to overreach like this. But he knew the reach and power of those in London. If they wanted, they could have had someone slip this note. He took the note out of his pocket and looked at it carefully. At that instant, he had a moment of clarity.

The typeset letter of the note was familiar. The Moscow Station and the embassy in general were forced to source the typewriters from Soviet Russia. They were not allowed to import from England. As a citizen or as a diplomat, you could not regularly buy a typewriter. This was to limit anti-propaganda, free speech, etc. All typewriters were registered, their typeface recorded, and any reparation recorded (if the typeface was changed, etc.); any publication could be traced back to the owner of the typewriter.

The typeface of the note had a clear distinction. *It was typed inside the British Embassy in Russia.*

Henley realized at that moment that the traitor was most likely sitting in Moscow and not in London. *The enemy must be closer to home.*

"Chin up, Mike," Alvares said, taking stock of the situation. "We can make something of this. I want you to spend the next four days in Moscow walking to every corner of the city, always in random patterns."

"Every day?"

Henley looked surprised but decided not to interrupt Alvares.

"Every hour till you fall dead asleep," Alvares was clear in what he wanted.

"And report back to me every day at 9 pm," Alvares added. Henley approved the plan. He also had something else for Mike to do. But that was for later, and only if he deemed it absolutely necessary. Mike was better in Moscow and close to him than having him on the loose—hot-headed and damaging the exfil.

"Right you are," Mike said, and immediately headed out of the club, leaving Henley and Alvares to finish their drinks.

"Well, if someone is tailing him, why not send them on a wild goose chase?" Alvares said.

"Nice play," Henley said as they watched the incoming rush of young folks entering the club.

Impressive, Henley thought, finishing his glass of cognac. The priest was right after all.

Chapter 27
So It Begins

"My milaya, I have missed you dearly," the man with long hair said, over the phone.

"Why did you call me at home? Is it an emergency?" She had been clear that home was strictly off-limits unless it was a matter of life and death.

"Did I catch you at the wrong time? I thought he wouldn't be home at this time of the day."

"He's not the same person I told you about a few years back," she said.

"What does that mean?"

"Never mind," she was finding it difficult to keep him to the point.

"I need the General to do me a favor. The one I mentioned last time."

"Can this wait?"

"I fear not, it's time before my cover is blown. You have the details… in the file I gave you last time."

"Okay, milaya," she said, reciprocating his love for her was a key part of being a female handler.

She kept the phone and moved across to her kid's room. She moved the pink study table to reveal a small lever that was built right into the walls. There was a circular ring with number notations—a safe dial. She moved the dial a few times to key in the right codes. She moved the dial for one last time and opened the safe. She pulled out the thin red file he had given her a week back.

She read through the description of the agent he wanted dead.

Three days to Christmas

Red Square, Moscow

Aldridge was anxious. Tesla had dropped a note in the dead letter drop last night—the one next to the Moscow theater—one of the three drop sites they used over the years. The message was cryptic. *Kremlin Square. 1900. Look for the tomb.* Keith was sure that Tesla would come, but he had requested to meet at the Red Square and not Gorky Park. He was not sure what the tomb meant and most of all—why choose the Kremlin?

Aldridge and Wright looked up at the Kremlin contemplating how the night would unfold. They had spent the last day planning the operation and the entire afternoon today going black and dropping counter surveillance from the KGB. It took a little under three hours to do the surveillance run. They had been spotted by two KGB agents and had them in pursuit for a moment but soon got rid of the tail. This was the easy part, though.

Tesla had decided on the location. *He knew the KGB inside-out and may have considered Gorky Park to be a dangerous spot under the current circumstances,* thought Aldridge. Aldridge found it odd that Tesla would choose to switch the location last minute. It wasn't his style. Aldridge knew Tesla to be utterly cautious and someone who took calculated risks. He must have had a reason to move the meeting to Kremlin Square—the busiest spot in all of Moscow.

"If you say so, mate. Your agent, your rules," Wright said, as he leaned back into the car, trying to get as comfortable as he could. This was to be a long night. He and Aldridge had long been in a tussle for the best case officer at Moscow Station. Like Aldridge, he was ambitious and cutthroat and ran the next best gold mine of a double agent after Tesla. Wright was a maverick, and his approach to spycraft was boisterous, often callous, and bordering on luck. Practical, Wright would say. Aldridge wasn't sure he agreed. He had been raised to be a classic spy, his was a game of deception, patience, and grit.

"If I was Control, I would not exfil your guy," Wright said, looking at Aldridge, who was running through some notes he had picked up from the file room earlier.

"Why not?"

"If he's delivering gold like you guys think he is, then why would I not let him continue doing that? Keep him for a few more years…" Wright said, looking out of the window as a few police patrol cars moved about.

Keith looked at him with a straight face. Wright read that.

"Fuck me, don't tell me that Control has not approved it yet?" Wright said, a startled look covering his face.

"That's for Henley to figure out," Aldridge said, flipping the notes.

"Ballsy move, I give you that."

"What I don't get is the part about the tomb," Aldridge contemplated loudly, looking at his notes. He didn't expect Wright to take part.

"Is there a cemetery nearby?" Wright chipped in. Aldridge had passed through the Kremlin and Red Square umpteen times but never saw a cemetery. Inextricably linked to all the most important historical and political events in Russia since the thirteenth century, the Kremlin had been the Great Prince's residence and a religious center. At the foot of its ramparts, on Red Square, sat St Basil's Basilica—one of the most beautiful Russian Orthodox monuments.

They got out of the car and headed toward the Basilica. Aldridge took a quick look at his watch, a fine Jaeger Le Coultre Reverso with a buttery soft tanned leather strap—a parting gift from his father when Keith left for Istanbul.

"Ten minutes to seven, time to move. But, something's not right," Aldridge said, scanning the queues outside the Basilica to see if he could spot Tesla. Stuart Wright ran to the nearby bookstore and came back with a tourist guide.

"For sure, this should mention a tomb, if there is one," he said and handed it over to Aldridge.

Aldridge flipped through to the index. And there it was, entry number thirteen: the Tomb of the Unknown Soldier.

The Tomb of the Unknown Soldier, erected to commemorate Soviet soldiers who lost their lives during WWII was a solemn monument that stood on the western walls of the Kremlin. The modest memorial was made from dark red porphyry, a bronze sculpture of a laurel branch, and a soldier's helmet on top of a banner.

Aldridge looked at his watch again. It was almost time. If he made a dash for it, he could run to the western side of the Kremlin and be at the tomb in 5 minutes.

"Get in the car and be ready to roll," he told Wright and started to run. Wright left his side and walked back to the parking spot, a few hundred meters down the road.

The premises of the tomb were dimly lit, almost dark, with barely any crowds. A few late-evening runners were passing by. Now it all made sense. Tesla had picked a quiet corner right in the middle of the city. It would be easy to mix in the crowds at the Kremlin if they were to be followed after the drop.

As he scanned the northwestern section, the part of the area with a large section of empty open spaces, Aldridge felt a sudden tap on his shoulder. He turned around and saw Tesla.

"You made it, Otto."

"You had me confused for a bit," Aldridge said and shook Viktor's hands.

"Control has approved your extraction," Aldridge said. He saw the look of a relieved man.

"Thank you, Otto."

"But it will not be easy."

"I'm prepared, Otto," Tesla said.

"We leave the day after Christmas. But before that, we need you to run one last op," Keith said and handed over the camera.

"Get us the details on the KGB's Budapest operations. Anything you can find. But please, be careful."

"Tell Control I can still help. This brain can hold a lot of information," Viktor said as he dropped the camera into the pockets of his long overcoat.

Aldridge understood that Tesla felt the burden of diminishing returns.

"You have already done a lot, my friend. Let's get you out safely."

At that moment, Aldridge had a hunch, and he played it.

"Have you heard any of these names in the KGB circles you operate in?" Aldridge read him a list of the top players at the Moscow and London station.

"Sorry," Viktor shook his head. "Even if they were there, we'd have never used their real names. But…" he took a brief pause. "In the last few months, I heard some officers talk about a real asset we have in the enemy agency. I can't be sure if it's in the British or American agencies, but the codename is Lennon."

"Lennon… as in John?"

"We have a funny sense of humor," Viktor said, "Do you want me to find out more?"

"It's too risky with what we have going on," Aldridge was tempted to throw Tesla into the trenches to find out, but restrained himself.

"Hold tight, Viktor, for another few days," Aldridge said and handed him the note the team had prepared.

"One last thing, Viktor. The agency has approved the exfiltration only for you and not the whole family. I know this comes unexpectedly, but the stakes are really high."

"But, Otto," Viktor said, crestfallen at the thought of leaving his wife and kid behind.

"You know very well that if I leave them behind then they are going to face the brunt of me betraying the country. They will not see another light of the day, Otto."

"I will see if the team approves to exfil your family as well. I will drop the final details at the dead drop site tomorrow. We have to get you out safely first. We leave on Boxing Day," Aldridge stood firm.

Wright watched the faint silhouette of Keith Aldridge walking toward the car. He had been revving the engine, fearing the fierce Moscow winter would get the better of it.

"Let's go," Aldridge said as he got back in the car. There was excitement in his voice.

Wright pulled out into the Moscow traffic. Neither spoke for a moment as the visuals of an electric Moscow night passed them by.

"So, what's the verdict?"

With a hint of a smile, Aldridge turned to Wright. "We're good to go. We have an exfil on our hands!"

Chapter 28
Man Down

Neil Alvares turned to the corner of the street and parked his car. By now he had a fair grip on the intersections, routes, and directions around Moscow. He had had his fair share of driving around the city in the last three weeks he had been in this city. He loved it, probably a feeling that was not echoed by everyone coming to this city for the first time. If not on espionage business, he could see him spending time here—learning the culture, the people, and the romanticism of communism which was at the heart of Soviet Russia. A student of history and art since his days of spending time at the Romain Rowland Library in Pondicherry, Moscow fascinated him. When all the business of Tesla was done, Roslyn had promised to show him around town. He hoped that the events leading after the exfiltration would allow him to stay in Moscow for a few days. *Wishful thinking,* he thought. He had not had a single day where plans weren't being improvised, changed, or dumped.

He was to meet Ros later in the evening, but he planned a quick stop first to meet Mike Moore. A couple of days back, he had instructed Moore to drive around the city, in an attempt to keep the KGB chasing their own tails. He looked at his watch. 7 pm. Alvares opened the pack of cigarettes and lit one to keep him going in the cold. He had been leaning a lot on cigarettes since his arrival in Moscow—something he was not proud of.

The streetlight he stood next to kept flickering on and off, casting an unusual shadow on the street, as if warning him of an impending calamity. Alvares tried to move away from that thought, although not superstitious, thinking so was built into his Indian upbringing. He saw a familiar-looking vehicle slowing down and parking toward the curbside. *Moore,* he thought.

"Not the greatest spot to meet, sport," Mike said, trying to show his seniority in the city.

"As long as you didn't bring along a tail, this works," Alvares said and passed on a cigarette to Mike. He refused.

"Not my first gig," Mike said, struggling to remember the name.

"Neil Alvares, if that's what you are looking for."

"I have been driving around, like you and Henley said, and nothing sticks out, except…"

"Except?" Alvares leaned in.

"One of your guys, Stuart Wright, seems to have a second apartment in the industrial quarters of the city…"

"How do you mean?"

"Yesterday evening, I was driving around the industrial quarters in the eastern end of the city, the hillside with the large factories on one side and a plush residential quarter on the other. I saw Wright driving into an apartment. I stayed put for a few hours to see if he would come out. Seems he stayed there the whole night."

"Why is that a concern?" Neil asked.

"Come on, Alvares, you want me to lay it out for you? One of your agents has a second house at the other end of the city, and you don't think that sticks out?" Mike said, triumphantly.

"I will relay this to the boss. Anything else?"

"Rest all seems kosher."

"Stay put for now. Henley or I will be in touch," Alvares said and turned back toward the other end of the street. Alvares arrived back at his apartment for a quick change; his mind still racing with the seeds of doubt that Mike had placed about Stuart Wright. Wright, the man behind the case officer and a star agent, ticked all the boxes for a man who was behind the affairs they uncovered in India. He couldn't shake off the thought and left the apartment.

Despite it only being a short walk to Roslyn's apartment, Alvares had decided the fully padded overalls would be best. Alvares was still trying to find the right set of clothes to manage the extreme cold. He was planning to make a surprise visit to Roslyn's place. He bought a bouquet and a bottle of wine to thank her for the kindness and generosity she had shown him since he'd arrived.

As he approached the intersection just before Roslyn's, he spied a spot of commotion. A distant siren sounded in the distance, fast approaching. A bad accident, he thought. From a distance, it didn't look like a car crash. In India, by now a few hundred people would have already gathered. But winters in Moscow meant that there were less than thirty people bordering the location.

Alvares kept a safe distance. He was an outsider, on a fake passport, and working for British intelligence. Not the best idea to be caught in a pub brawl incident, he thought. Wright had given him a short speech on what to expect on Moscow roads, especially at night. Pub fights were common.

Alvares saw a few more people running toward the spot, shouting in Russian for help, he presumed. Probably a hit and run, he thought, considering the crowd was circling toward the middle of the intersection. He still couldn't make out if the person was dead or not. Nobody seemed to be making any efforts to revive, just cries for help.

As Alvares walked toward the site, he saw a sandal lay on the road, a trail of blood surrounding it. A hit and run, definitely.

It was a red sandal, Alvares noted. Roslyn had one. She wore it for the Christmas party.

His hands trembled and his head began to spin as he edged toward the site. The siren was now bellowing louder than ever. He had to make sure he got a look at the body before the ambulance or the police arrived. Between the crowds, he made his way to the center, hoping against hope.

A body lay motionless in the middle of the road.

Roslyn's.

In a state of panic and complete loss for words, Alvares left the site and ran toward the embassy.

Everything had changed.

꧁꧂

The British Embassy held a short memorial service. Roslyn was to be buried back home in England, next to her son. Simon Henley was grieving, and so were the rest of the station members. Although he knew her only for a short period, Neil felt a tremendous sense of loss.

Henley walked up to the billiards table to give a short speech celebrating the life and work of Roslyn Henry Ashby as the rest of the crew surrounded the boss.

"There never was and never would be someone like Ros. She was a brilliant spy and yet the warmest human you could find in the business we are in. She was the mother figure who kept us going through the toughest of times and silently celebrated every win this station had. These walls will forever be grateful to the glue that kept everything together. Here's to Ros."

It was short, inspiring, and purposeful.

John Marbury could see his friend struggling but held his ground as he went about the business. He watched Henley making a few calls. Roslyn's death, as per the official reports, was an accident. Marbury knew this was not the case. It was murder, and he was now about to exact his revenge—cold and calculated. A long-time servant of the service, a friend, had fallen on foreign soil.

The mood in the office was grim. They needed to restore a bit of normality and get the wheels turning again.

"Right everyone, Henley's office—two minutes," Marbury said. He had had enough.

"Lads, we've got to get started on our exfil plans." Marbury was ready to get to work. "Control has given us until tomorrow to come back with options... where's Wright?"

"Something came in that he had to rush out to," Darcy said. Alvares heard that and his face turned pale. The meeting with Mike came rushing back to his memory.

"Right," said Marbury, "So, Aldridge, what sort of risks are we dealing with, aside from the one we know already?"

Aldridge was pacing back and forth across the carpet in Henley's office. He gave Marbury a quick recount of the rendezvous he had with Tesla.

"When was the last time we did an exfil in Moscow?" Aldridge asked.

"The last we did was Gordievsky," Marbury quickly chipped in. "But that was also the first, and the Russians weren't prepared for it."

"This time it will be harder—the Russians are always expecting something now." Henley was weighing the risk.

"And we have to get his wife and kid out as well. That's trouble," Marbury asserted.

"Do you think he'll move without them?" Alvares asked.

"I already relayed the idea, he didn't take it well," Aldridge said. "But I don't see a way we could take them all out together."

"Under the circumstances, there is no way we can carry the whole family," Henley was clear.

"Ideas, people, ideas—not excuses. We're better than this," Marbury said, visibly frustrated.

"Alvares, any ideas?" Aldridge asked, hoping for some inspiration.

"Can we bring them in separately? Different timelines?" Alvares asked.

"The first sniff the Russians get, they'll lock up his wife and kid. Guaranteed. He'll never agree to it," Aldridge said.

"We send them on a fake holiday, pick them up there?" Alvares asked.

"Now, I like that..." Marbury said.

"Norway could work?" Aldridge remarked. "The Russians will be watching Finland after Gordievsky..."

Everyone took a brief pause. On first contact, it seemed this could work. A family of three taking a break, traveling to Norway, and never coming back. Plausible, yes; risky... yes.

"Do we have a station in Norway?" Aldridge asked.

"Not even an outpost. Those guys have been effectively neutral and never took sides once they came to know we used Finland to bring in Gordievsky," Henley said.

"Well, that's a problem, isn't it?" Marbury said.

"Not necessarily, Marbury." Alvares walked to the giant window in Henley's office. Overlooking the vast expanse of the snow piling up in the city in front, he carefully mulled things over.

"You have an idea?" Marbury asked.

"I have one word for you: bluff," Alvares said and moved over to Henley's desk. He pulled open a map of Moscow, scouring the edges of the city with his fingers.

"Look at the route we used for Gordievsky… Moscow to Leningrad and then Vyborg in Finland," He pointed his fingers to the small hamlet of Vyborg, at the northwest corner of the country. "That's where we ask Tesla to take his family for a vacation."

"How's that a bluff?" Aldridge checked in.

"Well, spies have a blindside, don't we? We look so hard outside our walls that sometimes we overlook our backyards. The Russians have guarded the Finnish border for so long and have seen zero activity, I can't help but believe that they have laid the guard down."

"And, we hit them exactly where they don't expect us to," Aldridge completed the thought.

"Exactly. We actually do the Finland route all over again. Play the bluff."

"There's still a lot to plan, especially with three souls to take with us and not just one," Marbury added. "But I think this has legs, Alvares. Well done." Alvares felt his chest puff up.

"Mind if I have a word, Simon," Aldridge asked Henley as the rest left the room to work on the exfiltration plan and route.

"Something Tesla told me, probably you should know," Keith said.

"What about?"

"He mentioned a double agent who is working for the KGB. Not sure which agency, could be us, could be the Americans…"

"Does he have a name?"

"Only the codename: Lennon."

"Thanks for this, Aldridge. Keep this information with you for now, will you?"

With Aldridge gone, Henley took out a wooden board engraved 'Chaturanga' with hand-etched chess pieces. A gift from the Turkish ambassador, it was one of his prized possessions.

Chess was his favorite game. It helped him to focus, think, and in some ways, meditate. He moved the pieces around in different formations. Father Samuel had made his first move. It was his turn next. He had to carefully plan and execute his side of the plan for this to work perfectly. There was no room for error.

Henley looked through the glass walls of his office. Roslyn was a loyal team player and confidante. She had taken one fine step at a time, careful and calculated, but had ended up a pawn. Someone had taken advantage of her, and he was not going to have any of it. His wrath will rain down on them.

The KGB had chipped into his fortress, bit by bit, and now the enemy had done major damage. Whichever way Henley put together the pieces, there was only one way to make this work. There was no place for emotions. This had to be done.

Henley left his office, determined and with purpose, and headed straight to Mike Moore's house. He knew the risk of running Mike for this job. But he had one quality that others didn't have. The KGB wasn't interested in scalp hunters. He was a nobody. And Henley needed a nobody to run this job.

Chapter 29
The Joker Card

The next day
Dec 24, 1982
Moscow Station

Father Samuel looked at the wide facade of the embassy building. He had been here many years back, before Henley took charge. This probably would be his last trip to this part of the world. At least he hoped so. His presence was not a favor from one chief to the other. He was here to set things right. Like Henley, Father Samuel's house was in disorder.

He had arranged for a quick breakfast meeting with Alvares before he officially took a position at the Moscow Center as an 'operation support'.

"Seems you have taken a liking to this place, Alvares," he said as Alvares brought a tray with two cups of coffee and some sandwiches from the pantry. The two spies from India had taken a corner table at the embassy staff restaurant for their quick meet-up.

"Sitting here, between the regular embassy folks, you wouldn't guess the rough seas the guys at the station are navigating Father," Alvares said as a large group of clerks, assistants, and bureaucrats played a merry-go-round to spot an empty table. The dining hall was full that morning—the last working day before the embassy staff would break for Christmas.

"How has the team taken to the news of Roslyn's death?"

"Henley seems to be the worst hit," Alvares said trying to hide his own battles with coming to terms with her death.

"The wire from Moscow said you spotted her body first, how did that come to be?"

Alvares recounted the events leading up to him finding her dead body in the middle of the street.

"Have you considered the fact that if it was the KGB; they would have stayed around to see if they could spot someone from the Moscow Station coming to check on her?"

Alvares nodded. He had not considered that.

"There could be a target on your back if they suspect you were a witness to their operation," Father Samuel said, concerned that his deputy's cover may have been blown open.

"I have to assume that they know I am an active member of the Moscow Station," Alvares acknowledged the gravity of the situation. He was no more a regular visitor to the embassy. He was now field operational.

"Alvares, there is something I need to tell you," Father Samuel said and leaned closer to Neil and whispered into his ears, *"A time will come when you will need to choose between two operations. Choose Aldridge."*

❦

"Samuel, old sport, how was your trip?" Henley welcomed his old friend into the office. The priest was in plain clothes. His athletic frame and crisp clothing took Henley by surprise.

"Strange times, but here we are," Father Samuel said. "I'm terribly sorry for your loss, Henley. Alvares spoke highly of Roslyn," he added.

"She would have liked you. Not the serviceman, but the priest."

Father Samuel smiled as he looked around Henley's impressive office. Commendations from the state, a medal from his time in the army, and a few photographs.

"Who's that?" he asked, pointing to a photograph of a younger Henley with another man in British khaki greens.

"John Marbury," Henley said and walked up to the photograph. "Runs our tech. But now his deputy runs most of the tech ops."

"Someone you deeply trust, Henley?" Father Samuel looked around for other members of his staff.

"With my life," Henley said. That was a bold claim in the business.

"I will count on him then. I hope to spend some time going through the files when you don't need me around," Father Samuel asserted. The devil was in the details. His network of spies had been built on that premise. He liked to plan everything to the last tiny detail. But the events in the last few weeks reeked of anything but detail. And he was guilty of this laxity.

The office was in a mad rush with preparations underway. The entire staff was working extra hours to put together the exfil that was to happen in two days. Henley called Marbury into the office for a quick debrief.

"John, this is Father Samuel," Henley introduced him to the priest.

"Appreciate you coming down and helping us," Marbury said and took a seat next to the priest.

"I have word from Vyborg," Marbury said and pulled a page from the file that he carried with him from the file room.

"My contact runs a car workshop in Vyborg. Good lad, Mikko. He is low-key and runs smart surveillance for me," Marbury said, ruffling through the papers, hoping to land the right piece of information.

"Here, look at his signal notes from last month," Marbury moved his fingers to the portion of the page that was highlighted in fluorescent yellow. Mikko's notes were meticulous.

Marbury then laid out the plan that the lads had worked out. The plan was to use the same Gordievsky route in an attempt to bluff the KGB counter-surveillance. *Moscow to Leningrad and then Vyborg in Finland and then a safe passage to India.*

"If you make it beyond Vyborg public stations, you're pretty much sleepwalking the rest of the way," Marbury said.

"How old is this report?" Father Samuel asked. "We can't rely on outdated information."

"Last month. I don't suppose much has changed," Marbury said, with little confidence. He knew the game had tilted on its head. Roslyn was the breaking point. The priest was here not to support, but to jointly lead the operations. It was a two-man leadership at the station now.

Stuart Wright came rushing into the office and barged straight into Henley's office.

"Who are you?" he said, looking at Father Samuel.

"Wright, this is Father Samuel, from India."

"Henley, I have something important. Can I have the room?" Wright gave a quick handshake to Father Samuel and got straight to the point.

"You can speak...he's one of us," Henley said.

"Well then, more the merrier, for this is some grade-A news... Eddie wants out, too." He walked toward the cabinet and took out a bottle of cognac.

Henley got up and went next to Wright, put his arm around his shoulders, and asked him to take a breath. Tell me from the start, he said. Father Samuel looked at Wright keenly, trying to assess him. *Alvares had conveyed his doubts about Wright based on Mike's revelation.*

"I got back home late last night and saw the sign on my garage door," Wright said. A small cross in yellow chalk was a signal from his agent, Eddie, indicating a drop at one of the dead letter boxes.

"I did the run, went through the regular dead letter drops."

"You're sure you didn't have company?" Henley asked.

"You bet. I was black through and through… Anyway, at the last dead drop box, next to the university, I found this," Wright said and handed over a brown bag.

Henley opened the bag and saw a small envelope with a note inside. *Cover blown. Need to leave Russia. Urgent.*

Dmitri Alexander Popov, codenamed Eddie, had been a key asset for MI6 in Moscow. There was a tussle, of sorts, between Tesla and Eddie, for who could become the most valuable asset. A key player in the Fifth Chief Directorate, the chief government agency of union-republican jurisdiction which carried out internal security, foreign intelligence, and counter-intelligence in the KGB, Dmitri had been providing intelligence to MI6 via his handler, Wright, who had built a long-standing, successful relationship spanning the last seven years.

Unlike Tesla, Eddie was a man of base needs and luxuries. At first, he asked for small wads of cash, luxury pens, and Western music records. *It will come back to bite us*, Henley had warned Wright, but Wright had fought hard. Once the favors, money, and Western goods started flowing through, Eddie's work rate and quality of work product increased.

When Eddie shared the naval treaty plans between Russia and China, that could change the landscape of the South China Sea, affecting the harbors of Hong Kong, Vietnam, and the surrounding islands, the intel from Eddie helped Britain to launch a counter, before the treaty could fully see its potential. But over the last two years, Eddie had slowed down and had been less willing to take risks. Wright had held on tight, and in the last two months, he found Eddie back in the saddle.

"John, we need to speak to Control," Henley said. Marbury started setting up the codes for the call and after several minutes, Henley was through to Control's office.

"Something major has turned up on our doors," Henley said, as Wright, Father Samuel, and Marbury listened in.

"Go ahead, Henley. Engels, Maeston, and Smith are here with me," Control said, his voice crisp and purposeful as it filled Henley's room.

Henley moved in closer to the phone. "We have a developing situation. We have reason to believe another asset has been compromised."

"Another one, Henley?" Maeston said, unable or unwilling to hide his mocking tone.

"You're right, Maeston. Another one. Wonder if there are celebrations being planned in London," Henley hit back.

"Don't be a child, Henley. We are all responsible adults here," Smith weighed in. A station chief himself, he knew the challenges they faced in Moscow.

"Thank you, Smith, but Engels might want to have his say here. We don't have the resources here to pull out two assets."

"That's correct, Henley. The exfil package counts for one, and even if we did provide the funds, do you have enough operational bodies to handle two?" Engels added. "And I'm afraid that there's nothing else that can be done on that front." There was a heavy silence.

"So… who is it you want out, Henley?" Control asked. It was time to make a decision.

Henley looked at Father Samuel and Marbury.

"Tesla," Henley said, eventually. More silence.

"Why?" Engels' voice sounded grim.

"Because, Engels, he deserves it the most. He has provided us the most valuable intel, consistently and of the highest quality."

"Eddie's work on the naval treaty earned us a lot of favors from the government," Maeston threw his hat in the ring.

"Favors that went into the foxtrot funds, which you used to pump up Panama station, Engels?" Henley pushed the narrative further. *Engels' godson was now running the show in Panama.* Simon knew Engels had played the backroom politics to throw Wright out of Panama to replace him with his godson. Henley winked at Stuart Wright and gave a wry smile. Simon always had his agent's back.

"Don't be a snob Henley, just because other stations are now catching up to Moscow," the discussion was getting heated.

"Stay on the topic, everyone!" Control commanded.

"Henley, who's got more to give?" Smith asked.

"Tesla," Henley said after a pause.

"Well, then that's that. Tesla is more valuable here, gentlemen. We cannot let emotions dictate this. Eddie is the clear candidate for extraction as he has run his course. We've got as much as we can from him. Tesla will have to stiffen his lip a little longer," Smith asserted his choice.

"Where is your moral compass, Smith? It's a death sentence, you know that," Marbury shouted into the speaker.

"We cannot be making these decisions based on emotions, Marbury. We've all seen where that leads," Maeston sounded furious.

"Is that what everyone wants out there?" Henley asked. It was important for him it was a unanimous decision from London. Each confirmation sounded like a nail being hammered into Tesla's coffin.

"So be it. Eddie gets the exfil package. Tesla remains behind the curtain," Henley said. The Big Three promptly left the room, an air of superiority following them.

"I believe Turner has joined you over there?" Control asked once he was alone in the room.

"Present," responded the priest.

"Henley, I need you to personally oversee the ground operations for this exfil. Turner, can you run the comms with London? I want minute-by-minute detail."

"As you command," Henley said and cut the call.

"Wrighty, we're going to need to prepare an exfil plan and get the specifics to Eddie pronto," Henley directed Wright.

Wright was flummoxed. He was now in the spotlight. Something he wished for from far away but now was a reality. He was now to run the biggest exfil in MI6's recent history, not Aldridge.

Wright left the room to pull the files on exfil routes they had prepared for Tesla, now seemingly an option to exfil Eddie.

There was a moment of silence in Henley's office. Henley looked at Father Samuel. Their plan had worked. Control had acted on the plan laid out by Father Samuel and executed the misdirection. Henley had already briefed Marbury if this came to pass.

"Marbury, if this goes to plan, you know what to do?" Henley asked.

"I do. But will Aldridge and Alvares take the plunge?"

"They will," Father Samuel said. He was confident in the plan he had worked out.

"I hope so, too, Samuel," Henley said, "and if we are lucky… the traitor in our ranks catches on, too."

At that moment, Aldridge barged into the office in his running gear.

"Sorry, who is getting defected?" Aldridge asked.

"Eddie, Wright's asset," Henley said and looked straight into Aldridge's eyes.

"Are you fucking kidding me?" Aldridge shouted.

"Do I look like I'm kidding?" Henley's heavy baritone almost shook the table and everyone in his sights.

"And what about Tesla? What do you expect him to do?"

"To wait," Henley said. "This has come directly from the top."

"I can't believe this! You're telling me that Control values Eddie more than Tesla?"

"Quite the opposite. I know he values Tesla much higher. That's why they want him to stay." Henley wasn't mincing his words.

"So, we just leave him to the dogs? He has a wife and child for Christ's sake." Aldridge was furious.

His outburst was met with utter silence. The chain of command was clear, the instructions clearer. But the morality was clear as mud. On balance, Tesla should have been granted the ticket to freedom. He had paid his dues, done more than what was asked of him and he deserved the loyalty back. And here they were, ready to squeeze him to every drop they could.

"I just don't even know who we are. Not even sure if we are better or worse than the commies!" Aldridge couldn't contain the explosion of emotions and stormed out.

Henley got up and followed Aldridge. The snowfall had intensified. From the ground floor, it was just a sea of white that had engulfed the city as far as one could see. Aldridge's silhouette stood out like a speck of dust on a white canvas. Smoke snaked from the end of his cigarette as he took a drag.

"Pass me one," Henley said, leaning against the wall. Aldridge obliged, lighting a cigarette and passing it to Henley without looking at him.

"I can't believe you agreed to this travesty," Aldridge said.

"Someday, hopefully, you will be in my shoes and you will be required to take such orders in your stride."

"Before I took this job, I went through some of the old case files. Yours in particular," Aldridge said.

"Many moons ago," Henley said, wistfully.

"Not really. You handled Gordievsky…you know why I took this job, Henley?"

Henley avoided the question and kept puffing away.

"You were in the same predicament as this. You were given no choice. Circus wanted to run Lupin longer. But you took a stance and fought for your assets. You made it happen."

"The circumstances were different."

"Were they? How is Tesla different from Lupin?"

"Lupin was our only agent. The only meaningful agent behind the curtain. We had to show we could take our guy out, right under the noses of these communists."

"Why?" Aldridge asked, still trying to figure it out.

"So we could show the future Teslas and Eddies of this world that they could have a safe passage if push came to shove."

"So, what has changed now?" Aldridge asked.

"We got greedy. We want more, and we have choices to fall on."

"Is it that simple?" It didn't seem to Aldridge who was finding it hard to understand the balance at play. Espionage had been always about protecting his country, at all costs. Yet, he stood there, arguing with his boss, who probably has been doing the same for much longer. Why was he so emotionally attached to his field agent, Aldridge was carrying a fight inside him; one between the angels and demons inside him. The angels seem never to catch a break.

"We are never black and white, Aldridge. We operate only in the gray areas," Henley said and threw the cigarette stub, stomping with his feet on the dying embers. He looked squarely at Aldridge. "You have a long career in front of you, Aldridge. Choose wisely." With that, he started back inside.

As he pulled open the doors, he turned back to Aldridge. "Do what your gut tells you, do what you think is right."

At that very moment, it all made sense. Aldridge knew what he had to do.

Chapter 30
The Butterfly Effect

Small, seemingly trivial events may ultimately result in something with much larger consequences.
– Edward Lorenz, 1960

Moscow Station

Father Samuel called in the core operational team- Wright, Aldridge, Darcy, and Marbury for a quick debrief. Everyone assembled at the billiards table, waiting in anticipation. The billiards table had become emblematic of the Moscow Station's recent woes. The green carpet of the once-illustrious single-wood carved table now had glaring holes and burn marks from cigarette embers flying over. So was the Moscow Station— once illustrious and known for its super tight operations, now had holes, spills, and blemishes.

"In exactly two days, I have the live drop with Eddie. I need the specifics of the full defection package," Wright said in a strong, determined tone about him.

"Two days isn't enough to make this watertight," shouted Darcy.

"Then fucking let's get to work," Wright said. The case officer in him was taking stock. He was not the casual, flirty, and flamboyant agent this afternoon. He was a man with a purpose. Whether he liked it or resented it, he was now thrown into the limelight, and he preferred not to be the deer caught in the headlights.

"You heard the man. This is our plan A," Marbury said and laid out two big sheets of paper. Everybody slouched in to see the plans laid out on the table.

John pointed at the left sheet, Operation Witchcraft written in bold letters. Plan B—the plan that was set aside for Tesla exfiltration.

OPERATION WITCHCRAFT:
Eddie goes to work as he usually does.
Takes off from work during lunchtime and goes black.
Reaches the Moscow Central Station by 5 pm.
Train to Sochi. Darcy accompanies him on the train, keeping a safe distance.
Arrive at Sochi the next morning.
Wright picks Eddie and does the surveillance run, goes black.
Wright and Eddie reach the port of Sochi.
Sochi to Istanbul by sea.
Istanbul to the Safe house.

"Holy Moly, I wish it were that simple," Wright said, looking at the overall plan.

"Aldridge, what do you think?" Marbury asked, knowing that they would need their smartest case officer to fully buy in with the plan and give his insights.

Aldridge thought deep and hard, "Wrighty, do you think your guy can manage to go black and make it on time to the train station?"

"That's the tough part. He is a nervous wreck."

"That's our single point of failure," Aldridge said, "Address that and we can manage the rest."

On the periphery, the plan seemed to make sense, everyone agreed. Henley had to sign off. Darcy, Marbury, and Wright got together to further drill down the plan with details, assignments, and plans for surveillance runs for the D day. Alvares joined them.

Aldridge hunched over to Father Samuel and softly whispered into her ears, "What about plan B?"

"Keith, your plan for using the old Gordievsky route is brilliant. But Wright has a veto, guess he is going with this," Father Samuel said with a hint of remorse. He could see Aldridge was suffering. This planning could have been for his agent.

"I agree with Wright, this plan is better," he said and gave a quick pat on Alvares' back as he left the room.

There was something about Aldridge this afternoon, Alvares thought. He had known him long enough. There was no way Aldridge thought that Wright's plan was better than his. Why didn't he fight it out? He should have been doing everything to push his idea forward. Marbury was going around in circles. Probably best to relay this to Father Samuel, he would know what to do, he decided.

Aldridge had a troubled twenty-four hours. Conscience, guilt, fear of failure, just plain disappointment, or probably all of them were weighing on his shoulders. He had been the star case officer for the MI6, running the biggest counter-surveillance operative in Tesla. And in one day, he had been relegated to a second-class officer. Wright and his agent were far more important. Not for once did he buy the premise that Tesla is more important to us, so he should continue serving us. *Bollocks,* he thought.

In a couple of days, he would be part of the team that would plan the defection of Eddie. But tonight, Aldridge was still working on his own plan. A masterplan that would catch everyone by surprise. It was bold, calculative, and may cost his job. But he didn't care. Tesla had been their greatest asset, and he intended to do right by him.

Aldridge had run an emergency dead drop for Tesla the previous night. He needed to let Tesla know the change of plans. Tesla was not going to be officially exfiltrated on Boxing Day. He dearly hoped that Tesla would keep a lookout daily on the drop sites. He needed to meet Tesla tonight and convey the change of plans and the bold strategy he had put in place. But he won't be able to pull off alone. He needed an ally, a third wheel: Neil Alvares.

Aldridge walked into the heat of the mission room. Marbury, Darcy, and Wright, all strangely gallant, were planning the Eddie exfiltration. For all their differences and shortcomings, they were all tuned in to one cause. Aldridge knew what he had to do.

Amongst the testosterone-filled clamor, stood Alvares, like a deer caught in the headlights. Aldridge walked past Henley's chambers and gave him the hint of a smile. Henley smiled back.

He came up behind Alvares and placed an arm around his shoulder, gently guiding him out of the cauldron and leaning in close.

"We have work to do, come outside," Aldridge whispered.

It was snowing outside, and the weather taking a turn for the worse. But Aldridge was sharp and focused on his thoughts and forgot his coat back in the station. Alvares followed him shortly, Aldridge's overcoat in tow.

He handed Aldridge his black winter overcoat, "What's troubling you?" Alvares asked.

"I don't buy this whole last-minute Eddie request," Aldridge said.

"You smell foul play?"

"It's like India all over again. Last minute the plan gets switched from Tesla to Eddie Doesn't make sense; too dangerous," Aldridge said, reminding Alvares they still hadn't uncovered who'd been switching the codes and diverting the operations into completely different directions.

"You could be right. But to switch an exfiltration request?" Alvares said. "It's on a different scale altogether. How could you convince an asset to request a full defection?"

"Exactly."

"Someone has played a really long game to make this change, or…"

"Or what?" Aldridge asked.

"Or it's just a coincidence…"

"You think it's a mere coincidence that two of our top double agents request a full defection within days of each other?" Aldridge said.

"What are you leaning toward? Someone in MI6 is selling us out to the KGB?" Alvares said. "If that's our working theory, then Tesla won't have long before the KGB catches and executes him."

This was the moment Aldridge was waiting for.

"Why don't we take him out?" Aldridge proposed.

"Take him out? Tell me you are not saying we help him defect?"

"That is exactly what I am saying."

"Henley and the rest won't buy it. That ship has sailed."

"We don't need to tell them. We can run it off the books."

"Let me assume for a bit that you are not crazy. How would that even work?"

"Hear me out," Aldridge said and pulled a sheet of paper. The sheet had a series of lines and curves, showing a map and movements marked in red.

"This is a copy of the Gordievsky defection route. I have changed a few details, given the operational challenges we have running a two-man team."

"You already had worked this out before I came!" Alvares suddenly realized he was being set up.

He looked through the sequence. On paper, it looked like they would be able to manage the show by themselves. But then there was a problem. Not one, but two.

"Even if you convince Tesla to defect alone, how do we excuse ourselves from the Eddie defection operation?"

"With some luck, I should have a smaller role in the operation. We will only know that later. But you...?" Aldridge said, hoping for an inspiration. They were quite close to forming a clear operational blueprint to make this work. But if both get stuck in Operation Witchcraft, then the plan would fail even before liftoff.

"The open case from India!" Alvares said, with a sudden jump.

"What about it?"

"I can speak to Father Samuel. Ask to be excused so I can spend the day in the file room and go through the registry. With some luck, I can then leave the station."

But first, they had a Tesla-sized problem. If he does not agree to defect alone, then this plan will not work. They only catered to one person. Any more, and the plan fails.

"We will know about that tonight," Aldridge said, looking at his watch. They had three hours to finish the work on Witchcraft, run counter surveillance, and go black before they met Tesla for the live drop.

Aldridge explained to Alvares the route they were to take. Drive to the nearby coffee shop, buy a cup of coffee, and read the newspaper for an hour. Leave the coffee shop, drive to the auto repair shop drop the car off for a quick tire change, and take the bus to the department store in the Metropolis section of the city. At the department store, they would split. Aldridge would buy a couple of stuff for his daughter and then take the taxi to the *Oktyabrskaya* metro station. From the station, he would buy a ticket back home, only to get off at the *Park Kultury* metro station. If he has gone successfully gone black, then walk the rest of the way to Gorky Park to meet Tesla. Alvares would circle back to the car repair shop and then drive his way to the Gorky Park east entrance and wait for Aldridge.

It took Aldridge a good four hours to go black and reach Gorky Park. He reached the designated bench, the same place where he had met Tesla the last time around. He rehearsed his delivery of bad news. Best to tell him straight to his face, he considered, knowing Tesla could see through if he bullshitted around. He wanted to see how Tesla would react. That would give me an idea of what to do next, Aldridge knew his plan depended heavily on Tesla's reaction.

Viktor had made it on time. He looked weaker than last time, showing that things weren't going well. Aldridge could see a man weighed down by his acts of betrayal of his country, and how it was affecting him physically and mentally. His memory of seeing Tesla for the first time, a healthy and confident man, felt distant and blurry.

"How are you, my friend?" Viktor spoke first.

"Could have been better, but nothing I can't manage. How are you holding up?" Aldridge said with genuine concern for his agent.

"How do you say in English…. umm…I have seen better days," Viktor said and lighted a cigarette.

"Do you have the plan ready?" Viktor asked

Keith waited for a few folks to pass by and said, "We have a problem, Viktor. Your trip has been delayed. Something else has come up that needs immediate attention."

"Something or someone?" Viktor asked with a sharp increase in his tone.

This was the moment of truth. Aldridge had promised himself to be straight and honest with Viktor.

"Someone. Another agent on our books has requested a full defection."

Viktor said nothing. He looked angry and crestfallen at the same time. Aldridge let him take in the news.

"What do you want me to do, Otto? I thought we had an understanding. I have asked nothing in return for my services."

"This came from the top, Viktor. Trust me, I tried."

"You should have tried harder," Viktor said. This was the first time he had shown his disappointment.

"I don't blame you for thinking so," Aldridge felt sorry. This was not on him but the MI6 had a different plan.

"It seems my body of work was not enough. The other agent brought you better intel than me I suppose," Viktor said and threw the cigarette stub and looked around.

Viktor gave a wry smile back and said, "This is it. I know I am never leaving Russia."

Viktor held Aldridge's hand and gave a tight squeeze "And I know you tried, sorry for taking out my worries on you."

Aldridge held his silence. He was waiting for the signs. He needed to know that Viktor could be ready for an off-the-books exfil before laying the plan in front of him.

"I think I should leave now. This might be the last time we speak to each other. One last cigarette together?" Viktor lit two cigarettes and gave one to Aldridge. The double agent and his case officer sat for a moment, no words spoken, yet the silence was loud.

At that very moment, Aldridge knew Tesla would take the risk of an unassigned, off-the-books defection.

"I can help you out," Aldridge said.

"Help for what."

"Take you out of Russia."

"Would your bosses approve?"

"They don't need to know."

"Are you sure?"

"Damn right, I am. But…"

"But what?"

"You have to come alone. For my plan to work, it has to be just you. We cannot risk taking you and your family without the support from the entire team."

"Otto, I cannot do that. Helena and my child Olivia… how can I leave them behind."

"I promise you we will bring them to you. But not right away, only once you are settled."

"What will I tell them?"

"Nothing. This has to be just between you and me."

Aldridge quickly shared the overall plan but left a few details out. For Viktor's benefit, he had to keep him dark on some details. They went back and forth, arguing the merits of him leaving alone. Aldridge prevailed. Viktor agreed to the plan and assured Aldridge that he wouldn't tell Helena.

"I still have some prep to do. Tomorrow evening, I will signal you at the dead drop. Look for the alpha sign. That should tell you we are good to go. I will drop the details of where to meet along with the travel arrangements," saying so Aldridge gave a quick handshake and walked toward the parking lot. He turned back and saw a fast-paced Viktor walking in the other direction.

"And, how did he take it?" Alvares asked, quickly opening the door and started driving as soon as Aldridge got into the car. Aldridge gave him a quick rundown.

Aldridge was feeling a rush of adrenaline. He was going to do something crazy, bold, and borderline sackable offense, even a jail term. He looked at Alvares and had a feeling he had a capable ally to see this through.

Chapter 31
The Queen's Gambit

"Tomorrow, it's happening," he said, keeping his voice low on the phone. Although he was in his office, he worried that such a sensitive call should have been made from his workplace. But this couldn't wait. He had been trying to reach her since yesterday.

"My milaya, it feels good to hear your voice," she said.

"Listen carefully, my love. This is important. This is the big catch that I want to show the general. The things I can do for him."

"Where can I find the details?"

"From here I cannot find a dead letter box, so listen carefully to what I say," he said.

"I am listening," her voice was even more seductive on the phone. She had him on a short lease.

"Tomorrow, ask your people to be at all the major railway stations. Keep an eye...a close eye on the Moscow agents of the MI6. If there is a chance, I will find a way to send a signal."

"What will be the signal?" she asked.

"If the operation is a go, I will send give three quick calls to your telephone, in quick succession. Make sure you stay close to the phone."

She understood.

"If we catch them and if it is a big fish, the general will be very happy, my milaya," she comforted him.

"The General will see my true worth. If all goes well, you will be with me here, seeing my rise in the service."

"I am always with you my love."

"Together, we will rule," he said and cut the call. He had work to do. This was his pièce de résistance. His magnum opus.

※

Moscow Station

Christmas Day, 1982

"Silence!" Father Samuel shouted, "If chaos theory had a middle name, it would be you lot, I swear!" He wasn't having it. The office was in a mad rush, for the biggest double agent exfiltration was to happen. Marbury, Wright, Darcy, Aldridge, Alvares, and Father Samuel, the director of the operation—all had spent the night working on the two dead drops this afternoon: one for Tesla and the other for Eddie. These dead letter drops would detail the operational plans for the next day. Only with Tesla, it would be an apology letter from the MI6. They were planning to leave him out in the cold.

Operation Witchcraft: The moniker coined for the Eddie defection plan. Neil and Keith had secretly coined Operation Cricket for their covert plan. Aldridge was running the show off the books, not even Henley or Father Samuel had a sniff. Yet, the meticulous spy in him wanted to document every bit of their operation. For when the time comes, he would know exactly what to tell Control and those at the Circus. He wasn't going for glory; all he wanted was to take Tesla out securely and then use the operation notes to explain the need for an unauthorized covert op and hope to buy the resources to get Tesla's wife and kid out. He and Alvares still had work to do and plan the route. But he had to play his role in Operation Witchcraft first.

But there was a complication. Aldridge was assigned to travel with Wright to Sochi, ensure he had support, and if needed, cover. Aldridge was to oversee the part where Eddie is safely ushered into the ship at Sochi Port and off to Istanbul. He was good friends with the captain aboard the Claire *deLune*, a Turkish passenger vessel, from his time as the cultural attaché to Turkey for the British government. For Operation Cricket to work, it had to be on the same day as Operation Witchcraft. When the KGB catches wind that Eddie has defected, the security would go tenfold and it would become almost impossible for a two-man team to exfiltrate another KGB officer in Tesla.

Alvares was worried. This whole plan goes kaput if Aldridge cannot excuse himself from the trip to Sochi. He looked over at Aldridge worriedly, something has to change quickly, if not, they will have to abort Operation Cricket completely. Henley walked into the meeting. Alvares had already laid the groundwork to excuse himself from the line of duty in Operation Witchcraft. Father Samuel gave him the permission, rather too quickly, he thought.

"What's the status quo? Someone bring me in quickly," Henley said as he thumped on the table, seeking answers.

Wright stepped in, "Operation Witchcraft is scheduled to start tomorrow at 2 pm. Once Dmitri goes black, he will board the train to Sochi at Moscow Central at 4:45 pm."

There was a sudden silence in the room. In that moment of haste and high-voltage discussions, Wright slipped and for the first time mentioned Eddie's real name.

"Who is making sure he goes black?" Henley asked, realizing the slip.

Wright raised his hand and said, "Darcy will shadow Eddie, make sure he is not being followed. Once back, he will board the train with Eddie at Moscow Central, making sure of safe passage," Marbury said.

"I will take the train tomorrow morning to Sochi and wait for Eddie and Darcy at the Sochi train station the next morning," Wright chipped in.

"Charlie boy, get all the sleep you want tonight. I don't want you to lose sight of Eddie, even for a minute." Henley was clear in his instructions.

"And who is at the port?" Henley continued to map the operation in his mind.

"Will be me, boss," Aldridge said. He was now seriously worried. If Henley approves this operation as is, then he would need to excuse himself from this. That would throw an entire world of suspicion on him.

Henley paced around the billiards table while the rest looked at him. He stopped, turned his head slightly toward his left shoulder, and waited.

"Watch this, he is going to change the plan," Marbury said to Father Samuel. He had seen his friend work for decades and knew the telltale signs when he made a big change.

"This is too big an operation, both outside the walls of this building and inside," he said and looked at Aldridge. "Aldridge, trade places with Darcy."

"But why boss," Darcy said, "I can do the job."

"Aldridge is our senior most case officer. It is important that the operation starts strong."

"I second that," Father Samuel said.

"Aldridge, once you have dropped him off at the station, run back and go through our usual surveillance routes and look for KGB activity. If you see something that needs attention, make sure Father Samuel and Marbury are aware of it."

"We need to make sure that London knows the operation is underway. Marbury will be at the office all along tracking the teams and running comms with me," Father Samuel said.

"And I will go to the port, instead of Aldridge," Henley said. There were shocked faces around. It had been years since Henley had even been part of a dead drop, let alone an exfiltration.

"But Henley, you don't need to..." Father Samuel said.

"This has come directly from Control; he wants this to be crisp and clean and wants me at the end of it," Henley said. He looked at Aldridge. Aldridge tried hard to suppress his bout of surprise and happiness. He had caught some luck, finally.

"Finally, Wrighty, you have the fake passport and tickets for Eddie?"

"Yes."

"Wrighty, are you clear?" John asked, making sure the final plan was clear.

"Not my first rodeo, but yeah, I have it on lock, boss. Aldridge shadows Eddie to the station, and Darcy joins Eddie on the train, I am at Sochi station and bring him to the port, and then boss welcomes us with flowers and vodka at Sochi Port," Wright said with his usual pomp and charisma.

"He is ready," Marbury whispered into Henley's ears.

"Take care of my house while I am away, will you..." Henley said to Father Samuel and went back to his office.

Darcy, Wright, and Marbury got together to plan the last dead drop with Eddie. Aldridge stood around with them to understand the nuts and bolts of the plan and his part in the play. A few hours later he was to run his own dead letter drop to let Tesla know the details of Operation Cricket.

Alvares walked over to Aldridge and softly whispered, "What do you want me to do?"

Aldridge took him to the side, "Go to the file room and find the files on the Gordievsky extraction. Read and understand as much as you can."

"And, circle back to me in exactly five hours. Downstairs at the guest diner."

Aldridge saw Wright and Darcy leave for the dead drop. He hated doing this alone, dead drops required a protocol that could only work with two in tandem. For a moment he pitied himself, for only a couple of weeks earlier he was the star of the show. He was the case officer for MI6's biggest asset in Russia, but now, reduced to a mere team player. He opened his wallet and stared at the picture of his wife Clarise and his daughter Esther. He mustered some courage and pumped himself up. It was showtime.

Aldridge opened the contents of the dead drop handed to him by Marbury. There were a few hundred in cash, a microdot film, a camera, and a typeset letter from Henley. *Classy bastard,* Aldridge thought. He read the note.

It is extremely difficult to say this, but at this moment, we do not have the resources to bring you along. We hope you continue to have faith in us. If not us, trust Otto. He will know what to do.

He will know what to do? The letter seemed incomplete. It was not typical of Henley to leave a note of this kind. Maybe he wants Tesla to know that he might not be taken out after all. Tesla was right; he is not going anywhere, Aldridge surmised. It was not the time to be emotional. He pulled himself to get going. He removed the note and put it back into his pocket. Instead, he kept one train ticket in the drop box—*Moscow to Leningrad, 26th December, departing at 5 pm.*

Later that evening.

Aldridge drove his car through the streets of Moscow for an hour, on random routes, and always checking his rearview. There was a black wagon that followed him for a while then moved off-road. He was now on the expressway. Quite a long way from where he was to drop the package. He took the first exit, circled back into the city, and drove toward the 2nd bridge on the Moskva River.

He parked the car along the curbside and walked through the hedges and under the footbridge. This was one of the many dead letter drop locations he and Tesla had used in the past. He took the box, placed it in a black trash bag, and carefully kept it next to the Douglas fir tree. He plucked some leaves and grass and some stones and placed them on top to conceal the bag underneath, camouflaging the box. The drop was done, now to make the signal so Viktor would know about the drop location.

Aldridge again took the route back into the city, drove for another hour, and circled back to Gorky Park. He went to the same bench where he would meet Viktor, placed a pine cone from the fir tree underneath the bench, and marked the sign of 'Alpha' and an 'M' on the back side of the bench. Viktor could either spot the pine cone or look at Alpha M and know the drop was at the Moskva River footbridge, next to the fir tree. The alpha was an indicator that the plan was On.

Now he hoped Viktor would make sure to visit the bench at Gorky Park tonight and find the drop. *I hope he is ready for tomorrow*, Aldridge thought and drove back to the office.

Anatoly's Bakery.

8 pm, the day before Operation Cricket and Operation Witchcraft

"Two sandwiches, darling," Aldridge shouted to Victoria, the lovely server at the diner. He saw Alvares sitting at the table with a glass of water and some cold sandwiches.

"I am starving, let's eat first," Aldridge said as he took out his overcoat and neatly placed it on the chair. Alvares was famished himself. They ate the meal in peace, not a single word spoken about the operation the next day. For almost an hour, they spoke about families, friendships, and the curveballs life had thrown at them. *A friendship was born.*

"Now for some work, shall we?" Aldridge said as he ordered two cups of coffee.

"I have been going through the Gordievsky operation as you said."

"And?"

"It's genius. But..."

"I still doubt if it is a two-man job," Alvares said.

"You are right. It's not a two-man job. But this is the hand we have been dealt with."

Alvares opened the map of the USSR and spread it on the table. He looked around to check if any of their colleagues were around. The diner was empty, except for the lovely Victoria who was busy closing down the diner.

He pointed to a small dot that showed Leningrad and circled it with a red marker. He drew a line with the red marker between Moscow and Leningrad. He then took the green marker pen and located Vyborg, a small town on the Russian-Finnish border. He drew a line from Leningrad to Vyborg.

"That red line, that is you and Tesla traveling by train tomorrow," Alvares said, as Aldridge caught onto the specifics of the operation, impressed by the attention to detail.

"Once I have shadowed and made sure that Eddie is safely on the train to Sochi, I will double back and rush to the next platform and take the train to Leningrad. Hopefully, Tesla would be there too," Aldridge said.

"How would you know he is on the train?" Alvares asked.

"Because I booked the tickets. My seat is in the same coach as his, further away."

"That green dot, Vyborg, that is where you get down and meet me. It's a few hours' bus ride from Leningrad."

"Have you figured out your route to Vyborg?" Aldridge asked.

Alvares took a few tickets and put them on the table. "Here ... the train and bus tickets for me to reach Vyborg from Moscow." Alvares was ahead with his planning. While the teams were away, he had already put together the operational plan and made the necessary arrangements.

"Are you carrying your camera?" Aldridge asked

"Positive," Alvares said and looked at the tickets. It was all in Russian, all he could make out was the time stamps. He had memorized the route and time for his bus and train interchanges and stops. Now, he had to trust the timeliness of the Russian railways and bus transportation systems.

"Good, carry that, for tomorrow you are just a tourist in this country."

"That is my cover, sure. At Vyborg, I am to meet Mikko. I need his address and a small note from you to verify that we are in this together."

Aldridge took a small strip of paper with an address written on it. He had managed to snick off Mikko's details from Marbury's case files.

Alvares folded the paper and kept it in his trouser pockets. "Neat. I will take a car from him and drive to Vyborg Central Train station and wait."

"Copy. From Vyborg, it's a Hail Mary pass. We will figure out once we get there," Aldridge said. He had a kamikaze plan in mind. But he couldn't risk it all. He needed to do this alone, without Alvares, if it came to that.

Aldridge explained to him the tickets and the timings and a brief layout of the city, in case he lost his way. They went through the plan a few more times.

"You are to leave early in the morning tomorrow. Have you figured out what to tell the priest?"

"He bought the India story and the need to follow up, pretty easy," Alvares said, still suspicious at the ease of that discussion. It was unlike the priest. But there was no time to worry about semantics. *When the time comes, choose Aldridge—the priest's words ringing in his ears.*

They both got up to leave. Keith turned and said, "And Neil, if we don't turn up at 6 am at the Vyborg Train Station, then leave immediately and take the same route back to Moscow and to the office. Don't wait for a second beyond 6 am."

"Aye aye, captain," Alvares said and walked out of the diner.

The Queen had made the move.

Chapter 32
One-Man Cavalry

Moscow Station

11 pm

Alvares left Aldridge at the bakery and headed back into the office.

Father Samuel and Alvares were the last ones left at Moscow Station. The rest of the crew had retired for the night. Alvares needed a moment of solace before everything began again. This was the home stretch.

He had chalked out his own little master plan. He was in Moscow for two reasons: to help Aldridge and to find out what happened to Kate Miller. If the Tesla operation went successfully, then he would head to Budapest. Before her death, Roslyn had set Alvares up with Peter Vaughan, the station chief at Budapest. Alvares knew the answers to Kate's disappearance lay there.

Alvares contemplated telling the priest about Operation Cricket. He had always confided in him. But Operation Cricket needed complete secrecy. The last few weeks at Moscow had been full of adrenaline rush but now, in the calm before the storm, it felt like the old days at Indian station—just him and the priest running everything.

"Plain black with two sugars, Father?" Alvares said as he brought them two cups of coffee.

"Thank you, Alvares. What a week this has been…"

"Anything I can help with?"

"I needed some time away from all the hubbub," Father Samuel said and took a sip from the steaming cup of coffee. "And something is bothering me."

"Something to do with Witchcraft?" Alvares asked.

"Not particularly. I have been drawn into thinking that the dead end you faced in India..." he took a deep pause. "What if the troubles you had at Shakuntala had a connection here in Moscow?"

"You think the code swaps were done from Moscow?"

"If it was one agent, it would be counted as an anomaly. But here we are dealing with four. There could have been more from other stations. There are only two locations with the power to pull off something like that. Moscow or London."

"You don't suspect someone from this team?" Alvares was trying to gather his thoughts.

"I could be completely wrong, and we could all just laugh about it when it turns out to be a wild goose chase."

Alvares had his doubts as well and Father Samuel picked up on them, in his silence.

"It's just a hunch, but I have this feeling that we are looking at it completely wrong."

"Kate Miller was in Moscow and Berlin before she came to our station. Maybe something from her past can give us a bit of direction?" Alvares said. He pulled out a file and handed it to Father Samuel.

"This details the assignments she had here and shows notes from the agent she was running in the field."

He was like a man possessed, running through the pages, giving a recount of Miller's time, almost verbatim. Father Samuel at that instant figured it out. Alvares was not just looking for a missing agent.

"I'll take it on from here, get some rest," Father Samuel said, snapping Alvares out of his monologue. He took some files from the registry and prepared for the walk back home. Alvares had given him something to think about. Kate Miller and her time in Moscow, after all, might be the way to go searching in these files.

Aldridge looked at his family sleeping next to him on the bed. This was the most peaceful time of his day—spending a few hours of silence in the comfort of his family, knowing they were safe.

He checked his watch: 0200. In an hour, he would have to jump into action. There was a small window in the dead of the morning when security would be at its lowest at the railway station. He had to be there to drop off travel documents for Tesla in the lockers before the rush of early-morning commuters.

He quickly changed, locked the door behind him, and checked the duffel bag he had prepared. It contained wads of cash, a Norwegian passport, a diary with important numbers, and a Walther PPK handgun—a cult favorite amongst MI6 agents. The route to the station would take him at least an hour. He couldn't risk driving straight to the station. He picked up a wet diaper that Esther was wearing before going to sleep and put it inside the bag.

The highway was unusually busy. Patrol vehicles were checking cars every few kilometers. He had not seen this before, although it was unusual for him to be out at this time. At the checkpoint just before the diversion to the railway station, the patrol vehicles asked him to stop. This was a problem. The last thing he wanted was to get caught with fake passports and a gun.

"Your papers, please," the officer said. Aldridge handed over his ID, car registration, and driving license to the officer, hoping that this would be quick.

"You work in the British embassy?" the officer asked as he spotted the diplomat signage.

"Yes sir, just a sanitation and janitorial officer," he explained in Russian. That was his official title at the embassy. He was a low-level employee on paper.

"A lot of shit in your embassy is it?" the officer joked. He may have caught a break here, Aldridge thought. He maintained his composure. The bag was in plain sight as the officer stuck his neck inside the car.

"Where are you going at this hour?"

"The pharmacy at the station," Aldridge said. "My kid is not well, and it's the only 24-hour pharmacy I know."

"Where is your address?"

"Arbat District, Smolenskaya."

The officer looked at his fellow officer at a distance, signaling something with his hands. Aldridge couldn't spot it—it was below the car window level. Aldridge knew the police were now suspecting something.

"Why come so far from your home? There is one pharmacy closer than this."

"I was not aware officer, thanks. I will remember next time," Aldridge moved a bit, and at that moment the police officer spotted the leather duffel bag on the floor of the passenger seat in the front.

"What's in the bag?" another police officer came into the passenger window and tried to unzip the bag.

Aldridge quickly put his hand on the bag. "Careful, officer. If you open that, your day is ruined."

"Why?"

"Because it's full of shit and diapers that I need to throw away," Aldridge said and laughed. The first officer instructed the second one to open the bag, one hand on his holster, ready to take out his gun if Aldridge made a movement.

The second officer opened the bag, and the promised waft came flying out.

"Sorry officer, we are actually full of shit. I tried to warn you," he said, playing it casual and low-key.

The officers let him leave. That was a close call.

⁂

Henley had found it nearly impossible to catch any sleep. He couldn't shrug off the feeling of an enemy lurking in the shadows. He played out the sequence of all events leading up to the night. And he arrived at the same conclusion. It would be almost impossible for someone in London to pull so many threads, including ordering a hit on Ros. The traitor was right here in Moscow, he could sense that.

The misdirection play worked out by Father Samuel had held its ground so far. But the second play—the one Henley planned was still out in the open. It would require a tremendous leap of faith to make it work. But he was not a man of faith. Henley was a man of action and he knew he had to find a way to reinforce the second play.

He walked through to his front room and searched for the call logs in the diary, hoping to find the numbers that Roslyn had kept ready for him to use when at home.

"Did I wake you, Samuel?" Henley asked as he heard a crackling sound on the other side.

"Not at all, Henley. I was just about to offer my morning prayers." Father Samuel hadn't slept either, reading the files that he had brought home. "What's troubling you?"

"We are going to burn Eddie, can't see any other way, are you sure we're doing the right thing?"

"We had no choice. This is the only way to smoke out the rat," Father Samuel assured Henley.

"You think our second play would work…we have left them short," Henley asked.

"What's on your mind, Simon?" the priest said.

"I think we need to send a one-man cavalry to help them out," Simon said.

"I know who you have in mind. So be it…" Father Samuel said.

"Thanks for the reassurance, Father. I'll leave you to your prayers."

"I'll make sure to offer one for you, Henley," the priest said and cut the call.

Henley got up to heat water for coffee. He had one more call to make. To John Marbury.

Chapter 33
The Man in the Yellow Tie

Cafe Pushkin Patisserie

1:30 pm

Aldridge sat outside Cafe Pushkin nursing a coffee. The baguette he'd ordered went untouched. Eddie's reaching the station on time was the key to both Witchcraft and Cricket. He scanned his surroundings, looking for any KGB. A few families were gleefully enjoying their lunch, a couple of old friends were playing chess, and a few regular-looking people were having a break at the cafe.

A few minutes later, Eddie walked in. He was a lanky, unassuming man with a cleft lip—the only thing that distinguished him. He wore a suit and carried his work briefcase. Smart, Aldridge thought. Eddie ordered his lunch and took a table right at the window. He kept looking out of the window, anxiously. Not a good sign, Aldridge thought. He had to wait until Eddie made his first move.

Without eating much, Eddie paid the server and started walking out of the cafe. Aldridge waited a few moments before he followed suit and set off after Eddie. In less than fifteen minutes, Eddie had walked past his office, which on any other day would have been his final stop post-lunch, and kept walking toward the bus stop. Aldridge was on his heels, keeping a safe distance to ensure Eddie didn't spot him. The last thing he would want is for Eddie to feel he was being followed, get cold feet, and throw the entire plan into disarray. The bus to St. Basil's Cathedral arrived, and Eddie boarded. So far, so good. Aldridge waited.

Just as the doors were coming to a close, Aldridge squeezed himself inside the bus and took a seat near the exit with a clear view of Eddie on the crowded bus.

As they got to St. Basil's Cathedral, Aldridge remembered the drop he and Wright had done last year at the same spot. That drop was one of the references Henley made when he made the claim of a traitor amidst their ranks. He felt a weird sense of *Déjà vu*. Eddie alighted and started walking across the street, to the other side of the road, for the next leg of the journey. *He'll take the bus to Bolshoi Theater, spend fifteen minutes on a tour of the theater, and then take the train to Moscow Central.* As they waited, Aldridge had a sudden feeling that they were being followed. He looked around, trying to spot any familiar faces, or worse, a KGB agent. Just as he thought it was his mind playing tricks, his eidetic memory kicked in. Across the street, next to the lamppost, a stout man in a suit with an oddly matched yellow tie. *He had been at the cafe.*

If his hunch was correct and the man was a KGB operative, then they were walking into an ambush. He made a quick calculation. If Eddie continued with the pre-determined route, the KGB man would either intercept him or continue following and run straight into his MI6 colleague, Darcy, at the train station. He had to drop the KGB on Eddie's tail before it was too late.

Aldridge looked over his shoulder. Eddie was still standing at the bus stop, waiting. The KGB agent was about twenty-five meters away. He had to alert Eddie. But he had to be careful. If the KGB agent got wind that Aldridge was involved, that would be the end of Operation Cricket as well.

Aldridge walked up to the bus schedule board and looked over the routes and timings. His memory of having seen the map of Moscow countless times served him well. He made a quick calculation and figured out an alternate route that could get Eddie to the Central station on time, but with a different route. But he also had to make it on time, via a separate route.

He inched closer to Eddie, waiting for the perfect moment. Aldridge checked his watch. 1525. There was one more bus before the one Eddie was waiting for.

The 1527 bus arrived. *On time, for once*, Aldridge thought and made his way right behind Eddie. As the passengers moved up and down the bus, rushing to find seats, Aldridge quickly whispered into Eddie's ear, "This is Viking's friend, don't turn around. You are being followed. Take this bus to Lenin's Museum, and from there walk to the Central Train Station."

Eddie nodded and immediately got into the bus and was momentarily immersed in the sea of passengers. Aldridge crossed his fingers. As soon as the 1527 left, the next bus started approaching the curbside. He stepped into the stream of passengers, hoping to catch sight of the man in the yellow tie and suit. There he was, lurking, trying to spot Eddie. By now, the bus had left with Eddie safe inside. Tail me, you commie bastard, Aldridge thought as he moved along the queue and entered the bus. He stood in the front section, ready to alight if need be. The bus started moving, Aldridge looked anxiously around for the man in the yellow tie but he couldn't spot him. The bus slowly started treading along the roads, and Aldridge heaved a sigh of relief.

Moscow Central Train Station, 4:30 pm

At the bookstore, Charlie Darcy had the perfect vantage point to spot incoming foot traffic. He was scanning the crowds, hoping in anxious anticipation to see Eddie walk through. This was his first covert operation in the field. He was a genius behind the secure walls of Moscow Station. But this was new territory, a new challenge, and a faceless enemy.

Darcy was surprised to see Aldridge entering platform one from the west end. *He was not supposed to be at the platform at all.*

"What are you doing here? I thought you were leaving once he's on the premises," Darcy asked, looking around to see if anyone was trying to spot them.

"We hit some traffic on the way. Eddie had to take a different route."

"Is he clean?" Darcy asked, worried that the operation had already stumbled.

"Should be, let's see if our man makes it to the station." With that, Aldridge walked toward the telephone booth next to the bookstore.

The announcement for the train to Sochi blasted through the intercom at the station. Aldridge looked at his watch. If Eddie didn't make it in the next five minutes, both operations would fall through.

The train trundled onto the platform. This was the moment of truth. Aldridge gave a glance at Darcy who picked up his luggage and made his way toward the carriage. Darcy was about to move when they both saw... Eddie was walking onto the platform and boarding the train.

With Darcy and Eddie boarding their train, Aldridge ran to the next platform. He had a fifteen-minute window to pick up his duffle bag from the valet box, spot Tesla, and board the train to Leningrad. He suddenly remembered he had to make a call to the embassy to Father Samuel and let him know the operation was underway.

He found the nearest phone booth and dialed in and heard Father Samuel on the other side.

"British Embassy, how can we help?"

"Witchcraft is a go!" Aldridge said and hung up before heading back to the lockers.

Aldridge fumbled through his pockets to find the key. He located the valet box, pulled out his bag, and walked toward the spot for coach number six of the incoming train. He kept looking around until, eventually, amidst the crowd of men, women, and families, he saw a familiar face. Tesla. *Operation Cricket was underway.*

On the other train, Darcy started moving through the coach, in search of his seat. He had got a place just in sight of their asset. As he was approaching his seat, three men brushed past him, throwing a tiny briefcase onto the overhead shelf.

Ugly fucking ties…who wears a yellow tie these days? Darcy thought and took his spot on the train as the three KGB men sat right in the middle of the coach, between Darcy and Eddie.

Chapter 34
Needle in a Haystack

Father Samuel was manning the station alone, Operation Witchcraft was underway, and he had the loneliest seat in the house. Marbury had left the station to continue the surveillance runs in Aldridge's absence and an errand to run at Henley's behest.

By now, Wright and Henley should have reached Sochi. He had last received word from Aldridge in the afternoon and since then there had been radio silence. These were the dead hours of the operation. All he could do was wait for the chips to fall and the agents to reach their designated areas on time, as planned.

He had made a startling discovery in the file room, however. After her recruitment, Kate Miller was immediately drafted into Moscow Station as an understudy for another case officer, George Barkley. Case officers requesting understudies to help them with operational workloads were not new. But to have a rookie join you made little sense, unless Barkley really wanted her, specifically, by his side. And now Barkley was dead and Miller was missing. She had either shared a similar fate to Barkley or had gone looking for him in Budapest. Alvares would want to know this. *But it could wait.*

He went back into the registry, looking for files on Tesla. There was a huge stack of files and case materials that Roslyn had prepared just before she was killed.

He was amazed at the quality of output from Tesla. It was immaculate, consistent, and of the highest order. No wonder the Circus wanted him to continue serving. He was invaluable to MI6 counter operations. Father Samuel marveled at the level of personal risk Tesla had undertaken. Aldridge had handled his agent very well through the years. The case notes on the dead letter drops, live drops, and brush passes, all documented perfectly, gave a clear recount of the five-year partnership between the two. There was no mention of any money deposits or material requests from Tesla. That seemed odd; for someone with a family to not seek recompense and financial security. He found it impossible to countenance that he had never requested anything in return for his services. Until now, that is, and they'd let him down.

It was clear from the notes, though, that Tesla's incentives came from a different place. He traced the origins of Tesla's hatred toward the Soviet government. The medical emergency and the trip to London changed the trajectory of this rising star in the KGB.

But how could a known KGB operative make it to London if Circus did not have a look at him?

There was little information in the files on their covert treatment in London but if Tesla was in London with his family, immigration officers would have alerted MI5, who handled domestic security. Who from MI5 handled the case? For sure, they would have documented the secret medical procedures for Tesla's kid. There were some burning questions. But the MI6 only caught wind of Tesla when he reached out to them at the Budapest Station, months later. *What happened in London?*

Father Samuel rushed back to Henley's office. This was above even his pay grade. He called Control.

"Tell me, this is about Witchcraft..." Control sounded tired.

"We are in the middle of it, nothing major to report so far." Father Samuel answered.

"What, then?" he asked.

"I know we've put Tesla on the back burner, but I have been going through the files on his time in London."

"The lads at MI5 handled it."

"So I presumed… can you help me get the files?"

"Why are we looking at MI5 files?"

"I'm interested to know who handled the case."

"Does this have something to do with the other problem we are having?" Control asked.

"I don't know. It's a long shot. It may prove nothing. Can you get it for me, tonight?"

"Let me see what I can do."

"I just need the names of the officers assigned to the case."

"I'll call you back," Control said and hung up. Father Samuel could sense a sudden change in Control's tone.

Father Samuel paced his way around the office. He was hoping this thread of investigation wouldn't have the same fate as Alvares and Aldridge had at Shakuntala. The traitor amongst their ranks had clearly made clear, concise, and clever moves to hide his identity.

"Samuel, I am calling you from the duty officer's room." That was Control.

"Can you manage to pull the log files? Let me find you the dates."

Father Samuel quickly looked at Tesla's files and browsed through the section that highlighted Tesla's visit to England.

"Here. July 7th, 1978."

Father Samuel could hear Control flipping through files and pages and waited patiently.

"Samuel, there is an entry here—a cable from the immigration alerting the MI5 for a possible high-ranking Russian diplomat entering England."

"We need to assume that was Tesla. How likely is it that we have two diplomats flying into England?"

"And Control, can you see if the cable mentions the departure destination of this diplomat in question?"

Control took another minute and spoke, "Budapest."

"That proves it was Tesla."

"What do the other entries say on this log?" Father Samuel asked, anxious that he may have the mole by the neck.

"We may have a problem here, Samuel."

"What about?"

"The log pages have been ripped up," Control said, his voice sounding low.

"God, dammit!"

"The last entry is dated 15th July—Tesla's kid being discharged from the hospital and MI5 trying to make contact."

Father Samuel thought through for a minute. He wasn't letting this go, not after having come this close.

"Control, if someone had to come down and rip those pages off, definitely there must be a list somewhere of the people who visited the building in the days leading up to Tesla's return from England."

"Well, if not the official registry logs, then there is one last place we could look into," Control said. Samuel could sense that Control had caught on and was now fully vested in this needle-in-a-haystack search.

"Where?"

"The janitor's roster."

Father Samuel thought hard and fast. That would make sense. The file room and registry were in a completely different wing and someplace that not MI5 and MI6 operatives would visit every day. This was a place for the secretaries.

"That could be it, boss. Can you send me the list of names that spurt out related to the MI5 that entered the building on those dates?"

It took an hour or so before a few codes started to sputter through in Marbury's room. The message contained a list of three names. That's what he was hoping for.

He checked the name against the log files that Roslyn had prepared.

This couldn't be, he thought. As he read the names, tremors went through his body. There was one name that matched Roslyn's files with the list Control sent in. This was it. This was the connection he was looking for between Tesla's time in England and the list of people who were actively involved in the operations here.

But he needed more proof. He wanted to nail the bastard dead in the heart.

This was the needle in the haystack he had been looking for.

He couldn't risk informing Henley right away. He wanted to make sure first.

Chapter 35

Bus to Vyborg

Aldridge stood up and stretched. He had been sitting in the same position for almost five hours. Russian train carriages were small compared to those in Britain. He sat with three more passengers, a young family: a bespectacled man in his thirties, with his blonde and attractive wife, and an infant. He had offered them a hand with their luggage as they'd boarded and made small talk, attempting to keep the mood as casual as possible.

Tesla was in the same coach. Aldridge had to make contact, check if Tesla was holding up, and prepare for what was to come next. In the chaos, he had given Tesla only enough information to make it to the train to Leningrad. After Leningrad, the sailing was less plain. Aldridge was prepared for it. The gun in his bag was the last resort. He hoped he wouldn't need to use it.

Aldridge walked along the aisle, watching through the large windows at the fast-moving scenery outside. He knocked on the door of Tesla's cabin. A tall Russian gentleman opened the door.

"Lighter?" Aldridge asked in Russian. He hoped the man didn't carry one.

"I have one…" A voice said from inside.

"Thank you, mine just ran out of fuel… care to join me?"

"Sure. I'd like some fresh air too," Tesla said and slowly followed Aldridge as they moved to the end of the coach, next to the bathroom and the vestibule that connected the other coaches of the train.

"How are we doing?" Tesla asked. He looked anxious.

"So far, so good. But this was the easy part," Aldridge took one cigarette.

Tesla was in a somber mood. A deep sense of guilt pervaded everything. Aldridge empathized that leaving his family behind was not what he wanted, but circumstances had become dire. Survival was primal.

A few passengers passed by. Aldridge immediately started telling Tesla some nonsense about an imaginary friend he was to visit in Leningrad.

"We can't be seen together for much longer," Aldridge said, refocusing them on what lay ahead. Tesla kept looking out at the wide expanse of the Soviet countryside rushing past. An endless blanket of snow with a few trees and houses adorned the landscape. He soaked in as much as he could. It would be a long time, possibly never, before he got a chance to return to his homeland.

"In about three hours, we reach Leningrad. Head over to the main platform. Buy some food, if you can. Hit the washroom, change your shirt, and then wait for me at the exit."

"Are you sure we are not being followed?" Tesla looked nervous.

"Just a few hours more. Once we're in Vyborg, we have more help. Hold tight."

"Alright, Otto."

"It's Aldridge. Keith Aldridge," he said. It was the first time he had given his real name to Tesla. He had enjoyed their partnership and a sort of friendship for the better part of half a decade. In a few hours, it would all be over. It was only right that Tesla knew the real name of his handler. He had placed enormous trust in him. It was only befitting that Aldridge returned a small share of that trust.

An onboard announcement woke Aldridge with a start. Aldridge looked at his watch. 0045. They would shortly be arriving in Leningrad. Aldridge went to check if Tesla was awake. The last thing he wanted was to leave him on the train. He walked briskly along the aisle, glancing at Tesla's cabin, and saw him sitting ready, peering through the windows as the train started to slow.

The train trudged into the station and stopped on the platform. A few guards were doing the rounds but Tesla was on his own until he reached the main exit. Aldridge alighted, and walked over the bridge, keeping an eye out for Tesla.

The bridge was dimly lit. A good place for Aldridge to linger as he looked for his man. He peered through the iron railings as the last few passengers alighted. And then came Tesla, walking slowly with his briefcase by his side. Aldridge let Tesla catch him up but as the other man got onto the bridge the lights suddenly illuminated as a group of security guards marched up the stairs. Aldridge couldn't wait any longer and got down to the main platform.

It was enormous, and surprisingly—given the time of night—was flooded with guards patrolling the platform. *That was odd.* Aldridge went to the announcement board and checked if there were any major trains making it to Leningrad later that night. Theirs was the last.

Aldridge made his way through the security gates and waited at a bookstore, close to the exit. When Tesla didn't arrive, Aldridge ordered a coffee and took cover. He checked his watch. It had been almost thirty minutes since they'd gotten off. The bus to Vyborg was due in less than fifteen minutes. Aldridge couldn't afford to go back to the platform; it was too dangerous. All he could do was wait.

Five minutes left. Aldridge couldn't leave him behind. Aldridge paid the cafe owner and turned back toward the platform when he felt a hand rub his shoulders. He turned and saw Tesla making his way through the exit door. He quickly followed him through the doors and outside the Leningrad railway station.

As they boarded the bus to Vyborg, Aldridge took a moment to gather his thoughts. His hands hadn't stopped shaking. He was seated behind Tesla who sat still, waiting for the bus to move.

"What took you so long?" he asked Tesla, slightly leaning forward, making sure only he could hear.

"We may have a problem…" Tesla said, without flinching his head.

"What happened?"

"I bumped into someone from my days in Budapest. He immediately recognized me. We used to be close."

"So, what's the problem?"

"He asked me what I was doing in Leningrad…"

The ticket collector came to collect the fees for the trip. Aldridge gave him a fistful of Rubles and waited for him to move on.

Aldridge leaned over again. "And what did you say?"

"He caught me by surprise. Without thinking, I told him I was in town to meet my in-laws."

"That sounds about alright. What's the problem?"

"My wife's parents are not in Leningrad," Tesla took a deep pause. "And he knows that."

Chapter 36
The Wrong Man

Sochi, 1:00 am

Hotel Continental

Stuart Wright checked into the hotel using his Czech identity. He was a journalist covering the rise of football in the Soviet states as part of his cover story. The Continental was the biggest of its kind in Sochi—a place for affluent businessmen, politicos, and the elite class of Soviet Russia, often acting as a getaway from Moscow and a spot for amorous activities and shady business deals. It was the perfect cover for Wright, who had a taste of the high life and women. But although he carried his usual swagger on the outside, he was at his anxious worst inside. He hated Istanbul. A deputation many years ago had resulted in many a drunken stupor, polygamous relationships, and a failed marriage; all of those memories came back rushing in. Now he did everything in secrecy—the drinking, the hookups, away from the glamor—at his second apartment in Moscow. A place that was completely private, almost sanctimonious, hidden in plain sight from his colleagues and enemies alike.

It was Henley who handpicked him from the gutters of Istanbul and brought him to Moscow, giving him a second chance. Wright owed a successful operation to Simon for doing right by him and ensuring safe passage for his asset. He had to make sure Eddie was delivered in one piece to Istanbul. *Thereafter, he is not my problem,* Stuart comforted himself. He was different from Aldridge—this was strictly business and not a place for friendship, especially when you are a case officer.

The bar was bustling with activity—burlesque dancers plied their trade, and hordes of men cheered them on. Wright got a few drinks into his system and waited. He had an hour before he was to head to the train station, run a surveillance check, and prepare for Eddie's arrival in the early hours of the morning.

᠅

Wright was confident of a fairly easy night. Sochi was a quaint town in the grand scheme of things, with very little-known KGB activity. The only challenge was the security clearance at the port, but Henley had sorted that. The architecture and the layout of the small cramped spaces of Sochi station on the platform reeked of the Soviet emphasis on infrastructure. All their national funds went into defense and counter-intelligence. The Cold War had sucked their coffers dry.

He walked around the train station, along the length of the platform. There wasn't much of a rush given the time of night. A few families with luggage being towed around by hapless porters, a group of kids loitering, smoking cigarettes, and a crowd of people waiting for an express train to make a brief stop. He ran a second lap, slower and surer. A few police had gathered to pick up the kids; other than that, the scene was still the same.

Wright was secretly superstitious—something he hid from his colleagues. He liked the persona he had created in front of the others; it worked for him. He liked to do everything in threes. Three dogs at home, three separate covert identities with unique backgrounds, three baths a day, knew three languages, three houses to his name, and to round things up, three failed relationships.

Just as he took a turn, ready to take the third lap of the station, he suddenly realized something. There was a pattern, something he didn't catch before. The unusually short man at the telephone booth, the man with a black hat at the bookshop, and the tall, bearded man at the coffee shop hadn't moved. And they all were in suits—odd, given the time of the night.

He had to be sure. He kept moving, trying not to raise attention. But he had no luggage. Roaming around the station in the dead of night was a risk, but he had to make sure.

Wright held his composure and kept a steady gait. He lit a cigarette and crossed the telephone booth. The same man was sitting next to it, moving his head from left to right. Wright kept walking. This wasn't looking good. The man at the bookshop was also still lingering. Wright saw him flipping through the magazines without looking at the pages. It could still be a coincidence, his mind playing tricks, or the men were too drunk to not move around, he thought. He cursed himself for having a drink too many.

He paused, looked at the blank tracks, and gave himself a moment to think. He had to get this right. He didn't want to jeopardize the entire operation just because he got spooked. It was time to be brave.

There was only one way to be sure. Wright slowly walked toward the coffee shop, right next to the tall, bearded man in a suit, and ordered a cup of coffee in his best Russian accent. He looked the man directly in the eye and asked, "Are you also going to Leningrad on the next train?"

The tall, bearded man looked startled. "Yes, should be here shortly," he replied, and gave a slight nod to the man at the telephone booth, behind Wright's shoulder.

"*Spasibo*," Wright thanked the man in Russian and slowly moved away with his coffee. He knew the train schedule by heart. There was no train to Leningrad; the last one had left at 2100. They were definitely KGB!

Fuck, Wright said to himself and tried to move away from the line of sight of the KGB agents as quickly as possible. He looked over his shoulder and he saw them convening. They, too, knew that Wright was a British spy. He could sense that and was almost certain they were hot on his heels.

Wright made his way into the parking lot. He patted his pocket for the keys to the car he'd had dropped there. It contained his Turkish passport, a fake passport for Eddie, and a few key papers that were to be given at the time of handoff. He couldn't afford to get caught. He had to drop the tail and alert Henley. He looked at his watch. He had a couple of hours. If he played his cards right, he had enough time to drop the tail and find Henley.

Wright decided to not take the car because that's what the KGB would think he would do. But he couldn't stay the whole night in the parking lot either. Like Aldridge, he too was blessed with a photographic memory. At 0330, a train was to reach platform six. He could take that to the next stop, get a taxi back to Sochi station, take the car, and dash off to Henley. It could work. All he had to do was to enter the station again in time for the train.

He waited a few minutes before quietly moving toward the ledge of the first floor of the parking lot. "I hope this doesn't kill me," he said out loud to himself and then stepped off the side of the building.

He felt a sharp pain in his knees as he landed. He gave himself a second before he stood up and, keeping his head down, edged along the wall to the other side of the parking lot. There was no way to make it to the platform via the footbridge. The only way was to cross the tracks on foot and then run onto the other platform. But he had to time it right. The train was due in exactly three minutes.

Hobbling slightly from the drop, Wright made a run straight to the tracks. A patrolling officer spotted him and gave a yell, but Wright kept running. There was a light in the far distance. The train was coming straight at him. He mustered all the energy he could and leaped onto the platform. Just as he found his feet, the train entered the platform, blocking the view of the KGB agents on the other platform.

Stuart Wright took the first door and entered and shoved his way through the coaches to the front. He had made it. As the train gathered speed, he saw one of the KGB agents—the guy from the bookshop—sitting waiting for an ambush.

And then he realized.

It wasn't just Eddie he had to protect. Charlie Darcy was on the train, too.

That place is red hot, he thought. His head was spinning, his knees bleeding, and his ankles ready to give up.

How did the KGB catch wind that something was going to happen in Sochi? Had Eddie turned? Or was there a mole? Either way, someone was going down.

꩜

6:30 am, the day of.

The Grand Budapest Hotel

Stuart Wright paid the taxi driver and got down a few blocks from the hotel where Henley was staying. He walked across the street and stood right opposite the lobby. From across the street, he scanned the area. The lobby looked bright and possibly the only well-lit place along the whole street. A few taxis had arrived, dropping off some early-morning passengers. The place looked kosher, devoid of any suspicious movement.

But just a few meters away, under the dimly lit lamppost, Wright spotted someone suspicious. A tall man in a suit stood right there, barely moving in this cold, without a jacket, and not a good reason to stay outdoors. He had to be KGB, Wright concluded—the attire and general demeanor of the man had an uncanny resemblance to his three friends at the station. Wright was thinking of different ways he could give the man the slip and find his way into the hotel lobby when suddenly he felt a tap on his shoulder.

"It's a cold night, no?" A beautiful, slender, long-haired girl asked him in Russian.

"Now that you are here, it isn't," Wright replied, turning on his charm, in an instant.

"Maybe, I can help to keep you warm?" she said.

Wright took her arm, and they walked together across the street and straight to the hotel lobby. The KGB man hadn't flinched. His ploy had worked. The KGB clearly didn't suspect a man with a prostitute walking into the hotel to be an MI6 agent, at least not this time of day.

"Sweetheart, wait here while I find us a room," Wright said to the girl and walked over to the lobby receptionist.

"Could you help me and my lovely friend with your finest room?" he asked the receptionist.

"Of course, sir," said the receptionist. As she turned her head away and went looking for the rooms in the roster, Wright quickly flipped through the check-in sheet that lay in front of him. He had to find Henley's room number. *Oleksander*. Henley's codename. There he was, room fifty-three.

"Can I make a quick phone call to my friend while you're looking?" he said and dialed into Henley's room without waiting for an answer.

"Who's this?" Henley answered, his voice sounding grumpy and tired.

"Front desk, sir. This is your wake-up call," Wright said as softly as possible.

"Wake-up call?" Henley asked, and then he recognized the voice. "Oh… yes, thank you."

"Welcome Sir. Mr. Oleksander… breakfast will be served at 8 am. Our hotel is full this morning and I suggest you leave early and avoid a big rush. Perhaps you might try one of the breakfast places nearby?"

"Oh, is it? Thank you. I think I will go to the bakery at Stoleshnikov Lane."

"Very well, sir," said Wright setting the receiver down.

"Thank you, I will come back in a bit to book the room," Wright told the receptionist and quietly handed her a 100 rouble note for her troubles.

He walked up to the blonde girl and asked her to meet him later. He handed her another note and told her to take care of his friend standing outside near the lamppost. Wright was in his element. He never shied from giving one back to the commies at the KGB.

⁂

8 am, Pushkin Bakery, Stoleshnikov Lane

"What the fuck happened, Wright?" Henley asked. Wright apprised him of the details, but it was a rhetorical question. The details didn't matter. Henley knew what had happened. *The ghosts of previous such botched operations came rushing back to him.* Wright looked at Henley, expecting fury, but his boss kept calm, sipping coffee and in a state of deep concentration.

"You did well but we still have to get Charlie out without walking into the ambush ourselves. Which is the station before Sochi?"

"Dagomys," Wright promptly replied.

"How far's that from here?" Henley asked and traced the route on the map.

"About 50 km."

"Right, and can you find me two women—friends of your young woman from earlier, to accompany me?"

Wright looked surprised. "I sure can, but what's the plan here?"

"I will take a taxi to Dagomys with the two ladies, and catch the same train that Charlie and Eddie are on. I'll find a way to have the ladies tell our boys to stay on past Sochi. You will meet us at Adler at the post office. Be ready with the car."

"Why don't I come with you?" Wright said, looking grim that his boss might not pull it off alone.

"They have seen your face, Stuart. Can't risk you to be seen anywhere near Sochi, or Adler station for that matter," Henley said, reading the look on Wright's face. "And, don't worry. There's still a field agent alive inside this old body, I will handle it," Saying so, Henley went to the restroom.

Wright sat at the coffee table, figuring out his route to Adler and the best way to find some girls in the early hours of the day.

Wright felt a pat on his back and turned around to look. Henley was almost unrecognizable in his new ensemble. His normally gray hair and mustache were jet black, hair slicked back and oversized spectacles adorned his face. The old spy still had a few tricks under his sleeve. Classic espionage was never out of fashion, Wright thought.

"That should get the girls excited for the night," Wright said.

Chapter 37
Bait and Switch

Bus to Vyborg, 5:30 am

Keith Aldridge thought hard. Failure would mean Tesla getting caught and being sent to Lubyanka prison. He would have a trial without a lawyer and be shot dead soon after. Failure was not an option.

Aldridge had been in the clandestine services for a decade and a half, and he regarded it as a job. But, somehow, this time it felt personal. Henley's words came ringing back to him. *There is a mole, Aldridge, a Russian mole right here in MI6.* He looked at the back of Tesla's head. The man sat motionless, peering through the window, probably wondering if he had made the right decision.

Aldridge felt a plan coming together, daring yet simple, but Neil Alvares had to be the man to do it. If the KGB were on their tail, most likely, they knew what Aldridge looked like. He couldn't risk seeing leaving the bus together with Tesla. But they didn't know Alvares.

The young family from Aldridge's coach was traveling on the same bus. He had caught some luck. They were the perfect cover for his plan. He went up to them, spoke to them for a few minutes, and came back to his seat. He scribbled in his diary a short detail of the plan, tore the page, and slipped it into Tesla's overcoat pocket.

He leaned over and said, "Viktor, we need to split up at Vyborg. I can't explain in detail, but look for a handsome Asian guy. His name is Neil Alvares. He will carry a camera with him, which should make it easier for you to spot him.

Walk up to him and give him this note. When you leave the bus, that couple with the baby will join you."

"When will you join us?"

"I will find my way to you, don't worry. I need to make sure you reach the borders safely. All you have to do is find Alvares and make sure the couple stays close to you. I will find you at the border," Aldridge assured him.

He planned to stay on the bus all the way to Lappeenranta, a town forty kilometers beyond Vyborg, just before the Finnish border. He would walk the rest of the way if he had to. He trusted Alvares to find his way to the border and from there, he planned to cross over with Tesla, alone. He couldn't risk taking Alvares. He checked his duffel bag again for the pistol.

The bus conductor announced Vyborg as the next stop and Tesla slowly made his way to the exit where the cheery couple joined him and got down.

Keith Aldridge was the last passenger on the bus as it pulled into Lappeenranta. There was not a single soul in sight. He walked briskly toward the town center, hoping to hitch a ride toward Alvares and Tesla. By his count, he had about an hour before they reached the Finnish border. The distance from Lappeenranta to the border checkpost was about forty kilometers. It could take him less than an hour if he made a dash for it. He couldn't afford to wait for a hitch. The only way he could be there on time was to drive as fast as he could.

Keith Aldridge looked around for houses with cars. It seemed like an agricultural town, with trailers and tractors everywhere. Eventually, he found an old compact four-wheel-drive LuAZ vehicle parked in front of a townhouse. He moved toward the car and tried the handle. His heart leaped as he heard the clunk of the catch. Lucky break. He got in, found the wire panel cover next to the steering column, and started connecting combinations of wires. After a few tries, the engine coughed to life. He made the connection true and quietly pulled away down the street. As he made his way to the main road, he put his foot down.

⁂

Neil Alvares was ready and waiting at Vyborg. Mikko, Marbury's contact, had given him a brown Lada Niva for the drive to the border. He had been at the stop for several hours, anxiously waiting for Aldridge and Tesla to arrive.

Another bus arrived, but Aldridge was nowhere to be seen. A couple with a baby and a tall gentleman walked right up to him. The tall man tipped his hat and handed him a note.

He opened the note:

N, this is K. Meet at the last crossing before the Finnish Border at Lappeenranta. Cover: Tesla is your tour guide, and he is taking you and the couple to Finland to see the northern lights. Don't go beyond the crossing without me. P.S: And if the baby poops, put the poop in the boot.

Alvares understood almost all of it, except the baby poop part. He wondered if it was a code. He treated it verbatim. He took Tesla to his side and quickly explained the plan. Tesla took the wheel, with Alvares in the front and the couple and the baby at the back.

"So nice of your friend to offer us a free hotel stay in Finland," the young man in the back said, unaware that he and his family were part of a major spy operation. "He also gave us some money and said he was starting a new business and needed some fresh faces for the tour catalog. You're a photographer, right?"

Neil Alvares turned back and gave a wide smile. He kept looking through the rearview mirror. His instincts had kicked in. If Aldridge had a reason to not join them, then it only meant one thing: *the KGB was onto them.*

It was now up to him to take them across the last stretch. But there was a small problem. Right from the time he got off the train at Vyborg and took the car, he had a sense that he was being followed. He had gone around the town for an hour and dropped the tail. But with the changes in plan and assuming Aldridge was being followed too, he had the feeling it would be coming back sooner than later.

Tesla drove at a steady pace. Alvares had the map in his hands and gave Tesla the directions to Lappeenranta as the couple tried to feed the crying baby. They stopped momentarily and Alvares took the poop-filled diapers and put them in the car's boot as Aldridge had instructed. The smell had engulfed the car and Neil had to roll down a window.

As they continued through the town, dawn breaking in the sky, Alvares spotted the same car that had been behind him at Vyborg. Fearing the worst, he kept it to himself. He couldn't afford Tesla to get off plan and do something stupid. Not only that, he could endanger the lives of three innocent civilians in the back.

It took them just under an hour to reach Lappeenranta. This was where Aldridge had asked them to stop. But for how long? Alvares asked Tesla to park at the curbside and wait. He explained to the couple that the car had become hot and needed to wait for a few minutes. Tesla tried to keep a straight face.

Alvares looked around and saw the same black car that had followed them all the way, parked a few cars behind them. Across the railway crossing, a squad of policemen was checking through each car passing through the signal crossing. The situation was getting tense.

There was nowhere to hide. They were marooned in the middle of a wide expanse of fields, sandwiched between the KGB tailing them and the police at the checkpoint.

Tesla was fidgeting on the steering wheel, with an abject look about him. *I need a plan B if Aldridge doesn't make it in the next twenty minutes*, Alvares thought.

Fifteen minutes and two trains had passed, yet Aldridge was nowhere to be seen. The black car behind was waiting to pounce on them if they moved. The couple inside were getting anxious, wondering why they weren't moving. The husband threatened to call off the entire idea and leave. Alvares convinced them to stay on for a few more minutes and promised to leave after the next train passed by.

If Aldridge didn't turn up, Alvares prepared himself for a maverick plan. There was a narrow track running across the fields that the tractors probably used for sowing seeds. When the next train crossed the signal, he could drive the car parallel to it, at full speed, and cross the tracks to the other side. But he would have to time it perfectly, or else he could drive himself and Tesla to a certain death. Was it worth risking their lives? Alvares considered as the minutes ticked by. There was no way he was going to pass through the security upfront without Keith.

And then he heard someone calling his name. It was Aldridge.

"Thank goodness you made it," Alvares said, relieved that he needn't go with his action-fueled kamikaze plan.

"Tell me you weren't about to do something crazy?" Aldridge appeared at the window of the car and gave him a smile. He had dropped off his stolen car on the other side of the field and run through until he reached the border crossing to find Alvares.

"I wouldn't say it was crazy…" Alvares said and then let him know about the black car that had followed them.

"That's a fucking problem," Aldridge said and took a pause. "Ask the couple to come out for a breath of fresh air."

Alvares urged the couple out of the car and they started stretching their legs at the edge of the field and the narrow dirt road.

"Did you collect the nappies?" Aldridge asked as he got back to the car.

"Yes, I meant to ask you about that…" Alvares said, but Aldridge had already moved round to the driver's side.

"Viktor," he said, opening the car door.

"Aldridge…" Tesla said as he exited the vehicle.

"If you wouldn't mind following me…" Aldridge said and made his way to the back of the car. He popped the boot and indicated to Viktor to get inside.

"You're serious?" Viktor laughed.

"Deadly…" said Aldridge and then helped the big man get inside the car. Once Viktor was in, he covered him with the plastic sheet that Mikko had provided. He then neatly arranged the baby poop in front of him. For onlookers, all they would see is some baby poop-filled diapers and a big plastic film behind them. He had remembered the trick that helped him evade the police patrol on his way to Moscow Station a couple of days back when he dropped his duffel bag at the station lockers.

"Now what?" Alvares asked.

"You head back to Moscow. I will take it from here," Aldridge said and gave Alvares the directions to the car he had parked.

"But there are security guards at the checkpost. There's no way you're making it out of there. They know your identity by now."

"Let's hope they buy my story of being a tourist guide," Aldridge said.

"No, they won't, you have no fucking clue about Finland… but I do!" John Marbury came out of nowhere and stood behind Alvares and Aldridge.

"What are you doing here? How, who…" Alvares asked, equally shocked and pleased to see a friendly face.

"We don't have time for that. You both take the car," he pointed to the car that had followed Alvares, "and leave for Moscow. Now." John Marbury had taken control of the operation.

"Are you sure?" Aldridge asked, still surprised at the sudden change of events.

"Damn right, I am. Leave it to me. I will take it on from here. They don't know who I am," he said and asked Aldridge the state of play and the plan he had in place.

"You're a lifesaver, Marbury," Aldridge said.

"Don't thank me. It was Henley's plan all along," Marbury said and took the wheels. Alvares ushered the family back in, and Aldridge explained to them that Marbury would be their host at the hotel in Finland.

John Marbury immediately started joking around with the young couple in Russian, easing their fears. Inside the boot, Viktor tried to stay motionless. The stench of the baby's poop was nauseating, but he had to survive the next couple of hours.

Keith Aldridge and Neil Alvares made their way to John's car—the black car that had been following Alvares all along.

"You can drive," Aldridge said to Alvares and tossed him the keys.

As they pulled off and started back toward Vyborg, silence ensued. It wasn't until they were well on the highway that Alvares spoke up.

"So…" he brought in Alvares on the day's events thus far.

"And that baby poop, my friend, is for the sniffer dogs at the checkpoint. That smell should steer them well away from checking further inside the boot," Aldridge said.

Satisfied, Alvares put his foot down and they were on their way back toward Moscow.

Aldridge had a few questions himself. Particularly how Marbury and Henley had gotten wind of his operations. But that could wait till they were back in Moscow. Whatever it was, he was thankful that the old dog had their backs.

Chapter 38
Old Dog, New Trick

Moscow Station,

The day of. 7 am.

Father Samuel had a pile of files in front of him. He had gone through every file, transcript, and record he could find on the name Control gave him. So far, he had been clean. There was no way to tie him to being a mole besides a janitor's roster, and that he was involved in the MI5 operation with Tesla's kid. All of this could just be a pure happenstance. He could not say on authority that this person was the one who tore apart the pages from the registry, nor could he link him to being. a Russian mole.

Everything was squeaky clean on the books. But that was suspicious in itself. No one had such a clean history unless you had systematically wiped out any evidence of foul play. That gave him hope. He was obviously missing something.

His theory was simple. Somewhere between MI5's operation to help Tesla and the agent moving to MI6 in Budapest and then to Moscow, the KGB must have recruited him. How? He didn't have the answer to that. But he just knew. He had a role in Moscow Station and had every tool available to make the switches at Shakuntala to divert the agents to Budapest. The mole had access to the system and the knowledge to run a deep cover operation.

Father Samuel went through everything, trying to find a piece of evidence that could give him some sort of link. There was none. Out of desperation, he ran through all the agents' desks. Same result. All that was left was Roslyn's.

He rummaged through her desk. Her personal items were still intact. A lot had been going on at the station, and no one had bothered to clear her stuff out. Father Samuel neatly arranged her personal items into a box as he went. In the last drawer, he saw a file. Roslyn had made a request to the London office asking for details on the fake operation that she and Henley had conjured up.

He went through the notes. She had asked London for a copy of the submarine technology that the Indian station had prepared for the fake operation. Three copies were sent to London and three to Moscow. *Roslyn had impersonated Henley in making this request to Control.*

Was she the mole? Had the KGB figured out she was a liability and assassinated her?

Anything was possible.

Father Samuel continued to read through the notes. She had all six copies of the fake technology papers and workshop locations that the engineers in India had prepared. This was almost the proof he needed. She could have passed on the copies to her handler at the KGB. But why would they kill her if she just handed them the details of the most important piece of British technology? *Maybe they realized it was chicken feed and that's what had led to her death.*

Father Samuel had cleared out her desk. All evidence pointed to Roslyn. He thumped the desk in anger. Suddenly, the top of the desk opened up. He squeezed his hand inside and pulled out a thin file that was concealed under it. It was a file from Tesla.

At the top, there was a sticky note with a date. It was the day of the last drop that Aldridge had met with Tesla. Tesla had handed over a file to Aldridge before they parted ways.

He figured Aldridge must have handed the file to Roslyn for indexing and filing in the registry and forgot about it.

He opened the file and there was a single piece of paper—a copy of the submarine technology. And then it made all sense.

Roslyn had figured out that the agent who had the same copy as the one Tesla sent back to Aldridge, must have passed it to the KGB. To make sure, she must have requested all the copies, to confirm that all six copies were different. She wasn't the mole. But she'd found out who was.

And now so did he. He knew who was given this copy of the submarine tech, which made its way to his KGB handlers.

It was Charles 'Charlie' Darcy.

Father Samuel immediately rushed to find a phone to reach Simon Henley.

༺ ༻

Henley replaced the receiver and came out of the phone booth. He was shaken to his core. If the priest was right then it was a massive failure on his part. His legacy was in tatters. He couldn't understand why Darcy would betray his country and his colleagues like this. Business, maybe that's what it was for him, Henley thought. If any consolation, Darcy was the only agent in Moscow Station that had not been handpicked by Henley. And maybe that was the problem. There was only one way to find out—catch him off guard and have him taken to a safe house for questioning. There was one bad apple that they knew of. There could be more.

The switch that he and Father Samuel planned had worked to perfection until now. Marbury had called him from Vyborg a few hours earlier, confirming that Alvares and Aldridge had taken the plunge to extract Tesla on their own. Their plan was working. They had successfully diverted the attention of the mole and the KGB to Eddie, rather than Tesla. It was meant to look like a real operation, or else the mole or the KGB would not have bought it. That had meant sacrificing Eddie. But now the game had changed again.

If Eddie was caught and Darcy made a run for it, then they would never know how far the KGB had infiltrated the British secret service. They needed to get Darcy out, without him suspecting anything. They would have to see Operation Witchcraft through to its conclusion. Wright would have to wait before he knew everything. If they were lucky, they could still save Eddie. But he knew, deep in his heart, that Eddie was going straight into the hands of the KGB. Darcy had played his part perfectly. He had stayed closest to Eddie, giving him the ability to alert the KGB at any point of the operation.

That son of a bitch was ruthless.

Simon Henley had one trump card—the one he kept closest to his chest, that no one knew of. Not even the priest. Mike Moore. Henley had secretly asked him to travel to Sochi and run the surveillance at the port. He still had time before Wright was back with the girls. He rushed to the port to find Moore. He knew exactly how to take Darcy out of Moscow and to a safe house.

Mike Moore was at the loading docks, next to the port. The *Clair de Lune* was docked right near the first aisle of the port. From the small cafeteria overlooking the docks, Mike had a clear line of sight to the ship. He could keep an eye on any KGB movement and was to alert Henley during the day if something came up. He was to make a cross in yellow chalk on the first gate that led to the first docking aisle at the port. That would alert Henley if he were to reach the port with Eddie and Wright.

"Boss, what are you doing here?" Mike asked, surprised.

"Mike, listen carefully to what I have to say."

"All ears, boss."

"Plans have changed. Buy two tickets to Istanbul on the Clair de Lune. One for you and for Charlie Darcy."

"Darcy?" Mike almost shouted.

"Yes, you need to pretend that you and Darcy are off to Istanbul as part of the operation. That is all you're to tell him. When you get to Istanbul, take him to the safe house. You know where it is?"

"I do," Mike said.

"Good. I will send word to the Istanbul station and make arrangements for you both to be there. Don't let him out of your sight till I say so, am I clear?" Henley asserted.

"Crystal, boss."

"Good man. See this through Mike, and you will have everything you need waiting for you in Prague," Henley said. As he left the shipyard, he saw Wright marching across the concourse, arm-in-arm with two exceptionally beautiful women.

"Henley, this is Irina and Nicola. Ladies, this is Oleksander," Stuart Wright introduced the two women to Henley.

"Ladies, thank you for joining us. I hope we are going to have a great time," Simon Henley said, looking at least a couple of decades younger in his black ensemble, head to toe.

Henley had his car ready and drove to Dagomys station with the two women in tow where they waited to board the train that was carrying Eddie and Darcy.

Irina and Nicola were noisy and giggly and cozying up with Henley on the train. A perfect camouflage, he thought, trying not to enjoy himself too much.

Henley walked from cabin to cabin, until finally he spotted Darcy. The traitor sat there, relaxed, not knowing the world around him was burning.

He was alone, the other passengers having disembarked already, and Henley walked into the cabin and sat in front of Darcy. The ladies kept laughing and speaking in Russian. Simon Henley stared directly at Charlie Darcy and gave a smile.

It took a moment for it to register, but Henley's deep blue eyes and the radiant smile soon gave him away.

"Boss, what are you doing here?" Darcy asked, surprised and unsettled.

"Keep it down, Darcy… and follow my lead," Henley told him to stick by and not make a move as they approached Sochi station.

"How far is Eddie from us?"

"A couple of cabins."

"Right, we need to move to the other end of the train," Henley said, "You take Irina, I'll take Nicola."

At the end of the coach, Henley grabbed Darcy closer and said, "Wright couldn't make it to the station. What's the play here?"

Darcy's facial expressions suddenly changed, caught off guard. He had not counted on the Moscow chief to be on board the train. He had to think fast.

"I think we wait for Eddie to get off and find his way to the exit. If the car is still there, then we can pick him up and head to the port," Darcy said. The girls stood around them, chatting to each other.

"Any KGB on the train?" Henley asked.

"It's been a clean ride, boss. Aldridge said that they ran into trouble, but the train's squeaky clean for all I know," he lied. Just two stops earlier, he had made a brush pass with the KGB agents on board and handed them a note confirming that Eddie was on board and to wait for an MI6 agent, Stuart Wright, at the Sochi station. The KGB agents were ready for the ambush to take an MI6 agent and Eddie the traitor.

"Good lad. Once the train stops, stay on. We're getting off at Adler, the next stop. I will give you a signal. Only then get down and head to the exit from the right end of the platform. There is an unmarked exit that leads to the parking lot," Henley said.

"And the ladies?" Darcy asked. This was all going too fast and too different from what he had planned for.

"What about them?" Henley hadn't thought that far ahead. He quickly had a word with them, passed them some money, and told them to find a seat with the men in suits a few berths behind. He could use any distractions possible to throw at the KGB men. Henley and Darcy crossed the connecting vestibule and moved a few coaches away as the train approached the platform. It gave them a clear view of when Eddie stepped down from the coach.

As the train came to a halt, Henley and Darcy were a few coaches away from Eddie. Henley got down onto the platform and trained his eyes toward his left, hoping to catch a glimpse. He watched Eddie get down. As soon as he set foot on the platform, two men in suits and ties moved discreetly toward Eddie. Eddie scanned around for Wright, but he was nowhere to be found. Henley signaled Darcy to stay put as the train announced its departure from the station, and he took one step back and stood on the stairs that led into the coach. As the train moved away, Henley watched as the KGB swooped in and rounded up Eddie.

That was the end of service for Eddie.

Henley was sure Eddie would never see the light of day again. Possibly exiled for the rest of his life behind bars, or worse, shot dead for treason at Lubyanka. Henley got back into the coach and shut the door behind him. They had just about escaped the KGB net.

Charlie Darcy saw the action through the glass windows. He had just handed the KGB their biggest traitor in years but wondered why Wright had not made it to the station. That would have been perfect. The General would have been extremely happy. But for now, this will do, he thought.

Chapter 39
Homecoming

Adler

7 pm

Stuart Wright watched Darcy and Henley get off the train. Darcy immediately moved toward the west exit. Wright was relieved that they had made it past the KGB. But then it dawned upon him. Eddie was missing.

"Where's Eddie?" he asked Henley, as they kept walking at a brisk pace toward the exit. In the car, Henley gave him the bad news. Wright looked crestfallen. This was the first time in his career that he had his agent caught. He kept a check on his emotions and revved up the car.

Darcy joined them in the car, and then Henley made his move.

"Darcy, I cannot risk you being in Moscow. We need to assess the damage Eddie could do. He might give you away if he has seen you on the train. Same for you, Wrighty."

"What's the plan, boss?" Wright asked.

"We already have two seats booked on the ship to Istanbul. Darcy, I want you to board that ship with someone I trust. He will help you across the border in Turkey and take you to our safe house in Istanbul. Stay there till I say so," Henley instructed as Wright kept driving on. He was not sure if he understood what the boss was playing at.

"And you, Wright, you will head to India with Alvares."

Henley gave them no chance to respond. Darcy didn't have time to think or to retort. *This might actually be good*, he thought. If he played his cards right, he could land a big role in Istanbul. He envisaged his rise to the top of the tree. For all he knew, he had burned the Moscow operations to the ground. *She would be so proud of him. The love of his life, his milaya would need to know somehow that he was going to Istanbul.* He decided to wait till he was onboard the ship and then find a way to pass the information.

Wright got out at the Continental Hotel, and Henley took the wheel and drove straight to the port with Darcy in the car.

"What the hell is he doing here?" Darcy asked as he saw Mike walking toward them at the port entrance.

"You know Moore?" Henley asked as Mike shook Henley's hands and looked at Darcy with a smug face.

"I very well know who he is... bloody scalp hunters," Darcy said.

"Just doing my job, Darcy," Mike said. Something that Henley didn't know: Mike and Darcy shared a past. When Darcy was at Budapest Station, before his big money move to Moscow, Mike and Darcy had become close. Darcy used their friendship to gain a favor from Mike's boss—Steve Smith. That favor had been for Darcy to be moved to Moscow Station from Budapest. Darcy had betrayed Mike—a betrayal that almost cost Mike his job and his family. Mike had two problems—women and alcohol. Darcy used both to his advantage and assisted Steve Smith on an operation while Mike went on a holiday with his mistress.

"Whatever it is between you two, keep that low and easy till you have made it to Istanbul," Henley ordered. "Mike is being transferred to Prague and he will be your only company till you make it to Istanbul, Darcy."

Simon Henley watched them head toward the ship. He had taken a huge gamble in running with Mike. Repeatedly, Mike had done a half job, and he had hesitated to hand over a dangerous double agent to a low-level operative. But Mike had qualities that no one else in his team had. He was handy, flew under the radar, and knew the workings of the system, and best of all, Darcy would suspect nothing—his ego would get the better of him and cloud his judgment.

Three days later

Moscow Station

Simon Henley had just got word from Mike. Darcy was now at the Istanbul safe house, closely watched and under house arrest.

Stuart Wright, Keith Aldridge, and Neil Alvares had assembled at Simon Henley's office. This was the first time they all had come down together to the office since the two operations had concluded. Wright paced around the room like a madman. He had lost his agent. Aldridge and Alvares looked distraught—no one had had word from Marbury yet.

"Henley, line three… It's him," Father Samuel called from the comms office. Simon Henley took the phone and put it on speaker.

"John? Are you safe?"

"Pretty much…" They could hear John Marbury loud and clear.

"Is Tesla with you?" Aldridge asked anxiously.

"He's doing fine, don't worry, Aldridge."

"Rest easy, John. It's not safe for you to be back in Moscow yet. Father Samuel will head to you in Finland and take you both onwards to India."

"Ok, boss. Much deserved holiday, I suppose," Marbury said.

"Something like that. Send us your hotel coordinates." Henley said and cut the call. Aldridge and Alvares wrapped one another in an embrace. It had worked. They'd got Tesla out. Operation Cricket was a success.

Henley looked at Father Samuel. They knew it was time to let the lads in on their grand plan.

"I suppose you might be wondering…"

"How the bloody hell did you know what we were up to?" Aldridge said.

"Over the years, we had a feeling that we had a mole in our ranks. We had operations going wrong, our regular drops getting hit by the KGB surveillance, and the movements being tracked much beyond our liking," Henley started putting together the pieces of the puzzle for everyone around.

"And then Control dealt us the hammer blow. We had a few agents missing or dead, and it led straight to our door. It was our problem to fix. The working theory was that there is a traitor amongst our ranks."

"We went through all of your files, history, your spouses, friends for any associations with the Soviets…" Henley winked at Father Samuel, "… to see if you had any reason to sell yourselves to the KGB."

"But, you all came out squeaky clean," Father Samuel added.

Henley continued, "I then reached out to Father Samuel to help flush out the mole and we devised a scheme by which we created a fake technology, each of you getting a different version of the plans."

"That's why I went to India?" Aldridge asked.

"And I went to London…" Wright added to the story.

"Right. But it was cut short when Tesla reached out to us, and we couldn't bury the mole then. With Tesla needing extracting, there was every bit a possibility of putting the entire operation in danger if we didn't catch the mole first."

"Henley reached out to me, and we hatched a plan together," Father Samuel continued the story.

"We had to kill two birds with one stone. Extract Tesla safely, yet catch the mole red-handed."

"So, we laid a plan," Henley said. "A plan to steer the KGB in the wrong direction while the real action happened somewhere else."

"How did we do that?" Wright asked.

"Father, would you care to explain?"

Father Samuel cleared his throat, "I arranged with Control to send a considerable amount of money to Wright's agent, Eddie, to thank him for his services. We told him that we had received word from our network that his name was doing the rounds of the KGB corridors and that we should bring him to England pronto. We asked him to make immediate contact with his handler, Wright."

"Mike Moore helped to tail him and make the drop. We also told Eddie that we feared for his life, to speed up his defection," Henley said.

"We asked him to inform Wright that he wanted out, and the rest would be taken care of," Henley said, looking straight at Wright. Stuart Wright, at the moment, understood that Eddie was used as a bait.

"At that point, we still didn't know if the mole was in Moscow or London. Everyone was a suspect," Father Samuel continued. "So, we had to make the Eddie exfiltration seem as real as possible. That way, if there was a mole, the KGB would try to kill Operation Witchcraft."

"And while the KGB was busy focusing on Eddie... Tesla would have a free run, hopefully, to make it out of Moscow without the traitor knowing that an operation was underway to defect Tesla."

"But how did you know that Aldridge would run a covert op to bring Tesla out?" Wright asked.

"Leap of faith," Father Samuel said and smiled.

Henley looked at Alvares and Aldridge and said, "You two... this entire operation was built on the hope that you would take the extreme step. We knew that with no support if you were to do it all by yourself, you could only take Tesla so far. That's when I had Marbury tail you guys and support the operation when the time comes."

"And I am sorry about your guy, Wright. Collateral damage. Tesla has done a lot for our country. He is one of us. We had to do everything in our power to bring him home," Henley said.

"What happened to Eddie… What was the mole's doing?" Wright asked.

"I am afraid so."

"And did Eddie help find out who the mole was? Say he did Henley, else we sacrificed him for nothing," Wright said, visibly upset. He took this professional loss on the chin; he took one for the team.

Simon Henley took a deep pause, "Look around the room. Who is missing?"

"Fucking *Darcy?*" Wright suddenly realized. They had forgotten that Charlie was not in the room. Almost always, everyone assumed he would be in the comms room.

Henley gave them a recount of the events and how he used Mike to get him to Istanbul's safe house. He had received word from Istanbul station chief and Moore that Darcy was kept safe, hidden from the KGB and not allowed any outside access. He was under house arrest. Henley was to head to Istanbul soon to interrogate him.

Simon Henley walked up to Aldridge and placed an arm over his shoulder, "Well done, son. You're ready for the big league. Tighten your belt, being the station chief of Moscow will be some ride."

Aldridge understood. Henley was passing the baton to him. At that moment, he thought of his wife Clarise and his daughter. This was not just a professional triumph but a personal one too.

"And him over there, watch him carefully," Henley said, pointing to Neil Alvares.

"Why?" Aldridge asked.

"Eventually he'll be Our Man in India," Simon gave Alvares a quick wink and joined the rest as they cheered and celebrated through the night.

Keith Aldridge knew Neil Alvares's story was not over here, yet. He knew Alvares would continue his search to find Kate Miller. If she were not dead already, in part due to Darcy's betrayal, he would help Alvares find Kate Miller. And he had his own trail to follow—Vince Gilligan.

Chapter 40
Occam's Razor

Occam's razor-all things being equal, the simplest conclusion is usually the correct one.

A month later

MI6 safe house, Istanbul

The MI6 safe house in Başakşehir, a well-heeled suburb of Istanbul, was as nondescript as a house could be between an array of rich households. It was the standard fare of two stories, a gray facade, white windows, and a small porch. Nothing suggested it was a citadel of espionage for the British in Turkey. The dynamics of the clandestine business in Istanbul were the polar opposite of those of Moscow. Where Moscow demanded restraint, cunning, and guile, Istanbul was loud, brash, carefree, and a playground of debonair spies and undercover agents.

Charles Darcy had been a prisoner there for more than a month now. On the second day of reaching Istanbul, he realized he was caught. *The game was over.* The old bastards at Moscow Station had caught him. He had always been careful, only ever switching the codes when a full system reboot was done, always directing the agents to Budapest *as his Russian masters ordered.*

From the communications desk of Moscow Station, Charles Darcy had a vantage position. He could tap all the incoming and outgoing communications. Over the years he had figured out the secret codes and knew them by rote. Tesla was the only agent he could not lay a finger on. Eddie came out of the blue. It was an opportunity he could not pass up. A full defection program to happen right under his nose; it was the perfect opportunity to show the General what he could do. *And she had assured him he could do it. Eddie with Wright in tow was to be his pièce de résistance.*

Just before he and Mike left Sochi, he had tipped off a note to his handler that he was being taken to an Istanbul safe house, along with the address. *She would be worried sick and would want to know If I was safe and well,* he had thought. He hoped the deputy captain of the ship, who was staying back at Sochi for the next ship, would find the dead letter box and drop off the note. But it had been a month and there was no news. *Maybe she never received my note,* he thought.

Simon Henley had visited him a few weeks back. Their meeting had been short and to the point. Henley wanted to know who else from the Circus was involved. Darcy gave him nothing. *Not without immunity.* He knew Simon Henley's weakness. He had too much pride and would protect his legacy at all costs. He knew Henley would not want him to be executed. Henley would do everything possible to find out if Darcy knew more and had help from someone in the Circus. *The English were different from the Russians in that way.*

And now Henley was back. Another round of interrogation.

"It seems we are treating you well," Henley said as he walked into the room. It was spacious enough for one person, cramped for two, and was adorned with pictures of the countryside, books to read, and an iron grill that covered the window that allowed a small bit of sunlight to come in.

"Food could be better, but nothing I can't handle," Darcy said, looking worn out, beard outgrown and his long hair growing longer. His spectacles were hiding the emotions in his eyes. *Darcy did look like John Lennon, Henley thought, as he recounted the conversation between Aldridge and Tesla when Tesla tipped off a foreign agent working for the KGB codenamed Lennon.*

Henley took a seat on the couch and kept a file on the table.

"That is the immunity you asked for."

"Great..." Darcy said, waiting for Henley to pitch.

"But prove your worth to me, just like you did to your Russian masters."

"I serve no one!" Darcy shouted. "I did this for myself and for my future."

"What future, Darcy? Look around you."

"Top of the Circus, Henley. Just like you, Aldridge, and the rest of you, I too had ambitions."

"And look where that's landed you," Henley said, feeling sorry for the misguided young man.

"Who's signed the immunity... is it Control?"

"It will be from who you want, Darcy."

"You can't play me on this, Henley. I know you. This is above Control's pay grade. I want Tilbury to sign it."

"You want the undersecretary to the Prime Minister to sign it?"

"If you want what you came for, Simon, then it has to be from Tilbury."

"Well then, you will have it, Charlie. Make sure you put down everything, no chicken feed," Henley said.

Henley got up to leave and then turned back to ask, "One last question, Charlie... Roslyn, was that you?"

Darcy turned blue. That was the only regret. She had found him out and he needed to shut her down. He said nothing and just looked away, through the small window to hide the deep guilt on his face.

"I thought so," Henley said and stood up to leave. "Give us everything you know. Try to make some good out of all this."

With Simon gone, Darcy wrote the key players he knew at the KGB and the help he had to run the double agent operations. He gave the details on the dead letter drops, live drop locations, KGB surveillance techniques, and the tonnage of information he had passed on to them over the years. He wrote it all down, except the codename of his case officer, his love, *his milaya*. **H**. That was all he wrote. *One letter—that could do no harm,* he thought.

He had played both sides. He had filled his coffers with money from the KGB and hoodwinked MI6 for years. With this last roll of the dice, he could restart and slowly build a new life with H by his side. She had promised. She was his lover first, case officer second.

A hot plate of food was ready for him in the dining area. The maid, who took care of the safe house and his needs, was away. Someone else had dropped in the food.

He took a bite of the kebab and switched on the television. He tore the piece of bread and was about to take a bite when he saw a note tucked inside the piece of Elmek.

He opened the note.

Nothing personal, my love. This was business.
-H

As he reread the note, trying to make sense of it, he felt a scratch in the back of his throat. He reached for his top button and opened up his collar. He was finding it hard to breathe.

—The End—